A Most Unlikely Hero

Volume 8

Written by Brandon Varnell

Illustrations by XuaHanNin

A Most Unlikely Hero Volume 8
Copyright © 2020 Brandon Varnell & Kitsune Incorporated
Illustration Copyright © 2020 XuanHanNin
All rights reserved.

To see Brandon Varnell's other works, or to ask for permission to use his works, visit him at www.varnell-brandon.com, facebook at www.facebook.com/AmericanKitsune, twitter at www.twitter.com/BrandonbVarnell, Patreon at https://www.patreon.com/BrandonVarnell, and instagram at www.instagram.com/brandonbvarnell.

ISBN: 987-1-951904-14-2

DEDICATION

This page is made in dedication to my amazing patrons. Without them, my characters would never get lewded by so many wonderful artists:

Aaron Harris
Alarinnise
Alexander Rodriguez
Amando Pastrana
Benjamin Morgan
Brennan
Bruce Johnson
C.L. Holgrahm
Chace Corso
CosmicOrange
David
DeseriDeri
Dhivael
Edward Lamar Stephenson
Emery Moore
Feitochan
Forrest Hansen
Ine Airlcana
Jacob Flores
Jacob Wonjo
Jason Davis
Jason Grey
Jeremy Schultz
Jessica
John Patton
Joshua Garrett
Kevin
Lucid Fact
Mark Frabotta
Matthew Wallace
Max A Kramer
Michael Moneymaker
Nathan
Nathan S
Nicholas

Omegapudding
Patrick Burns-popieniuck
Phillip Hedgepeth
Rafael Eriksen
Red Phoenix
Red Viking
Samuel Donaldson
Sean Gray
Seismic Wolf
Shotgunr12
Saudi Corp
Starwarsscout Jon
Thomas Jackson
ToraLinkley
Travis Cox
Trevor Ward
Victor Patrick Baur
Virgil Gardner
William Crew
Yuriy Snyadanko
Zachery

CONTENT

Prologue: Jāhilīyah Problem Solved

Chapter 1: A Troublesome Return Home

Interlude: The Not Quite Damsel in Distress

Chapter 2: Operation Save Jasmine Commences

Chapter 3: Blackmail for a Noble Cause

Chapter 4: Date and Disaster

Chapter 5: Kazekiri

Epilogue: Nyx's Surprise Birthday Bash

PROLOGUE

JĀHILĪYAH PROBLEM SOLVED

Jāhilīyah was a desert planet. Fierce winds ripped across its surface almost constantly. The sandstorm that ravaged Jāhilīyah had been going strong for the last one hundred years, and it was partially thanks to this sandstorm that their planet was suffering from a drought.

Al-lāt stared at the desert landscape from within her palace, a glittering structure of crystallized sand, a towering spire that pierced the sky.

This palace was not one created by her people. The Jāhilīyahns had discovered this structure many centuries ago. Her family, the royal family of Jāhilīyah who had led their people to prosperity in ages past, had been the ones to make use of this crystal palace, carving out the inside and turning it into their home. Despite being made of crystal, it was not easy to see through. The crystal was a thick white. Only the window panes, placed in specific sections that wouldn't ruin the structure's stability, allowed one a glimpse of the outside world.

It had been nearly three months, give or take a week, since Al-lāt had returned to her home planet with her two brothers in tow, but it wasn't a pleasant return. She had returned in failure.

They had gone all the way to Mars, a small planet in one of the most remote sections of the galaxy, their purpose to locate Princess Gabrielle and have her marry Al-lāt's eldest brother. If Ibn-Al Kalbi married Princess Gabrielle and became Emperor of the Galaxy, then it would be easy to gather a source of water for her people. They could order several planets to donate water to Jāhilīyah. Their planet would be saved.

But they had failed.

Princess Gabrielle had a suitor by the name of Alexander S. Ryker. According to the message that King Lucifer had sent across the galaxy, Alexander S. Ryker was a human, a populous being that littered every quadrant of the galaxy. Humans had no powers. They had no unique abilities. Defeating him and stealing Princess Gabrielle away should have been easy.

It wasn't.

Alexander S. Ryker was not human—at least, he was not fully human. During their battle, Alex had displayed two separate powers. The first one she had easily recognized as the Aura of Creation, a power unique to Angelisians.

The Aura of Creation was said to be one of the strongest powers in the entire galaxy. It was not just the power to create an aura. It was the power to use their aura for whatever purpose they desire, whether it was controlling different elements, or channeling the powers of the cosmos themselves.

King Lucifer was said to have the most powerful Aura of Creation in the last six thousand years. He was the one who had stopped the numerous wars spreading across the galaxy. The King of Angelisia had waged what amounted to a one-man war on the entire galaxy, beat it into submission, and told them that from now on, he was in charge. He had then proceeded to blow up an entire uninhabited solar system just to get his point across.

Al-lāt had not been born at the time, but she had seen the recording of King Lucifer addressing the galaxy. The power he had displayed still frightened her.

Alexander S. Ryker did not have King Lucifer's overwhelming power. His ability to use his Aura of Creation was limited. He had only been able to create simple things with his Aura, weapons and the like. It seemed that the more esoteric and powerful arts, such as controlling the cosmos and bending the elements to his whim, was something that he was not versed in.

That had mattered little.

Alexander had a second power, one that Al-lāt had no knowledge of. Even now she remembered that strange power, the red energy that had gushed from his body, the spine-tingling terror that his change had invoked in her. She had nearly lost her life that day. Were it not for Princess Gabrielle's intervention, she would have died.

After the battle had ended, she had been given the chance to speak with Alexander, and she had informed him of their plight. He had asked and she'd had no reason to refuse. Alexander had listened. When she'd finished explaining everything, he made a decision that surprised her.

He agreed to help.

He told her that he would become Emperor of the Galaxy and find a method of gathering water for her, that he would save her people. In return, he asked that she never try to kidnap Gabrielle again.

Al-lāt had agreed.

What else could she do?

"You seem to be in deep thought, Sis," the voice of her youngest brother reached her. She saw his visage appear in the reflection of the window.

Manāf was technically only her half-brother, but she had known him since he was born, and the bond they shared was definitely that of siblings. She had watched over him for years. In return, Manāf had supported and protected her from everything that sought her harm. It was thanks in part to his efforts that she was still alive today.

"I was thinking about how long it might take for Alexander to come through on his promise to aid us," Al-lāt admitted. "I wish to place my trust in him, but it is difficult. Even if he does come through for us, how long will that take? Will our people even still be alive by then?"

"Well, that is certainly a deep issue." Manāf walked up until he was right behind her. His chitinous face, with its mandibles and large eyes, were perfectly visible in the window. "I can see how that would cause you stress. Considering our situation, there's no telling how much longer our people will last in these conditions."

The death toll of her people was climbing every day. It had already gone up from ten deaths per month to about twenty. Her people were by no means populous, so every death hurt them. The last population count had put her people at a total of 104,548, but that number was steadily declining.

Al-lāt had done what she could to mitigate this crisis, from creating a new form of moisture vaporator to imposing a planet-wide water limit. Even she followed this limit.

Jāhilīyahns could survive without water for a long time. It was part of their biology. They stored water inside of their bodies and used it sparingly, allowing them to go for months without needing to rehydrate. Theoretically, it should have been enough to keep her people from dying long enough to find another source of water.

It was no use. Even with the limits imposed, too much time had been spent and they had yet to discover a source of water. Her people continued to drop.

What made the situation even more disheartening was that some of her people had resorted to crime, stealing and even killing to get their hands on the water that should have gone to their fellow Jāhilīyahn. The situation was rapidly degrading day after day. Not even Ibn Al-Kalbi's elite unit, which she had placed in charge of protecting her people, could stop this from happening.

"Al!!" A voice came echoing from down the corridor. She turned around. It was her eldest brother running toward her as fast as his triple-jointed legs could carry him, his scythe-shaped arms swinging back and forth.

"Ibn Al-Kalbi," she began, frowning, "is something the matter?"

"It's… airship…" Ibn Al-Kalbi gasped. "There's an… an airship from Camelot! They said they wanted to meet with you!"

Al-lāt frowned at this knowledge. Camelot was a solar system several parsecs away. It wasn't the closest solar system to her planet, but it wasn't the furthest either. Even so, it took about three weeks to travel from here to there. She had heard that Camelot was home to several beautiful planets, including a planet with the same name as its solar system and one planet made entirely of water. She would have liked to visit that planet.

"Do you know what they are here for?" she asked.

Ibn Al-Kalbi shook his head. "They only said that they wanted to speak with you."

"Have them land in the Crystal Palace's tenth docking bay," she instructed. "I shall greet them."

"Right!"

Ibn Al-Kalbi turned around and took off running back the way he had come, presumably to give the orders to let the Camelot ship in. Al-lāt ordered Manāf to gather her honor guard before heading to meet with the dignitaries of Camelot.

Docking bays in the Crystal Palace were merely large spaces that had been carved out of the crystal. They offered little in the way of an actual docking bay. There were no docking clamps, and each bay only came equipped with one fuel line. While fuel was not as scarce as water, it was still considered a precious commodity and was not to be squandered.

Al-lāt's bodyguards arrived before the ship carrying the Camelot dignitary came in. She did not recognize the ship's class, though it reminded her of an ancient bird of prey. It was sleek and smooth. The shuttle passed through the ray shield, which kept the desert storm at bay, and slowly set down on the ground. Blinking lights along the ship caught her attention. A couple of vents opened on the ship's aft and ventral sides, blowing out sand that must have been trapped in the ventilation. Before long, the boarding ramp lowered and several people stepped out.

They must have been guards. All of them were humanoids wearing streamlined silver armor over black unitards. Each one carried a sleek blaster rifle. She couldn't see their faces, which were covered by helmets, but these people were of secondary importance.

The woman walking toward them was the one who garnered her attention.

She walked toward them with a stance that radiated authority, commanding yet also beautiful, despite her human appearance. She had dark hair that trailed down her back in gentle curls, and eyes like obsidian. Olive-colored skin was partially hidden by a sleeveless white gown that fluttered as she walked. Her ears were slightly pointed, telling Al-lāt that this girl was not human. She did not recognize the species, though Camelot was said to be home to several different kinds of people.

To Jāhilīyahns, humanoid species were ugly. However, to the rest of the galaxy, humanoids were considered the most attractive of all species.

Al-lāt was half-human. No matter how hard she tried to deny it, she could never be rid of her human side, the side telling her even now that the woman before her was beautiful.

"You must be Al-lāt." The woman smiled upon greeting her. "I am Nimue, crown princess of Camelot. I am here on behalf of my husband, Prince Arthur, who has asked me to come here at the behest of Alexander S. Ryker."

A jolt traveled through Al-lāt's spine, causing her to straighten. Her multi-jointed fingers twitched sporadically, though she hid them beneath the voluminous sleeves of her robes. A good politician never let others know when they were flustered or surprised. It gave the other person an advantage during their negotiations.

"You know Alexander Ryker?"

Nimue's smile widened. "Indeed I do. He just recently helped stop a civil war from destroying our solar system, but let us speak of other matters. After all..." The woman's eyes gleamed. "I am here to talk business."

"I understand." Al-lāt hid her nervousness behind what she hoped was an affable smile. Given that she was a mixed breed, her smile probably looked more frightening than friendly. "Please follow me to my office. We can speak in private there."

"Thank you."

Since this was a diplomatic affair, Al-lāt led Nimue to her office, where she did all of her work. Everything was made from crystal. It had all been carved straight from the palace, so everything in this room was technically part of the room and not just additions. The bookshelves, the desk, the floor, the chandelier. Everything. Al-lāt walked over to her desk and sat down on her crystal chair. It wasn't the most comfortable chair, but it had been carved from the crystal, so she made do.

"Please, sit." Al-lāt gestured to the chair in front of the desk.

"Thank you." Nimue sat down, showing no signs of discomfort at sitting on a hard crystal chair. "This palace is quite marvelous. I've never seen a structure made entirely of crystal."

"This palace was naturally formed," Al-lāt informed Nimue. "Our people carved the palace out of the crystal, but it has always been here."

"Are these crystals rare?" asked Nimue.

"No." Shaking her head, Al-lāt explained more about these crystals to Nimue. "There are hundreds of crystal formations located throughout the planet. There are even more underground. The one I live in just happens to be the largest."

"Is that so…" Nimue murmured, shook her head, and then placed her hands on her lap and smiled. "I've come to speak with you because I've heard from Alexander that your planet is currently suffering a drought thanks to this sandstorm."

"Yes, that is correct." Al-lāt did her best not to show her surprise or confusion. "May I ask what it is you're here for exactly?"

"Of course. Before he left, Alexander requested that Prince Arthur aid you with your problem."

Al-lāt could not stop her eyes from widening. "Then…?"

"I have with me two plans to help your planet." Nimue swiped her finger through the air. A tear in space appeared. It looked like a small, black line that was warping the area around it. She reached in, pulling out a holographic projector. "The first plan is to supply your planet with enough water to keep your people from dying of dehydration. However, that's only a short-term solution. The long-term solution is one that Alexander came up with and asked us to help execute."

She placed the holographic projector on the desk. It was small and flat, a universal projector that most people across the galaxy used. After pressing a button on the side, Nimue sat back and allowed the holographic project to display its contents.

"This is…?"

"It's a terraformer," Nimue said.

The holographic image on display was of a device with six legs akin to a spider's, a cylindrical body that had several strange valves protruding from its surface, and an exhaust of some kind on top that was projecting light. That was what it looked like at first. As she watched, particles of something were sucked into the top and projected out the bottom as something else, a type of liquid or gas, it looked like. Her lips twitched involuntarily into a frown as the substance fell onto the ground and plants began to grow.

"Alexander made this blueprint and gave it along with a prototype of the terraformer to Prince Arthur," Nimue continued, though Al-lāt was only partially listening. "This terraformer takes nutrients and moisture from sand and wind energy, transforming them into a type of fertilizer that helps promote plant growth. I don't know exactly how it works. Alexander tried to explain it, but a lot of the explanation went over my head. According to him, this terraformer was designed specifically to work on a desert planet."

"Then... with this, my people can be saved?" asked Al-lāt, scarcely able to believe what she was hearing. She continued to stare at the terraformer in the holographic display. It kept repeating the same movements over and over, showing that this was just a looped projection. Even so, as she watched the machine commit to the same actions over and over, hope began to blossom in her chest.

Nimue nodded. "Yes. Not only that, but Alexander has given us a deal. If we help you terraform your planet, we get the rights to market and sell this product to other planets, so it won't cost you anything."

Al-lāt thought she might cry, she was so happy. Alexander really had kept his promise. Her people were saved!

"However, this is a long-term solution," Nimue added. Al-lāt looked back at her. "It won't solve the problems caused by your drought right away. It's going to take years, which is why Prince Arthur proposed that we send shipments of water, enough to last until the terraforming project is successful."

"I-I understand." Al-lāt tried to take several deep breaths to calm down. Her heart was pounding in her ribcage. "Thank you for the—"

"Hold on." Nimue held up a hand to stop Al-lāt from speaking. "Before you thank me, you should know that the plan to supply you with water is not going to be free. Alexander made us a deal to help you terraform this planet, but that doesn't include supplying you with water, which will be a costly endeavor."

Al-lāt did not allow herself to feel anger at these words; she understood. This was not Alexander, who did things out of the goodness of his heart, from a desire to chase some impossible dream of becoming a hero. This was the crown princess of Camelot, the future queen of a solar system. She didn't have Alexander's altruism. Everything she did was in service to the betterment of her people.

Just like Al-lāt herself.

Centering herself, Al-lāt took slow, deep, even breaths. They were about to enter negotiations now. Since her planet was not that important, and they did not have many resources, she had never done negotiations with another planet—certainly not one as powerful as Camelot. The thought of doing so now caused her chest to flutter and constrict at the same time.

"My planet does not have much to offer, as I am sure you know," Al-lāt said. "Is there any way we can broker a deal?"

"Of course there is." Nimue smiled, and it appeared both kind and dangerous. Al-lāt suppressed a shiver. "Do you mind if I ask you about those crystal formations you told me about earlier?"

CHAPTER 1

A TROUBLESOME RETURN HOME

It took seven days to reach Mars. According to Gabrielle, that wasn't long as far as space travel went. Even hyperspace had its limits, Alex had learned, and most of those limits involved being able to travel faster than light at a limited speed.

Of course, speed was not determined by distance. One could reach a certain quadrant of the galaxy faster despite the distance being shorter. Ultimately, the amount of time traveling through hyperspace took depended on the routes being used, the abilities of the hyperspace drive, and the talents of the navigator.

The one piloting the vessel they were on was Claudia, who, while not the greatest navigator around, could at least pilot a ship. She used already mapped out navigation routes, so she didn't actually have to do anything. Her job mainly involved taking them into and out of hyperspace every time they jumped to a new place.

It was a relatively easy task. Gabrielle knew how to do it, and she was able to teach Alex how to jump in and out of hyperspace.

While Alex had been told by Claudia that time spent in transit would be boring, he found that time to be very fruitful. Alex learned a lot about space travel, about the vessel itself, and he spent what time he had not learning with Gabrielle and Nyx, two people whose importance to him was becoming irreplaceable. It also gave him time to think.

Alex had a lot to think about.

His current thoughts were centered around his love life, and more specifically, just what he should do about it. There were no doubts that he loved Gabrielle. That had become obvious to him, and Alex planned on rectifying the situation with her. When they got home, he would take her on a date.

However, even though Alex had committed himself to Gabrielle, she wasn't the only girl in his life, nor was she the only one who was important to him. Jasmine. Kazekiri. Nyx. Selene. He didn't include Alice in this list, but that was only because she was family. Those four were important to him. While Selene might have shot him down, Alex was at least positive that Jasmine and Nyx liked him. Nyx had even confessed as much while they were on Camelot.

Actually, he still needed to talk to Nyx about that, didn't he?

For the past several years, ever since he had rescued her from some kidnappers, Jasmine had been visiting him, talking to him, and making obviously possessive remarks in regards to him. He had ignored it for all this time, playing the ignorance card. He'd been worried about what he might do to her. With how powerful his lust was, he had worried about hurting her by taking things too far. After what happened with Gabrielle, however, he couldn't really ignore it anymore.

I'll talk to Jasmine when I get home as well.

"You seem to be taking this matter so seriously."

Alex twitched as a seductive female voice echoed from within the depths of his mind.

What do you want, Asmodeus?

"Nothing much. Hehe, I was just going to give you some useful advice."

"I recommend not taking any advice she has to offer, Alexander," said a voice that sounded like him but was far more innocent.

"I was only going to suggest that he should accept her feelings."

That would be polygamy, which is illegal.

"Actually, that would probably solve all of your problems."

"Right?"

Oh! So now you're agreeing with her?! Whatever happened to not taking her advice?!

Before either Asmodeus or the other voice—Sachiel, he believed was that one's name—could say another word, a voice called out.

"Alex! There you are!"

The door to his shared bedroom with Gabrielle and Nyx opened, and Gabrielle walked in. Her silver wings, which protruded from her lower back, flapped several times, the light from overhead lamps reflecting off each glittering feather. They did that every so often. Flapped, that is. Likewise, her long and pointed ears caused her silver hair to part as they wiggled. She wore a crisis suit underneath her regular clothes, though it wasn't visible to the naked eye as anything more than a slight glossy sheen. Her skirt swished around her thighs as she walked up to him, and the pink T-shirt wrinkled as it stretched across her large bust.

"Gabby." Alex smiled as Gabrielle sat next to him. "Something up?"

Shaking her head, Gabrielle grinned at him. "No, I just wanted to be with you."

"That so?"

"Hm!"

Sitting there on the bed with the girl he'd agreed to marry, Alex wondered if now was a good time to discuss Jasmine and Nyx. This wasn't a decision he could make on his own. He was going to marry Gabrielle, he had decided, which meant that every decision he made now affected her. She had as much right to voice her opinion on this matter as he did.

"Say, Gabby..." he began, and then paused. Delicately. He needed to put this issue to her delicately. Swallowing the lump in his throat, Alex tried to center himself. "What do you think about the idea of me having more than one wife?"

Gabrielle stared at him, blinking several times as her head tilted left and right. It only lasted for a second. Her eyes soon lit up as she leaned forward, so close that their noses were touching.

"You're talking about Jasmine and Nyx, aren't you? You are, right?!"

Alex did his best not to lean back. "Erm… uh… yes."

"I knew it!" Gabrielle squealed, and Alex had to cover his ears, lest he go deaf. He hadn't realized she could make such a loud sound. His ears were ringing! Gabrielle was heedless of this as she continued. "This is so great! If you marry Jasmine and Nyx, that would make them my sisters!"

Rubbing his ears as if that would stop the ringing, Alex gave Gabrielle an uncertain look. "You're really okay with that? I mean, you know what that entails, right?"

"Of course I do!" Gabrielle said, still on her high. Even her ears and wings were flapping with excitement now. "It means all of us can be together forever!"

"Erm… well, that is true, but that's not…"

"This is so exciting!" Gabrielle continued, heedless of the fact that Alex was trying to speak to her. "I'm going to tell Nyx the news right now!"

"What? Wait! Don't do that! Gabby!"

But it was too late. Even as Alex stretched out a hand and told her to wait, Gabrielle was already rushing out of the room. He stared at the door as it closed behind her. Several seconds passed with him just standing there, his hand still outstretched as though grasping at nothing. Slowly, he lowered his hand and sighed.

He really wished she would listen to him.

Since Gabrielle was no doubt running off to find Nyx—it probably wouldn't be hard, considering how small this vessel was

—Alex decided to speak with Claudia. Part of him wanted to find Gabrielle and stop her. However, maybe this was for the best. He was already having a hard enough time dealing with this particular issue. Besides, Claudia was one of King Uther's eleven wives, which meant she had experience with polygamy. He wanted her advice on how this whole matter worked.

Claudia was in the cockpit, sitting in the pilot's chair. Her blonde hair, normally long enough to trail down to her butt, was tied into a tight bun, allowing her elegant neck and slender shoulders to show. She wore a black pilot's suit. It was basically a skintight bodysuit that conformed to a person's contours like a second skin. Since Claudia was quite voluptuous, Alex could see pretty much everything.

The cockpit was very much in keeping with standard shuttles. The pilot and co-pilot seats were up front. Meanwhile, the communications station was located on the left, behind the co-pilot's seat. The right simply contained a vast array of panels that covered the ship's mainframe. Gabrielle had informed him that this was where the technology for inputting hyperspace coordinates and flying the shuttle was. The panels could be easily removed in the event that repairs were needed.

"Claudia?" Alex asked.

"Oh! Alex!" Claudia turned her head, grinned at him, and patted the co-pilot's seat. "We're just about to pull out of hyperspace, so pop a squat!"

Alex did as he was told. It wasn't like he had anything better to do. The co-pilot's seat was pretty soft, and the crash webbing was a lot better than what the humans of his solar system had.

"Dial up the inertial dampener for me, will ya?" requested Claudia.

"How high?"

"Mm… eighty-five."

Alex placed his hands on the console and manipulated the inertial dampener, which was used to dampen the inertia that came from high-speed maneuvering. It was the inertial dampener that also allowed them to move at faster than light travel without turning into bloodstains on the wall. The inertial dampener could be raised or lowered to suit the passengers' and pilots' needs.

"Ah! That's much better." Claudia grinned as she placed a hand on the hyperdrive lever and began counting down. "We'll be leaving hyperspace in five. Four. Three. Two. One."

Exiting and entering hyperspace was one of the most amazing sights Alex had ever witnessed. Hyperspace looked a lot like they were traveling through a tunnel of light. When they reverted back to real space, the streaks of light surrounding them on all sides distorted, slowed, and then reverted back into small pinpoints of light. Seeing that happen always took his breath away.

"We'll be making one more jump through hyperspace," Claudia said. "Then we'll arrive at Mars."

"Right."

Alex leaned back as Claudia tapped away on the pilot console. She was adding in a pre-recorded route that would let them safely jump through hyperspace, though she could also input her own coordinates if she wanted.

Hyperspace travel was exceedingly dangerous. Inputting the wrong coordinates could result in your ship flying through a star, or crashing into a planet. Hyperspace took ships into a space that was "out of phase" with the rest of the universe. However, that did not mean they weren't still in the universe. They were, and as such, if they collided with a star or planet while in hyperspace, their shuttle, along with them, would suffer a terrible fate.

Fortunately, if they died that way, at least it would be so fast that they wouldn't even notice.

It wasn't much of a consolation.

"Say, Claudia, you mind if I ask a question?"

"You just did."

"Hahaha, mind if I ask two more?"

"Shoot."

"Do you… like being a part of King Uther's harem?"

Claudia didn't answer at first. She had finished adding the pre-existing coordinates, but she hadn't gone into hyperspace yet. Alex wondered if he had said the wrong thing. However, a moment later, Claudia pushed on the lever, and the pinpricks of light that were billions of stars suddenly became incandescent streaks that surrounded them on all sides like a tunnel.

The pilot's chair squeaked as Claudia leaned back and crossed her arms. She looked at him with calculating eyes, studying him as she tapped her right index finger against her left forearm. Alex wanted to look away. In fact, he almost did. The only reason he bore through her silent staring was because he wanted an answer to his question.

"I feel like this has less to do with me being part of Uther's harem and more about your own relationship problems," Claudia said at last. Considering this woman had been cracking jokes for the last week, it was pretty insightful.

"Well… yes…"

Claudia tapped a finger to her lips, seemingly in thought. No sounds entered the cockpit save for those of the many consoles' soft beeping and the gentle thrum of the hyperdrive. Alex wanted to say something, wanted to break the silence, but he feared that doing so might cause the world around him to break.

Lights from outside the viewport and the blinking consoles cast shadows on Claudia's face. It made her seem older somehow. The shadows gave her face a deeper appearance, as though it was revealing that she wasn't as young as she appeared. That made him wonder… just how old was this woman?

"I get the feeling that I'm not going to be the best person for you to talk to, but I've never had any problems with being a part of Uther's harem," Claudia said at last. "I love my sister wives… even Iggy, despite how she kidnapped Arty and used me. All of them are important to me, and all of us have a great time. In fact, thanks to them, I'm not bored whenever Uther goes off on his quests."

"You mean like he's doing right now with the mission he received from King Lucifer?"

Two years ago, or thereabouts, King Lucifer had requested that King Uther go on a mission. No one knew what that mission was.

Alex only had the barest details. Apparently, the King of Camelot and Gadreel, King Lucifer's first wife, had gone off together on a task assigned to them by King Lucifer. They had not been seen or heard from since.

"Just like that!" Claudia looked at the stars as they streaked by the viewport. "The eleven of us always like to go out and do our own thing. Our children don't think we keep an eye on them and just let them roam free, but the truth is that we really like spying on them and taking bets to see who will screw up first." Claudia paused and tilted her head. "Now that I'm thinking about it, Bedi technically screwed up first since he lost his planet to Lanci... Izzy owes me one thousand gauld."

Alex could feel the sweat trickling down his scalp. That did not sound like the kind of thing a mother should say. Then again, he didn't even know his mother, so it wasn't like he had room to talk.

"Does that help you at all?" asked Claudia.

Shaking himself from his stupor, Alex looked at Claudia and smiled. "Yeah, it does actually. Thank you."

"You're welcome. So, what was your second question?"

"I already asked it."

"Huh?"

Claudia looked at Alex with a questioning gaze, which he returned with a mild-mannered smile. She stared at him, brows furrowing, eyes squinting, as though trying to figure out his angle. Finally, after nearly thirty seconds of silence, the blonde woman's eyes widened with realization.

Her laughter soon echoed through the cockpit.

1

From bow to stern, the ship that Alex, Claudia, Gabrielle, and Nyx were on was, give or take, one hundred meters. It was about a third of that in width.

The ship only had four rooms. The engine room was the largest, and the engine was what made up most of the ship. Of course, he called it an engine, but it looked nothing like the engines he was used to. After the engine room was the two living quarters. The master room was where he, Gabrielle, and Nyx slept. Claudia had given it to them since there were three of them and one of her. She slept in the guest quarters. The next largest room was the cockpit, and the smallest room was the shower.

Alex was currently in the shower, though even that term was inaccurate. It wasn't a shower so much as a sonic cleaner and a tub. The room, which consisted of a changing room and a shower room separated by a thin, sliding door, was less than ten meters in length and five in width. There was no showerhead. The sonic cleaner was a room that hit you with ultraviolet rays that killed harmful,odorous bacteria. Technically, the tub wasn't needed, but like most humanoid species, Arthurians were fond of baths.

It was good that so many species had at least that one thing in common.

Alex didn't take a bath after cleaning himself off. He wasn't feeling up to it. After letting his crisis suit crawl back up his body and synchronize with his nerves—a still painful process—Alex wandered back into the master's quarters.

Gabrielle and Nyx were already there, and the moment he entered the room, their eyes turned to him.

He paused. The silence that entered the room wasn't awkward; there was no tension, no anxiety coming from either Gabrielle or Nyx, but he still felt a bit weirded out by their stares. Why were they staring at him so intently? He didn't know. Not knowing was what made him so nervous.

It was fortunate that Gabrielle was so good at breaking the ice.

"Alex!" She beamed at him. "I was just telling Nyx that you agreed to marry her, too!"

... Or not.

"Ah ha ha ha! I might actually like this bitch despite her being angelisian trash!"

"Hmph. Gabrielle is a pure-hearted young woman... unlike you."

"And yet she can say things like—"

Alex slammed on his mental shields hard, then took several deep breaths to calm himself down. This wasn't unexpected. He had already guessed that Gabrielle had been telling Nyx about their "conversation" while he'd been talking to Claudia. Dang it. This was not how he wanted to bring this particular topic up. He felt like slamming his head against the wall. However, that would have been immature, and he had already promised himself that he would confront this issue head on. He wouldn't run anymore.

"I wish you would have waited for me."

That didn't mean he wouldn't complain.

"Tee-hee!" was Gabrielle's response.

With a sigh that belonged to someone twice his age, Alex wandered into the room and sat down on the chair opposite the couch that Gabrielle and Nyx had taken up. While his fiancé—he still wasn't used to calling her that—pouted at him, Nyx revealed none of what she was thinking. The girl just stared at him impassively with her crimson gaze, framed by dark hair and set on a beautiful, porcelain face. While Alex still considered Gabrielly to be the epitome of beauty, Nyx's perfectly symmetrical features and doll-like appearance were nothing to scoff at.

"So... um..." Alex felt like he was grasping at a shock baton as he tried to think of something to say. "Er... Nyx... what do you... think of all this? I mean... like... relationship stuff."

The beautiful assassin shifted ever so slightly. The folds of her thigh-high skirt wrinkled around her legs, the black leather making a creaking noise as she lightly clutched it between her fingers. Alex couldn't stop himself from staring at her pale legs for a second longer than was probably appropriate. While Nyx's face remained impassive, her cheeks did turn a little pink.

"I do not know much about relationships," she confessed. "Being an assassin, I have never spent any significant amount of time with a single person... until you came along." The color on her cheeks darkened just a bit, but her face still remained the same as she stared at him. "You took me in despite not knowing a single thing about me, gave me a place to call home despite how I tried to kill you, and helped me understand what it means to feel like you belong somewhere. That's why I have decided that I belong with you."

For a girl who didn't talk often, when she had something to say, Nyx sure said a lot.

Alex figured this was Nyx's way of saying she consented to this, but he still wanted to be sure. This entire situation was already uncomfortable for him. The idea of being in a polygamous relationship rubbed his human sensibilities the wrong way. He understood, logically, that it was because of how he was raised. The solar system he lived in was monogamous. Polygamy was not legal, so the idea of marrying more than one wife made him uncomfortable. At the same time... at the same time...

If this will make them happy, why shouldn't I do it?

More than anything else, Alex wanted to make the people in his life happy. He wanted to make them smile every day, wanted them to feel safe and loved and secure, wanted to give them a place they could belong—a home. If marrying Gabrielle and Nyx—and potentially Jasmine, Selene, and Kazekiri—would make them happy, then he would at least present that option to them.

And some small part of him, a part that he still refused to acknowledge, admitted that the idea was appealing.

He continued to stare at Nyx. She stared back. Nyx had a way of making him feel like he was being pierced with daggers. Her impassive gaze was enough to make most people look away in discomfort, though he'd grown fairly used to the feeling of being penetrated by her eyes.

"Are you sure you're okay with this?" Alex asked. Nyx continued to stare. Alex finally became uncomfortable. "What I mean is... Nyx, will you, er, marry me?"

Even though he knew it was merely his perceptions, time seemed as though it had come to a standstill. Alex couldn't believe he was doing this. He couldn't believe he was asking someone besides Gabrielle to marry him—heck! He couldn't believe he was doing this in front of Gabrielle!

However, for as nervous as he was, Gabrielle seemed perfectly content. She sat there, a big smile plastered on her face, eyes shining with anticipation. He envied her for that. Just a little. Alex was holding his breath over here! A cold sweat had broken on his skin as his left leg bounced with nervous energy. If he hadn't been so busy gripping his pants, he would have been biting his nails!

He waited with bated breath.

And then...

"Yes," Nyx said simply.

Alex must have been leaning forward without realizing it because her word, so simple and straightforward, made him fall off the chair and smack face first into the ground. On the other hand, Gabrielle leapt from her seat and pumped a fist into the air.

"Yes!" she shouted as her wings flapped excitedly. "I have a new sister! I'm so excited!"

Alex sat up and tenderly touched his nose, hissing when pain stung him. It felt like the skin of his nose had been rubbed raw. Damn. His nose was probably going to be red for quite some time.

While he was on the ground, Gabrielle had pulled Nyx to her feet and hugged the girl for all she was worth. To her credit, Nyx didn't judo toss the alien princess like she used to do to him when he touched her, but neither did she return the hug. Alex found out why moments later.

"Princess... I... can't breath... you're... breaking... my spine...!"

Alex wondered if he should get between them. It looked like Gabrielle really was about to break Nyx's spine with her hug. Was that ominous cracking noise coming from the girl's back? Yes. It was. Okay. He really did need to put a stop to this.

"Okay, okay. That's enough hugging, Gabby." Alex stood up and pried the two apart—tried to pry the two apart. Gabrielle was stuck to the poor assassin like they were bonded at the molecular level. As the cracking in Nyx's spine became louder, he began to seriously worry about her health. "G-Gabby! That's quite enough hugging!"

"Huh?" Gabrielle looked at him, still hugging Nyx, who appeared ready to start frothing at the mouth. "Why? I love Nyx and want to hug her more!"

"Because you're killing her!"

"What are you talking about? I'm not—"

CRUNCH!!!

A loud sound echoed around the room, coming from Nyx, or more precisely, her spine. Alex and Gabrielle looked down at Nyx as her eyes rolled into the back of her head and her body went limper than soggy udon after it had been left to sit in boiling water for a day. The assassin's arms and legs dangled as her head lolled back and her spine arched in Gabrielle's grip.

"N-N-Nyx! Are you okay?! Talk me, Nyx!"

"Stop shaking her, Gabby! That's not going to help! You're only making the situation worse!"

"No, Nyx! Don't die on me now! We still have to get married to Alex together!!"

"Stop talking about marriage and help Nyx! There's some strange white stuff coming out of her mouth!"

"IS THAT HER SPIRIT?!"

"Don't say something so unscientific! You and I both know spirits don't exist! Just hurry up and help me put this stuff back into her!!"

"STAY WITH ME, NYX! STAY WITH ME!"

"DON'T PANIC, GABBY! YOU'RE GONNA MAKE ME PANIC TOO!"

After much struggling and panicking, Alex and Nyx did eventually manage to put the strange ethereal white stuff back into their friend. Nyx recovered soon after. Seconds after she recovered, Alex and Gabrielle found themselves sitting on the floor, a lump protruding from their heads where Nyx had hit them. The glare on her face was enough to leave them speechless, though whether because it was her first time glaring or because it was so scary, Alex didn't know.

"Please listen to me next time, Princess Gabrielly," Nyx said. "That really hurt."

Gabrielle lowered her head, and even her wings and ears drooped. "I'm sorry."

Nyx sighed. It was the first time Alex had heard her do that.

"It is... fine. Let's just go to bed."

"Okay!"

Her mood sure improved quickly. I guess not even nearly killing someone can keep Gabrielle down for long.

With that dry thought in mind, Alex also got ready for bed. They should be arriving on Mars tomorrow. He wanted to be refreshed when he greeted Alice, Jasmine, Kazekiri, and Selene.

2

It took one more day than expected to arrive at Mars, owing mostly to an uncharted comet that had forced them out of hyperspace. Alex had not done much during that time except think. It wasn't like he could do anything else. He and Gabrielle were banned from inventing while in the ship, and he couldn't spar with Nyx since there wasn't enough space.

During this time where he did nothing but think, Alex had decided that if everyone else agreed with it, he would go with the idea of taking on multiple wives. Of course, this was only if he wasn't mistaken in thinking that Jasmine and Kazekiri liked him. He hadn't talked with either yet. However, thanks to Gabrielle's intervention with Nyx, he could no longer just afford to sit still. He was already committed to this.

"All right," Claudia said as she maneuveredmaneuvered the shuttle, orienting herself toward Mars City. "I've never docked in a domed city before. Eh he. What a quaint way to live"

"Thank you for calling my home quaint," Alex muttered.

"Don't worry. I didn't mean that in a bad way."

"And what way did you mean it?"

"Oh, look! Someone's coming to greet us!"

"Don't change the subject!"

Everyone was in the cockpit. Alex was sitting in the co-pilot's seat. Gabrielle was at the communications array, while Nyx stood back and watched. She probably would have been better as the co-pilot, but when Alex had offered her the seat, the assassin had shook her head and said it would be good for him to experience handling this shuttle. Apparently, this craft's design was fairly standard, so if he could fly this, then he could fly most shuttles.

Outside of their viewport, another ship was coming up alongside them. Alex recognized the boxy shuttle. It was one of the Galactic Police Force's security shuttles. They must have sensed a new ship entering planetary orbit and come to investigate.

It's probably startling to have a ship suddenly appear like this. We don't have hyperspace capabilities.

"They're hailing us," Gabrielle announced.

"Put them on," Claudia said.

Gabrielle tapped on the screen for the communication system. Seconds later, a voice emerged from a set of speakers.

"Unidentified transport, state your name and business."

Claudia pressed a button on her pilot's console and began speaking, "This is Claudia Pendragon from the solar system Camelot. I'm just coming to drop off Alexander S. Ryker."

There was a long pause. In fact, it was so long that Alex wondered if something had happened on the other end. However, after what must have been at least five minutes of absolute silence, the voice came back.

"Roger that. You have received permission to enter. Please follow us and do not deviate from our course."

"Will do."

Claudia took her finger from the communication button, while Gabrielle shut off the outside communication channel. Leaning back, the woman in black leather grabbed the controls and eased them forward.

They followed the shuttle as it descended through Mars' atmosphere. Mars didn't have much in the way of ozone, so the atmosphere was very thin. Claudia didn't even need to release the ablative gels that kept the shuttle cool during atmospheric reentry.

The shuttle they were following hailed them again. Gabrielle put them back on.

"We have informed Commander Karen of your arrival. She has informed us that she is too busy to currently meet you, but that someone will be present to greet you once you've docked."

"Thank you for letting us know," Claudia said before the communication ended again.

After passing through the light wave barrier, they were directed toward one of the many docking bays at Mars City Spaceport. Claudia eased the shuttle into the hanger, which was a good deal smaller than the ones the Arthurians used. Because her shuttle relied on gravity repulsors instead of thrusters, she was able to easily spin the ship around once it entered the docking bay.

Alex helped her shut the engines off and begin the cooling process. Thanks to Claudia and Gabrielle, he had a clear idea of how to handle the ship. Once all of their systems had been turned off, they exited the cockpit and opened the boarding ramp located on the left aft section of the ship.

Alex disembarked with everyone else. As they emerged from the lowered boarding ramp and onto the docking bay, the doors on the far side opened, and Azazel rushed out with Kane and Abel behind him.

Azazel was tall, easily standing at around 244 centimeters, if not taller. His shining silver and segmented breastplate clattered against his thick shoulder pauldrons as he ran. The grieves that he wore went up to his knees, creating a loud clang as they banged against the durasteel floor. Hair the color of dirty snow bounced up and down, and his dark purple eyes shone with an almost disturbing joy. Two massive, white wings jutted from his back, currently retracted so they didn't bump into anything, but Alex could see them quivering with what he hoped was merely excitement. Likewise, his long and pointed ears wiggled as though they had a life of their own.

He skidded to a halt in front of them. Kane and Abel, the two bodyguards dressed in black suits, stopped behind him.

"Princess Gabrielle! Groom-to-Be!... Nyx." Once again, his greeting of Nyx was much colder.

"Stop that," Alex said.

"P-pardon?" Azazel suddenly stared at him in befuddlement.

"Stop glaring at Nyx." Alex narrowed his eyes. "I don't know what she did to earn your dislike, but she doesn't deserve it, so stop."

"Erm, but... Groom-to-Be, she tried to kill you."

It was a fair point. Nyx had tried to kill him. Her entire reason for coming to Mars had been because someone had hired her to assassinate him. She had also nearly succeeded. However, through a combination of luck, him not being a tyrant like her employer said he was, and the fact that he had saved her life, Nyx had ended up living with him instead.

"It doesn't matter," Alex said. "Nyx isn't after my life anymore. What's more, she's very precious to me. Any insult to her will be like an insult to me."

"And me," Gabrielle added. "Nyx is my friend now. I won't let you be mean to her."

Azazel stared at the two of them like they had just said something that he couldn't comprehend, but Alex didn't think this required any special way of thinking. Azazel was a soldier. He should understand that sometimes people did things, not because they wanted to, but because they were ordered to.

It was the same with Nyx. She hadn't tried to kill him out of malice. She'd done it because she was hired to. Alex didn't blame her for that, and while Gabrielle had for a while, she had eventually forgiven and accepted Nyx. It probably helped that Nyx was the reason they were still alive. King MacArt would have killed them if not for her.

I have heard that old saying about how facing adversity together causes bonds of friendship to form. I guess there is some truth to it.

Azazle sniffled once as tears began leaking from his eyes. His shoulders shook. The pauldrons clicked against his breastplate so rapidly that the noise reminded Alex of the sound an old-fashioned motor made when running. He looked ten seconds away from crying.

"I see how this is," he said. "You two... like Nyx more than me..."

Alex wanted to say that Azael didn't know what he was talking about. He wanted to say that, but he couldn't. It was kinda true. Alex liked Azazel well enough. However, he did not consider himself to be as close to the angelisian general as he was Nyx.

"It's not that we like her more than you," Gabrielle soothed. "It's just that Nyx is going to become my sister when she marries Alex."

Azazel stopped crying. He looked at Alex with a burning intensity that almost made him take several steps back. The fire in his eyes was something that put Alex on edge, and not just because he remembered how strong this man was.

"Is this true?" asked Azazel.

"Is... what true?" Alex hedged.

The darkening of Azazel's face became even more fierce. "Are you really making Nyx one of your wives?"

"Erm... yes?"

Azazel frowned at him, and then turned his gaze on Nyx, who stood on Alex's left. To her credit, Nyx merely returned the gaze with her normally impassive eyes. She didn't seem at all bothered like Alex, who had broken out into a cold sweat.

"Are you really going to become one of the Groom-to-Be's wives?"

Alex knew he was in hot water. Sure, he, Nyx, and Gabrielle had all agreed on getting married, and he would eventually have to come out and tell everyone. This wasn't something that could be hidden. Even so, it looked like Azazel was ten seconds from trying to kill Nyx.

Nyx slowly reached out and grabbed Alex's arm, startling him. He looked down at the girl, who only came up to his chest despite being several years older than he was. Her cheeks were a slight red again. It was the only sign that she was embarrassed.

"It's true. With Princess Gabrielle's permission, I have decided to become one of Alex's wives."

"I see."

The threatening aura suddenly increased, the intensity so frightening that Alex felt his legs quiver just from being in close proximity with the angelisian.

And then, inexplicably, the aura of DEATH that hung over them vanished. Azazel's change in countenance was so sudden that it startled Alex. The cold hostility toward Nyx disappeared as a smile bloomed on the tall man's face. He straightened his back and looked at Alex, eyes glistening with unshed tears. Somehow, it looked like his chest was swelling with pride.

"I have underestimated you yet again, Groom-to-Be. Getting a woman who tried to kill you is no easy feat, but it can be done. Why, I remember when my second wife tried to kill me."

Alex sighed. "I really wish you'd stop calling me—wait." He paused. "What?"

"It was single combat," Azazel continued. "The two of us were locked in a deadly struggle, two warriors fighting for glory in the arena. Back then, the arena didn't have all of the safety features that it does now, so death was a very real possibility. I remember that one of my eyes had been gouged out, and my ribs were shattered, but I refused to give up…"

Alex was getting pretty disturbed the longer the story went on. Rather than stand around and listen as Azazel proceeded to go into excruciating detail about his fight with his second wife, Alex turned toward Claudia, who was looking around with her hands on her hips and a smile on her face.

"This docking bay looks so primitive."

Alex rolled his eyes. "Well, excuse my people for being so primitive."

"You're excused."

He rolled his eyes again.

After he, Gabrielle, and Nyx said their goodbyes to Claudia, who said that she might decide to visit them again sometime, Alex left Azazel to his talking. It looked like he was getting to the exciting part. Considering how gory it had become, Alex was sure he didn't want to know the rest of the story about how Azazel and his second wife had nearly killed each other in a duel. He was pretty much done with that conversation after learning that Azazel's arm had been ripped off and reattached.

Oh, the things one learned.

3

After leaving the Mars Spaceport, Alex, Gabrielle, and Nyx took a shuttle to the Outer District, called such because it had been built outside of Mars City and was not actually a part of the city itself.

Mars City had been built within a large crater. Formerly known as the Dollfus Crater, it spanned 363.1 kilometers. Because it was so small, the city had been built upwards instead of out, and as a result, the dome that protected the city had expanded both upwards and outwards to maintain its structural integrity.

The outer district looked nothing like Mars City, which possessed an artificial appearance save for the massive amounts of genetically modified flora. Sidewalks meandered along roads, grass covered the ground, and trees dotted a landscape of gently rolling hills. Several large canals ran through the outer district. These canals traveled through several processing plants, which used an advanced recycling and sanitation process to clean the water of impurities, and then distributed it to the residence of Mars City.

Water was Mars' most precious resource. Unlike Earth, which was made up of roughly 71% water, the only water produced on Mars came from the polar ice caps. Water mining was an important operation there, which was why Northdome and Southdome—mining cities at the north and south poles—had been created some fifty years ago.

Houses and convenient stores made up most of the buildings in the outer district. There were a few power plants as well, but they were further out, away from where people lived. This place was a residential district. While the power plants were necessary to give the outer district power, nobody wanted them destroying the scenery.

"I can't wait to see Alice, Ariel, and Michelle!" Gabrielle said as they walked home.

"I'm sure they miss their big sister," Alex added.

"I bet they missed you too!"

The three of them were walking alongside the road, on a sidewalk. Alex thought it was kind of weird that they had a road since no one drove cars, which were an invention from before the start of the new calendar, but humans had always been creatures of habit.

There weren't many people present. It was late. Most of the people who lived in the Outer District were probably at home, eating with their families.

The thought of family made Alex long to see his little sister, Alice, whom he had always adored since they became a family. Before Gabrielle entered his life, he and Alice had lived alone. Their parents were dead, so Alex had assumed the roles of brother, father, and mother. He cooked, cleaned, made sure Alice was keeping up with her studies, protected her, and tried to teach her the importance of hard work. He hoped she had been doing well while he was in Camelot.

He also hoped she had kept her grades up. There were going to be problems if she slacked off.

As they neared their home, a loud explosion rocked the area, making the ground rumble beneath their feet. Plumes of smoke billowed in the not-so-distant distance. Alex looked up, a jolt traveling from the base of his spine all the way to his brain.

He knew where that explosion had come from.

"Oh, no…"

Forgetting about Gabrielle and Nyx, Alex rushed toward his house, skidding to a stop in front of the fence, and staring at what he found with ever increasing horror.

The house was in ruins. No, it wasn't just in ruins. It had been demolished. The roof had collapsed. Parts of the roofing were visible, sticking up from behind the few walls that remained standing. It was like something had crushed the roof so that it caved inward. Many of the walls were also missing. The few that remained were full of holes. What's more, there were numerous vines and plants coiling around the now decimated structure.

"No, no, no, no, no!"

Hopping right over the fence, Alex rushed through the busted down door, leapt over several thick vines like he was playing hopscotch, and raced toward where he heard the sound of screaming.

"You bitch! You think I'm just going to let you continue to insult me like that?!"

"I didn't insult you. All I said was that having large breasts isn't everything you seem to think it is."

"You were just being condescending!"

"Ha… think whatever you want, you spoiled brat."

"Perverted slut!"

Alex ran into the living room. Like the rest of his house, the living room was in ruins. The couch was nothing but broken fragments and foam, the walls were destroyed, and pictoframes sat shattered on the floor. In the middle of this destruction, Ariel and Michelle stood several meters apart and were glaring at each other.

Ariel and Michelle were Gabrielle's younger sisters. They were the same age as Alice and Jasmine, fourteen, and despite being sisters, they looked completely different from each other. Michelle had long green hair that was currently tied into a ponytail, while Ariel had short blue hair. Both of their hair had a silvery sheen to it, a genetic trait of angelisians, their ears were pointed, and they had wings identical to Gabrielle's protruding from their hips. They were also wearing an angelisian crisis suit, which showed off their figures—or lack of a figure, as was the case with Ariel, who was, well, flat.

"W-what the hell happened here?!" he shouted.

Ariel and Michelle, who were about ten seconds away from renewing their fight, suddenly froze in their tracks. Their heads slowly craned in his direction. From the paling of their faces, Alex could guess that they had not expected him to return home.

"A-Alex?!" Ariel squeaked.

"Oh, my." Michelle began twirling a lock of hair between her fingers. "I had not realized you would be returning so soon. It looks like you've caught us in a compromising situation."

Ariel growled. "Why does everything that comes out of your mouth sound so vulgar?!"

"It's a gift."

"Both you! Sit. Down." Alex snapped. The response from the two girls was immediate. They sat on the ground, not even bothering to clear it of glasteel and whatever else was on the floor. Alex took several deep breaths, calmed down, and began again. "Now, you two are going to explain what happened here. We'll start with you, Ariel. You'll tell me what happened from your perspective. During this time, Michelle, you won't speak. You will have a chance to say your piece afterward. Is that understood?"

Ariel and Michelle nodded, their heads bowed as though unable to look him in the eyes. During this time, Gabrielle and Nyx wandered into the room. While Nyx merely observed the area with the same casual indifference he had come to expect from her, Gabrielle whistled in what almost sounded like admiration.

"Waa... this place is a mess," Gabrielle said.

"It looks like a warzone," Nyx added.

"Ariel," Alex began. "Please tell me what happened."

Ariel's eyes fluttered rapidly, but she quickly shook her head and directed her gaze at him. "Right. So, we were all just watching something on the holovid, and Michelle said that I was lucky that my... my..."

"Your...?"

"She said I was lucky that I have small boobs!" Ariel shouted.

Michelle gave her an aggrieved look. "All I said was that my bra was beginning to feel tight, and so you're lucky that yours aren't going to get any bigger."

"That's you being condescending!" Ariel snapped. "You've always flaunted how much larger your chest is than mine! Always!"

"I was just—"

"Michelle," Alex said in a calm, mild voice. Even so, Michelle froze. "I believe I said that you would not speak until after Ariel was finished."

"Uh… y-yes, you did," Michelle said, and for whatever reason, as Alex continued to stare down at her, the angelisian princess' cheeks turned a light shade of pink as she rubbed her thighs together.

He frowned but dismissed it. He didn't have time to deal with her strange response.

"Ariel, continue please."

"T-that's it," she said.

He raised an eyebrow. "That's all that happened?"

"… Yes."

"Then how do you explain this?" Alex gestured to the now destroyed house. Ariel winced but said nothing, causing him to sigh as he turned to Michelle. "Let's hear your side of the story."

Michelle nodded and, still blushing, began her tale. "M-my bras have been feeling tight recently. I mentioned how I might need to get new bras soon, and Ariel made a mocking comment about how it was so terrible that I had big breasts. She was obviously being sarcastic, so I told her that having a large chest isn't all it's cracked up to be, and that she was lucky her breasts wouldn't get any bigger because it meant she wouldn't have to go out and buy new bras every time she grew."

"I told you, that's—"

"Ariel."

"Eep!"

Alex took a moment to think about what the two were telling him. Meanwhile, Nyx was picking through the remains of the house. She was crouched by a broken wall and holding up a pictoframe, trying to see if it worked. On the other hand, Gabrielle already had Mr. Fix-it out and was using it to repair the walls. He was grateful for her quick response.

"It sounds to me like this is a case of two people misunderstanding each other," he said at last. "Ariel, I don't think Michelle was actually trying to be condescending this time. However"—he raised a hand to stop Ariel, who had opened her mouth, from shouting—"I do understand that Michelle has been known to bully you about this issue. Michelle, from now on, don't mention breasts around Ariel."

Michelle's eyes widened as she tried to stand up. "But—"

"This entire situation is a direct result of your constant bullying," Alex interrupted. "If you didn't keep picking on Ariel, she would have never misunderstood your words, and this would have never happened. Am I wrong?" Michelle said nothing, but Alex, unsatisfied with that response, continued to stare at her until she started squirming in her seat. "Am. I. Wrong?"

Her cheeks growing an even more fierce shade of red, Michelle looked at the ground. "Y-you aren't wrong."

"Thought so." Nodding, Alex decided on their punishment. "Both of you, go down to the lab. Do not touch anything. Once we finish repairing the house, you're going to be stuck in your rooms for the next week."

Neither of the girls said anything; they nodded like meek mice, stood up, and walked toward the ruined doorway.

Before they could get too far, Alex called out to them, "Where is Alice?"

Ariel and Michelle stopped, looked at each other, and then looked back at Alice.

"I believe she left when we started fighting," Michelle answered.

That did sound like something Alice would do. She never liked to get herself involved in things that she deemed to be "troublesome" and would actively avoid situations like that. If left to her own devices, Alex was sure that his sister would spend all day every day in front of the holovid watching *Titan Girl* and eating curry.

She'll be back soon.

"Gabby, Nyx," he said. "Would you two mind helping me repair the house?"

"Tee-hee! I'm already on it!" Gabrielle waved Mr. Fix-it through the air.

"I will also help you," Nyx said.

"Thanks." He looked at the still destroyed house, then up at the dome, visible because his roof was gone, and then he sighed. "Well, let's get to work."

It took two hours to fix the house, which was actually really impressive. Had this happened to anyone else, it would have taken much longer, but Gabrielle had inventions that could repair damage like this with little effort.

Most of his and Gabrielle's inventions were destructive in nature. Well, they weren't made to be destructive. It just so happened that very few of them worked properly and tended to cause mayhem instead of working like they should. Alex had not been able to make an invention that worked the way he wanted in years—outside of the more advanced mechanics. Likewise, Gabrielle could only really make things that exploded or stripped people of their clothing.

It was a wonder they had any inventions that worked at all.

The house that he, Alice, Ariel, Gabrielle, Michelle, and Nyx lived in was a two-story structure. On the outside, it looked like a regular house of about 750 square meters, but on the inside, it was the same size as a mansion.

The house possessed six bedrooms. All of them were located upstairs, which could be accessed through either the staircase, or an elevator that Gabrielle had installed. Unlike before, where the upstairs featured a hallway with doors, now it looked more like a circular lounge with seven doors—one was for the shower room— and an entrance for the stairs. Likewise, the kitchen was about three times bigger than it had been, and the living room, while still small, possessed alien furniture that was round and squishy instead of square and soft.

Alex couldn't complain. He kind of liked the changes.

Alice came home several hours later. Not only had she been surprised by his presence, but Alex had been surprised by her sudden hug. He was not surprised when she called him a troublesome idiot for taking so long to come back.

Alex had already made dinner by the time she'd come home, so he had Gabrielle grab her sisters, and they all sat around the dinner table. He had made curry. Since he had been gone for almost a month, Alex had wanted to make his little sister's favorite dish. She... hadn't been as enthused as he thought she'd be. He expected her to cheer and pump her fist into the air, but outside of a small smile, her response was muted.

As they sat around the dinner table, Alex frowned at his sister as she quietly ate her meal. Ariel and Michelle were subdued as they ate. He'd expected that, though. Alice, on the other hand, should have been gobbling the food he made at speeds that exceeded light.

Alice Ryker, fourteen years old, had doe-like brown eyes that were framed by brown locks of hair. Her hair was long and wavy. It wavered every time she moved her head. Adorning her body were pink pajama pants and a sleeveless top that wrinkled every time she moved her limbs. Her eyes were the same color brown as her hair. They were half-lidded and seemed to stare at everything with lazy indifference.

"I'll be visiting your teachers tomorrow," Alex said.

"Hm."

"I'm going to ask them how your grades have been."

"Hm."

"You remember our deal, right? If your grades dropped, you won't get any strawberry cheesecake parfaits for a year."

"Hm."

Alex frowned. "Alice?"

"I remember our deal." Alice sighed as if answering him troubled her. "Don't worry. I've been keeping my grades up." She stood up and grabbed her plate. "Anyway, I'm done."

Alex frowned as Alice put away her dishes and left the room. Even after she was gone, he continued to stare at the door.

Not only was Alice not the type to put her stuff away like that, but she wasn't the type to act like this. She didn't talk much. However, she was normally quiet because speaking was too much trouble. This felt more like something heavy was weighing on her mind, which made her current actions even more worrying.

Alice wasn't the type who liked to think about anything too deep or heavy.

When dinner was finished, Alex put away the dishes, started up the washer, and made his way to Alice's room. He knocked on the automatic door.

"Alice? Can I talk to you?"

There was a slight pause before the door clicked and slid open. Alex stepped into the room, which was large but not massive. His feet padded against the soft white carpet as he looked around. Alice's room was about what he expected. There wasn't much in the way of furnishings or decoration. A bed sat against the far wall, a closet was on the opposite side, a desk was situated next to the window, and there were several pictographs of Titan Girl hanging from the walls. There was also a large Titan Girl holograph hovering in the center of the room.

Alice was sitting on the bed, lying on her back as she stared at the ceiling with a blank look.

Alex walked into the room, sat down on the edge of the bed, and waited for several seconds.

Alice said nothing.

"Something is bothering you," he stated. "What is it?"

"I'm… not sure," Alice began, and then shook her head. "No, that's not it. I'm worried about Jasmine."

The moment she mentioned Jasmine, Alex felt a jolt race through his spine. Jasmine de Truante had been a constant presence in his and Alice's lives for the last few years. She was a noble. Normally, this would have made her unlikable on principle, but she was different. Kind and willing to stand up for others, Jasmine was someone that Alex considered a good friend—no, she was more than that. In truth, Jasmine was one of the girls who had featured prominently in his dreams after she started maturing.

"Worried about Jasmine? Is something wrong with her?"

"I don't know," Alice whispered. "Jasmine hasn't been coming to school. She stopped attending after you left. I tried getting a hold of her, but I haven't been able to. I even went to her house, but neither she nor Madison were home."

That was definitely worrying. Jasmine was not the kind of person who would leave without giving any hint as to where she was going or why. In fact, whenever she would be gone for a few days—mostly due to her parents' political functions—she would make a big show of telling them about where she was going. The fact that she had said nothing to Alice concerned him.

"I'll go to her house tomorrow and see what I can find," Alex promised.

Alice reached her hand out to him. Alex realized what she wanted and grabbed her hand. As they clasped their fingers together, she gave him a small smile.

"Thank you, Big Bro," she said.

"Hey." Alex grinned. "What are big brothers for?"

"For being troublesome," Alice responded, though her smile negated any harshness the words may have contained.

4

The day that Alex, Gabrielle, and Nyx arrived home was Sunday, which meant everyone except Alex and Nyx were going to school the following morning.

Because he wanted to get back into his routine, Alex and Nyx walked to school with the others. Alex needed to see Alice's teachers anyway, or at least Principal Tepes, to find out how his sister had been doing while he'd been absent.

Atreyu Academy was a massive building with a streamlined design. While it was shaped like a rectangle, there were numerous moving walkways trailing around the outer walls, along with elevators and warp pads. Since the academy was so large, nearly 200 square kilometers, these transportation methods were necessary for students to reach their classes on time.

If one were to look at the academy from a bird's-eye view, they would've also noticed the many gardens that dotted the interior. Alex had done just that once while testing out an anti-gravity invention. He'd almost been expelled, which might have been because he'd destroyed part of the roof when his invention malfunctioned, but that was neither here nor there.

Just like Alice had told him, Jasmine, who normally waited for them by the front gate, was not there when he and the others arrived. It was weird not being greeted by her. Alex almost expected the girl to pop out at any second, place one hand on her hip and the other near her mouth, and do her spoiled rich girl laugh.

Only that didn't happen.

Alex and Nyx separated from the others at the front gate. While everyone else went to class, they went to visit the principal.

Caridna Tepes was not only the principal of Atreyu Academy, but she was also a former member of the Mars Police Special Forces. She had been on his dad's team—not that one could tell by looking at her.

Despite being in her mid-30s, Mrs. Tepes didn't look a day over twelve or thirteen. Her cherubic face contained a youthfulness that belied her age. She was short, so short that her feet didn't even reach the floor as she sat in the straight backed chair behind her desk. With her blonde hair done up in twin-tails, she really did look like a little girl.

As he and Nyx entered her office and walked up to her desk, Mrs. Tepes placed her hands on the smooth surface, leaned back, and gave them a grin.

"It's been a long time, kiddo," she said. "I hear you went on an out of this world adventure."

"It was more like an out of this solar system adventure," Alex said.

Mrs. Tepes chuckled. "You'll have to tell me about it later. There's something you want to talk to me about, right?"

"Two somethings, actually," Alex said. "First, I want to know how Alice's grades were while I was gone. Did they drop at all?"

"A brother to the end, I see." Mrs. Tepes grinned before typing something into her IDband, a small yellow band around her wrist. A holograph suddenly appeared above it. Alice's name hovered over a graph that had several lines running across it. The names of Alice's classes were on the left. "As you can see, Alice has been keeping her grades mostly steady. They did fluctuate a bit last week, but they never dropped past the ninetieth percentile."

Alex nodded. He was pleased to hear that his sister really had kept up with her grades. He hadn't really doubted that she would, per se, but he knew that Alice, if given the chance, would slack off like nobody's business, especially if he wasn't there to keep her in line.

He looked at the days where her grades dropped. It really was a small drop, only sending her temporarily into the eightieth percentile, and they went back up, but it was the days they dropped that made him wonder.

"Does the drop in Alice's grades coincide with the time that Jasmine stopped coming to the academy?"

Mrs. Tepes placed a hand on her head and rubbed it. "I figured that was going to be what you wanted to know next. Yes, it does."

"Can you tell me what happened to Jasmine?" asked Alex.

The pained look on Mrs. Tepes face told him all he needed to know. "I... can't. Not fully, anyway. All I can tell you is that her parents pulled her out of Atreyu Academy."

Alex clenched and unclenched his fingers. His spine tingled as though a static shock had caused it to go numb. He looked at the shelf to his left, studying the trophies and knicknacks that sat on it, more to buy him time than because of actual interest. He needed to remain calm. Until he had proof that something bad had happened to her, he couldn't let himself get worked up.

"You can't tell me anything else?"

Mrs. Tepes shook her head. "Sorry, but I'm really only authorized to help you when it involves your princess' marriage candidates... or Alice's grades," she added after a short pause.

Alex knew he wouldn't get anything more out of Mrs. Tepes. It wasn't because he couldn't intimidate her into giving him the information he wanted. If she knew something, she would have already told him. He wanted to believe that.

"I understand. Thank you for your help."

Mrs. Tepes gave him a sad smile and waved him off. "Anytime."

Alex and Nyx left the office and headed for the nearest warp point that would take them closer to the exit. As they walked, their feet tapping against the tiled floor, Nyx grabbed his hand.

"What are we going to do now?" she asked.

"I'd like to investigate Jasmine's house." Alex looked down at her. "Will you come with me?"

"I will go wherever you go." Nyx hesitated before hugging his arm. While smaller than Gabrielle, she wasn't flat. Alex felt the softness of her modest twins press into him.

"You're being awfully clingy today," Alex muttered as they took a warp point that sent them to the academy's entrance.

As they exited the building and walked past the gate, Nyx hugged his arm more tightly. "That's you and I are going to be married." She paused. "Do you not want me to hug you like this?"

Even with a face that refused to express any emotions, Alex thought he saw sadness flicker through her eyes. It was only there for a second. Part of him wondered if he wasn't pushing his perceptions onto her.

"Not at all." Alex looked away. "I like being this close to you."

"Me too," Nyx admitted.

Walking through the Outer District, he traveled with Nyx to the nearest shuttle stop, and took a shuttle to Mars City.

Mars City was a massive community of towering skyscrapers that sprawled out for kilometers. With 1.2 million people living there, it was the largest city on Mars. Like every city that was situated on this inhospitable planet, it was protected by a giant dome, a bubble which protected them from Mars' harmful atmosphere.

Because Mars City was one of those "one section built on top of another" type of cities, it consisted of four levels: upper, middle, lower, and under. The middle level was where the normal citizens worked and lived. There were apartment blocks, shopping and entertainment districts, and various offices where blue collar workers spent hours sitting behind a desk. The various civil service departments also had offices within the middle district.

Jasmine was a noble, which meant she lived in the upper district of Mars City. The upper district was not accessible by regular means. The airspace was void of traffic because there were several laws that prohibited traveling above a certain height. This was ostensibly so people wouldn't accidentally hit the dome, but it was really because the nobles didn't want their view of the city blocked.

Alex had visited Jasmine's mansion before. He was keyed into the Truantes' private warp pad.

He could have taken a warp pad from the school to get there, but he didn't want Mrs. Tepes to know what he was doing, just in case she decided to inform Karen.

Nyx was not keyed in, but Alex had full access to the Truante's warp pad as well. Jasmine had granted him full access after he saved her. Her words at the time had been: *"Oh ho ho ho ho! For the man who has stolen my heart, I, the Queen of Loyalty, can do no less than give you everything that I possess."*

Apparently, everything she possessed meant he had free rein to come over whenever he pleased. Alex had never told anyone this, but before he had created Madison, he had visited Jasmine numerous times so she wouldn't be lonely. That was also how he introduced her to Alice.

The warp pad was located on a platform next to the Tower de Truante.

Given that her parents were some of the wealthiest nobles around, it was little wonder that their tower was also one of the tallest. Gleaming black like obsidian, the tower was made from highly polished durasteel and glasteel panels. The Truante's mansion only consisted of one floor, but the floor itself was massive, about four times the size of Alex's house before Gabrielle used her dimension warping technology to expand the space inside.

Alex and Nyx wandered up to the front door, which loomed over them, easily big enough that three of him could stand on each other's shoulders and still not reach the top. Despite its size, the door itself was innocuous. Metallic. Lustrous. There didn't seem to be anything different, other than its sheer size, from any other door. There was an access panel on the left side.

He pressed the intercom button and spoke into it. "Hello? This is Alex. Jasmine, are you there? I'm here to see you."

He waited for five seconds. No response. He pressed the button again.

"Hello? Jasmine?"

Still no response.

"I sense something wrong," Nyx said.

"No kidding," Alex muttered. "It's not like Jasmine to keep someone waiting."

Shaking her head, Nyx said, "That is not what I meant." She placed a hand on the door. Alex thought the door rippled. "I can detect no signs of life inside this house."

"There's no one here?"

"Correct."

If Jasmine was not at school, then she should have been at home. There was no reason for her not to be. However, her parents had taken her out of Atreyu Academy, which could mean any number of things, from they had decided to move, to they no longer thought schooling was necessary. Having only met them once, Alex didn't have much of an impression on them. He just knew that he didn't like them for not paying more attention to Jasmine.

"Shall I break this down?" asked Nyx. "I can transmute a hole in the door if you want."

"Hold on." Alex tapped on his IDband. "Let me try something first."

Every citizen on Mars City had their own IDband. They acted as a personal communication device, identification, and biorhythmic scanner. Some of the newer IDbands had really odd modifications, like the one that told someone how many steps they had taken, or the one that blasted music from a small speaker.

Alex's IDband had a number of illegal modifications on it. One of those modifications was a program that would allow him to control Madison remotely. He could input commands, shut her down, activate her, and even locate her when required. Right now he wanted to see where she was.

"Madison is inside," he announced.

"Really?" Nyx tilted her head. "Why has she not answered the door?"

"She must be deactivated." He pressed another button on his IDband. "I'm reactivating her now."

Alex reactivated Madison with a command, and then sent her a command to open the door. Barely two minutes had passed before rushing footsteps reached them. Not long after that, the door opened and Alex was startled when a wide-eyed Madison appeared before them.

Madison looked like a beautiful young woman with long, russet-colored hair and eyes like amethysts. She wore a standard maid outfit; a black and white dress with lots of frills, white stockings, and a bonnet. The outfit fit her like a glove, a second skin. When combined with the elegant way she moved, that natural grace, one would almost think that she was human.

But she wasn't. Madison was an android that Alex had built for Jasmine several years ago. Her eyes were made from synthetic materials that looked real, and likewise, she had fake skin covering every inch of her body. The only part of her that looked fake were her long, metallic ears, which jutted from beneath her parted hair.

There were laws against the creation of artificial intelligences. Alex had heard that it was thanks to a war that had broken out between humans and machines some years prior, though he'd never bothered confirming it. In either event, only people who had a licence could create androids. Alex had one such licence thanks to his many patents.

"Master?" Madison said, her eyes growing even wider. "Master! You must help Mistress Jasmine!"

"Help Jasmine…" Alex felt a chill run down his spine. "Why? What's wrong with her?"

"Jasmine has been taken away by her parents!" Madison said in a rush. "They're planning to marry her off!"

Whatever Alex had been expecting Madison to say... that had not been it.

5

Alex did not know what to do. In this situation, where he had no information, no idea how any of this had come to be, all he could do was take Madison back to his house.

No one else was home when he arrived at the house; Gabrielle and the others were still in school. That was probably a good thing. This conversation was one that would be best to have alone.

"Let's head into the lab," Alex said as he took off his shoes.

"Affirmative, Master."

Both Nyx and Madison followed his example, slipping out of their shoes and setting them aside. While Madison wore stockings, Nyx was barefoot, save the pair of bands that covered the arches of her feet.

The lab was a large room many times larger than the house situated above it. It had originally been much smaller, but thanks to Gabrielle's liberal use of Mr. Dimension—an invention of hers that could distort the fabrics of reality—the space had been separated into its own dimension and expanded to nearly four times its original size.

Much like any other workshop, advanced machines sat around the room, some lined in rows and others sitting by themselves. All of the technologies were upgraded variations of human technology.

Each one was a human device that had been modified with angelisian technology. They didn't look much like their originals, though, and instead of the hard angles found in human tech, these possessed the organic curves of angelisian models.

"Come this way," Alex instructed Madison. "I'm gonna perform some routine maintenance on you to make sure nothing's wrong. While I do that, I want you to tell me about what happened."

"Yes, Master."

While Nyx stood some distance away, Alex directed Madison to disrobe and lay down on a lab table. Madison didn't hesitate to strip.

Alex had created Madison to be as human as possible. Not only was she a true artificial intelligence, but her body moved and looked like a real human's would. Her skin was soft. He had created his own synthetic skin that was based on a baby's skin, so it was even softer than a normal person's.

Of course, her skin was not the only thing that appeared real. While she lacked the sex organs of a human, what, with her body being made up of metal parts, she still had the most prominent female sex organs: Breasts.

Alex sometimes wondered if he'd taken things too far when it came to Madison's physical appearance, and her breasts in particular. Perky and proud, Madison not only sported a modest bust, but her breasts were capped with light pink nipples.

"Maybe you were subconsciously trying to release all of that pent up frustration you have."

Asmodeus... I don't know if you couldn't tell, but I am pretty busy right now.

"Of course I noticed. I just don't care."

Tsk!

"I don't always agree with this daemon, but I do think it's important not to hold yourself back so much. Sex is a natural activity. You shouldn't try to suppress your own sexual desire."

You two have been agreeing more and more lately. What's up with that?

"Let's just say that we've come to an... understanding."

Alex grabbed a nearby tool, one that could be used for multiple purposes, as Madison laid down on her stomach.

He didn't know what to think about the understanding that Asmodeus and the other voice inside of him had come to. On the one hand, it kind of helped him because he no longer had to deal with their arguing. On the other, he was nervous about the idea of them working together.

Activating the precision laser cutter, Alex made a careful incision in Madison's back. The skin peeled apart easily. Underneath her skin was not blood, muscle, and bone. It was metal. Setting the tool aside, Alex grabbed the skin and peeled it back, revealing more of the metal body.

Most of Madison's back was made of solid metal. He'd created it from a form of mercury, liquid metal. It was very malleable, which meant he didn't need to create joints that allowed her body to move like a human's. The only part that wasn't solid was the single panel in the center of her back.

"Tell me what happened to Jasmine," Alex ordered as he unscrewed the panel, took it off, and set it on the table. Inside of Madison's back were a series of circuits, wires, and machine parts.

"Jasmine's parents arrived home while Jasmine was at school," Madison said as Alex grabbed the tool, switched to scanner-mode, and used the scanner to map out the interior. He could have used Gabrielle's Mr. Scanner, which was larger, but this wasn't one of his and Gabrielle's inventions. This was Madison. "After Jasmine came home, her parents told her... they told her that they were taking her out of school, so she could get married to a nobleman's son."

Alex stopped what he was doing. He closed his eyes and took several deep, slow, calming breaths. It didn't really help settle the anger that was beginning to seethe inside of his gut. However, it did help him focus.

He went back to scanning, locating at least two problems with the servomotor processors. That would need to be calibrated.

Madison continued. "The nobleman in question doesn't live on Mars. I... don't know where he lives, though. I only heard his name. I tried to stop her parents from saying anymore, but... but someone shut me off."

"Jasmine?" Alex asked.

Unable to shake her head because she was lying on the table, Madison merely blinked once. "No, it was not Jasmine. She was sitting at the table. Whoever shut me off had been behind me."

Which meant that whoever it was had not shut her off but forcibly deactivated her. It was entirely possible for someone to do that, but it required them to know the unique electromagnetic frequency used by Madison's main operating system. In other words, they needed to have a perfect map of her "brainwaves", and an EMP emitter that would scramble those "brainwaves".

It shouldn't have been possible.

"Do you know who Jasmine is marrying?"

That was the most important question Alex could think of. Nobles were all well-known owners of large conglomerates, or the mothers and fathers of famous idols and actors. They weren't just important people. Many nobles also had direct involvement with the Galactic Defense Force, the ruling government body of this solar system. The nobles backed the GDF, and the GDF in turn let the nobles dictate governmental policies.

Alex's father had been in direct opposition of letting the nobles dictate government policies. According to Karen, Farone S. Ryker had done his best to bust nobles of various crimes so their influence would lessen. It wasn't as hard as it sounded. Many nobles took part in activities that weren't exactly legal.

There were several more problems that Alex located in Madison now that he was aware of what had happened to her. It looked like some of the components that made up her "brain" were scrambled. EMP emitters fired off short electromagnetic pulses that fried electronic devices. Madison had protection against that, but it could be overridden if someone had perfectly mapped the electrical pulses that made up her brainwaves.

There was also a method of brute forcing her to shut down. It required someone to send a strong electromagnetic burst directly into her processing core. Thinking on it, that might have been what happened here. There were several powerful guns that acted like EMPs. It was illegal for anyone but officers to own one, but if this person was a noble...

"Before I was deactivated, I did hear the name of the man who Jasmine was being forced to marry," Madison said. Her eyes were open. She turned her head and looked at him from the corner of her left eye as Alex began calibrating her servomotor processor. "His name is…"

INTERLUDE

THE NOT QUITE DAMSEL IN DISTRESS

Jasmine was hungry and tired—hungry, tired, hurt, and lonely. She didn't know how long it had been since her parents had locked her up in this room, and she had lost count of the number of times either her father had come to visit, to try and convince her to sign the marriage contract. It didn't matter. She didn't care.

She had to smile at how frustrated they must have been. One of the laws regarding the marriage of a minor was that both the parents and the minor in question had to formalize the marriage with a signed contract that was approved by both the GDF and GPF. That meant without her approval, no marriage could take place.

And she would never approve.

The place where she had been locked away in was a large room, lavishly furnished with red carpet and golden designs decorating the walls. Statues sat on pedestals of marble. Paintings hung from the walls. These were not holographic creations, nor were they fakes; these were real paintings and statues. Jasmine could scarcely imagine how much they cost. Even her parents could not afford to decorate an unused room with this much artwork.

Her bed was large, comfortable, and soft. She hated it. There was a desk situated against one of the walls, and a wardrobe stood several meters away, filled to the brim with extravagant clothes that Jasmine refused to wear.

She was still in her school uniform.

As she stood by the viewport, looking at the vast blackness of space beyond, the door to her room opened. She didn't turn. Thanks to the reflection in the viewport, she could see who had come this time.

He was a tall man. At a guess, she would have said that he was about a head taller than Alex. His delicate figure was adorned with clothes of the finest velvet, a dark form-fitting vest over a long-sleeved white shirt. Black pants were tucked into black boots, which squeaked as he walked. Blond hair and blue eyes several shades darker than her own stared at her back. They were drilling holes into her with lust. She felt dirty just knowing he was looking at her. The smile that he wore, arrogant beyond anything she had ever seen, made her lip curl.

Caelum de Fénelon was the son of a wealthy noble family. The de Fénelons owned several dozen mines, all of which were rich in adamantium and polarite, which were the two types of base metal that made durasteel.

Caelum's family supplied the Galactic Defense Force with durasteel, and in turn, they used the durasteel to create warships. Thanks to the deals that the GDF made for durasteel, the de Fénelon family wielded a lot of power, both politically and financially. In terms of influence, their political power was even greater than the power her family wielded.

"Jasmine." He said her name, speaking with the smooth, aristocratic snobbery of a noble. It matched his snobbish, aristocratic face to a T. "I hear you are still being stubborn."

"What are you doing here?" Jasmine asked.

"How long do you plan on clinging to this vain hope that someone will come for you?" he continued. "Surely, you can see how senseless it is to hold on to hope."

She sighed. "Why have you come here? I thought I had informed you that I have no desire to speak with you."

With a great flourish, the young man bowed before her, a mocking bow that all but spoke of the condescension that he had for her.

Women were not treated well in noble families. While the son of a noble family was always the heir who would inherit the family legacy, the daughter was always sold off to be married, either as a wife or chattel.

Polygamy was technically illegal, but that didn't mean the nobles didn't practice it, and the GDF always turned a blind eye to it. Jasmine hated how corrupt this solar system was.

She thought back to how Gabrielle had informed her that polygamy was legal everywhere else. Jasmine was actually considering letting Gabrielle marry Alex as a second wife. Truthfully, she was not repulsed by the idea of being in a polygamous relationship. That said, she was repulsed by the thought of marrying Caelum.

"Naturally, I have returned to convince you of the benefits that are to be had from this marriage. Surely you can see how beneficial an alliance between our two families would be. Your family controls numerous shipping lanes. Meanwhile, my family owns more than sixty-five percent of this solar system's mines. If the two of our families were joined through marriage, we could expand to take control of all the other noble families!"

Jasmine said nothing as the young nobleman pontificated. She heard the words, but she wasn't listening to them. In one ear. Out the other. Nothing this fool said mattered to her. The only thing that she cared about was knowing when he would be finished.

"You know," she began once the nobleman grew silent, "you always speak of how our marriage will benefit our families, how it will allow us to control other families, how great it will be for our two families. Not once did I hear you tell me how this marriage would benefit me." Finally, Jasmine turned around and smiled at the now frozen noble. "I'm sorry, Caelum, but I, the Queen of Matrimony, have no intention of ever marrying you."

The expression on Caelum's face was amusing. His entire face twisted up like warped plasteel. It was the kind of look people gave when they had tasted or smelled something foul.

"Y-you... " Caelum gritted his teeth as he marched up to her. "Time after time, I come here and attempt to change your mind, and time after time, you rebuff my advances."

"That is because your advances will never convince me that a marriage with you is in my best interest," Jasmine said.

"Do not lie to me!" Caelum snapped. "I know the truth! I've heard all about it from your brother! Yes, I am perfectly aware of the boy you like. This... this Alexander S. Ryker. I even looked into him." By now, Caelum was standing right in front of her, so close that Jasmine could see the arrogant gleam in his eyes. "Oh, how the mighty have fallen. It is no wonder your parents decided to marry you into my family. For a noblewoman of your stature to fall for a mere peasant is sickening. Clearly, you need to be retrained in what it means to be a nobl—GOOOFF!"

Rage boiled inside of Jasmine as she bent her knees, lowered her center of gravity, and tightened the muscles in her stomach. Caelum didn't even realize what she was doing. He wasn't even paying attention. Of course, this meant that when Jasmine thrust out her foot in a high kick that caught up in the chest, he was unable to mount a proper defense.

Jasmine couldn't even feel satisfaction as Caelum staggered back in shock. The rage she felt was overpowering. All she could think of was how much she hated this boy, of how much she wanted to beat the crap out of him, to break that disgustingly perfect nose under her fist. She couldn't remember a time she'd been so enraged.

Right now, she was the Queen of Rage.

As Caelum fell to a knee and placed a hand against his chest, Jasmine put all the vitriol she felt into her glare.

"Oh ho ho ho ho! Listen to me and listen well, Caelum de Fénelon," Jasmine said, using his full name. "I am the Queen of Disinterest. I do not care if you insult me. I do not care if you insult my family. There are many things you can insult that I do not care about. However…" This time, when Jasmine snapped off a kick that slammed into the underside of Caelum's chin and sent him sprawling onto his back, she did feel satisfaction. "… I will never let you insult Alexander."

Caelum was still lying on the floor. Blood leaked down his mouth, but he seemed too shocked to notice. She felt some satisfaction when she saw how the underside of his chin was beginning to swell. It would be an ugly, black bruise tomorrow.

Jasmine turned around and went back to staring out the viewport.

"Get out of my sight," she said. "And don't come back unless it's to tell me that you conceded defeat."

Even though she was not turned in his direction, Jasmine saw when Caelum stood to his feet. She watched as he stumbled to the door. She even saw how he paused after turning the handle and opening it.

"I won't forget how you slighted me." He turned his head around to glare at her. "When you and I are married, I am going to have you trained in how to be a proper noblewoman."

"Doubtful," Jasmine muttered as Caelum left, slamming the door shut behind him.

Now alone in her room, Jasmine raised her right arm. Wrapped around her forearm was a silver IDband. While it looked like every other IDband, this band was special. Alex had added numerous modifications to it that were not necessarily legal. One of those modifications was a tracking beacon that Madison could use to track her location.

Her parents didn't know about that. If they did, they would have tried to remove it, despite how such an act was illegal.

The problem was twofold. Madison had been deactivated and couldn't track her. Even if she were activated, there was no telling if her tracking beacon was in range of Madison's sensors. In which case, she only had one hope for rescue...

"Alexander..." Jasmine placed a hand against her chest, clenching the fabric of her collared shirt. "... Please come and save me. Your Queen is waiting for you."

CHAPTER 2

OPERATION SAVE JASMINE
COMMENCES

Alex finished his maintenance on Madison, and then went to the grocery store with Nyx. Their fridge was depressingly empty. No one had done any grocery shopping since Alex had left, which he supposed didn't surprise him as much as he wished it. There was no way Alice would ever go shopping. At the same time, he had hoped that Michelle, at least, would go to the store for groceries. She seemed to be the most responsible of the group... when she wasn't picking fights with her sister.

He wanted to stock up on some of the essentials for Alice's, Ariel's, Gabrielle's, and Michelle's lunches. He also needed to buy ingredients for dinner.

He wandered through the aisles of a nearby convenience store. He planned on cooking pizza today, so he was gathering all of the ingredients he would need: flour, eggs, olive oil, tomatoes, and everything else. Nyx was with him. She walked by his side and helped gather some of the ingredients on his list. He was grateful for her help. While his body moved in accordance to his wishes, his mind was far from his self-appointed task.

Jasmine was being married off to a man named Caelum de Fénelon, a noble from the de Fénelon family, who were well-known for the many mines they owned and the deals they cut with the Galactic Defense Force. They were not stationed on any planet. The mines they owned were asteroids, and so most of their facilities were built inside of asteroid belts, or around lone asteroids within the solar system.

Unfortunately, that was all Alex knew about the de Fénelon family. Like most noble families, they were extremely well-known names, but no one actually knew anything of substance. Nobles liked to keep to themselves. That was part of the reason rumors about their corruption kept spreading. It didn't help that the only time normal folks ever learned anything about nobles, it was because some noble family had been caught dealing Redline, or smuggling sex slaves, or something equally heinous.

Alex was in the same boat.

That left him on lasers and hydrospanners.

"Thank you and come again," the cashier said as Alex, still running on instinct, left the store with Nyx.

"You are worried about Jasmine," Nyx said.

"Huh?" Alex looked down at her, jolting as he replayed her words inside of his head. "Oh. Yeah, I am. I can't help it. Jasmine is an important person to me."

"Do you love her?"

"I... I do."

"Are you planning to make her one of your wives?"

"I... want to at least give her the option." Alex paused as something similar to a graviton sphere settled in the pit of his stomach. "Do you think I shouldn't?"

"I do not have a problem with it, and I doubt Princess Gabrielle will mind if you marry Jasmine either." Nyx tilted her head to look at him. "Are you going to save her?"

"If I can." Alex looked at the canal that he and Nyx were strolling past. It was the same canal where he had fought Azazel, where he had fought that giant robot, and it was close to the bridge where Nyx had almost killed him. A lot of crazy stuff had gone down there. "The problem is that I don't know where she is. What's more, I don't know how to find her."

Nyx was silent for nearly a full minute, but then she slowly nodded. "That is certainly a problem."

Alex's smile was mirthless. "Yes, it is."

Arriving back at home, Alex wandered into the kitchen and put away the groceries. Nyx helped. When they were finished, the two of them decided to spar in the simulation room. They hadn't sparred in a while. Alex was worried that he might have gotten rusty after being cooped up in that ship for so long.

The battle started off strong as Alex rushed at Nyx, launching a series of furious punches and kicks that he hoped she would be too slow to defend against. Sadly, defend against them Nyx did. Her arms came up. His attacks were blocked. The assassin would even redirect his arms and legs around her body with wide, circular movements that were more graceful than anything he'd ever seen. They were barely a minute into their fight, and Alex's crisis suit was already covered in sweat, despite the suit's ability to regulate his body temperature.

Nyx was as strong as ever. As an assassin with over a decade of experience, her skills in hand to hand combat was unparalleled. Alex could scarcely keep up with her attacks. They were so fast that her hands and feet were nothing but blurs before his eyes, and that was just her skills when it came to fighting in close-quarters.

Her alchemy was something else entirely.

Nyx was a being created through artificial means. Instead of flesh, blood, muscle, and bone, her body was composed of billions of nanomachines. Of course, the nanomachines created her body so its physiology was nearly identical to most humanoid species. That didn't change the fact that she hadn't been made the way other people were made.

The nanomachines that made up Nyx's body were like batteries that had an unlimited supply of energy. No matter how long they battled, Nyx continued to fight at the same level as when they first started. Actually, it almost seemed to Alex like she began upping her game the longer their fight continued.

When they started off, Nyx had stuck mostly with using swords, which she transmuted from the bands around her arms and legs. Then she began transmuting the ground. Since their battleground was a desert setting this time, it meant a lot of what she created were pillars and hands made of sand, which tried to crush Alex. He would destroy them with his Aura of Creation, but Nyx could transmute faster than he could fire off energy blasts.

Transmutation worked by deconstruction something and reconstructing it as something else. A good example were the hands that Nyx made. Each hand was composed of sand, hardened to the density of granite.

Alchemy worked under the Laws of Equivalent Exchange, a law stating that in order to create something, a person had to give something of equal value. It meant that Nyx couldn't transmute more than what she gave. If she used sixteen kilograms of sand to make something, what she made needed to be the same value as sixteen kilograms of sand.

That said, Nyx had a lot more freedom when it came to her alchemy. She wasn't bound by a lot of the conventional laws. This was because her body was composed of nanomachines, which acted as a power source to fuel her alchemy. It allowed her a much wider range of more powerful transmutations that most alchemists could never hope to mimic.

Hands weren't the only things Nyx transmuted. Alex eventually got the hang of destroying the hands. He learned that if he continued feeding power into his beams, he could control their direction and use them to destroy the hands. It actually took less energy to maintain a beam than it did to make a new one.

But that was when Nyx upped her game again.

She placed her hands on the ground, and suddenly, like massive monsters rising from the abyss, several giant worms with gaping maws filled with sharp teeth erupted from the ground. About sixteen or twenty meters in length, with a width that was two times larger than he was tall, these monstrosities towered over him. Their bodies were composed of sand. There were six of them in total, and they were surrounding him.

"Oh... this doesn't look good."

Blinking the sweat from his eyes, Alex created a set of massive wings with his Aura of Creation, bent his knees, and launched himself into the sky. His lips, cheeks, and eyelids peeled back as the wind pushed against him.

The sandworms all tried to take bites out of him. Alex created a whip in either hand. Spinning around as he ascended into the sky, Alex sent his whips at the sandworms, gouging chunks out of their bodies, which exploded with sand. Two collapsed as their cohesion was disrupted, but the rest were reconstructed. He grimaced when sand crawled up their bodies and healed the wounds he had dealt.

Finally, Alex blew past all of the sandworms, moving out of their reach. Now floating above them, he raised his hands into the air. Inhale. Exhale. Alex's breath was hot as he dispersed his whips and directed his Aura of Creation to the spot above his hands. What appeared before him was small at first, just a tiny sphere, but as the seconds ticked by, it grew larger and larger, until it was around the same size as a human.

"Let's see how your worms deal with this!!" Alex roared as he pulled his hands down. As though it was tethered to his hands, the sphere also flew down before it was launched at the worms.

They didn't stand a chance. The giant ball of energy slammed into the ground and erupted. Alex gritted his teeth as a fierce wind threatened to toss him away. He raised his arms to cover his face as sand and rocks pelted his body. Peeking through the cover of his arms, he watched the havoc his attack had unleashed.

The giant dome of energy looked nothing like an explosion. It was like a swirling vortex contained within a dome. However, while the dome seemed to contain a good portion of the energy, the force it whipped up created a fierce gale that threatened to blow Alex away. When the energy disappeared, all that remained of the area was a massive crater.

"That was an excellent use of your Aura of Creation," Sachiel said. *"Remember this, the Aura of Creation creates, but creation and destruction often go hand in hand."*

"Hmph! He could have caused even more destruction if he'd used my powers."

"Your powers are too difficult to control. Even when he used them last time, it was only for a second. Anymore and he would have succumbed to darkness."

"You say that like it's a bad thing."

Could you two not talk while I'm training.

"Don't say that. We were just going to warn you that your assassin bitch is behind you."

What?

Alex didn't even have time to be angry at how Asmodeus had called Nyx a bitch; a sharp pain had erupted from his back and stomach. A glance down revealed the culprit. The tip of a sword was protruding from his chest. He blinked. Then he turned his head and eyed Nyx, who floated behind him, her clothing transformed into a pair of black wings.

"What...?"

His sentence was never finished. Alex died, falling face first to the ground. Then the world reverted back to a simple square interior made of tiles, and Alex groaned, coming back to life in that same instant.

The simulation room, created by Gabrielle, was a room that not only created a separate dimension that could replicate any number of different terrains, but it converted all physical damage taken into mental stress. It still hurt to get stabbed. That said, it wasn't nearly as bad as actually getting stabbed.

He rolled over onto his back as a shadow appeared above him. It was, of course, Nyx.

"You killed me again."

"You got careless," Nyx said. She held out her hand. Alex grabbed it, allowing her to pull him up. "Just because you can use powerful attacks doesn't mean you always should. You need to learn when it is and isn't appropriate to use such attacks. Had you found another way to defeat those Grecian Spaceworms, you might have noticed me sneaking up behind you."

Alex grimaced. "You're right, of course. I'll do better next time." Nyx nodded as they left the simulation chamber, entering the larger part of the lab. "I keep forgetting that you're an assassin, especially when you pull off big moves like when you created those sandworms with your alchemy."

"An assassin isn't just someone who uses stealth to kill people," Nyx lectured. "Sometimes a large and flashy attack can do more to distract someone than a subtle attack. I use different transmutations to suit the situation. You'll eventually learn that certain attacks are more effective than others depending on the situation you are in and the opponent you are fighting."

It was interesting how much Nyx talked when she was lecturing him on combat. She was normally so quiet, though he had noticed that she was talking more as time went on. He hoped that meant she was becoming more comfortable around him.

Then again, she did state that she's going to marry me... that has to mean something.

Alex took a quick shower before Nyx, and then went into the kitchen while Nyx took a shower herself. Madison was already in the kitchen when he arrived. She stood before the counter and was kneading dough. He should have figured she would be making dinner. That was one of her jobs when she took care of Jasmine. It was probably ingrained in her now, but he felt a little off-put. Cooking was his job in this household.

"Madison," Alex said as he walked to the counter, grabbed the ingredients for the tomato sauce, and got to work.

"Master," Madison greeted. "I apologize for taking over your job, but I thought it would be a good idea to get started on dinner early."

"You sure you're not just trying to kill time because you're worried about Jasmine?"

"… That could be it." Madison paused in her work before continuing. "My circuits are feeling odd, but I detect no anomalies."

"Odd how?"

"It feels like the circuits dealing with thoughts are shorting out."

"They aren't shorting. I've already checked. That sensation you feel is worry."

"Worry?"

"Yes, worry." Alex put the tomato pulp in a saucepan over a high heat, added salt, olive oil, tomato paste, garlic, basil, and bay leaf. "You are special, Madison. Unlike normal AIs, you are a true artificial intelligence. You can think for yourself, you can learn, and you have feelings."

"Speaking of, Master, I have always wondered…"

"Yes?"

"Why did you make me like this?"

"That's a silly question." Once the sauce started to boil, Alex lowered the heat to a brisk simmer and began occasionally stirring. "I made you specifically to keep Jasmine company, so I wasn't going to create some half-assed robot who could only follow orders.

I wanted you to be Jasmine's friend and companion, not someone who merely did as they were told."

"I see."

"Do you dislike that I gave you the ability to form your own thoughts and feelings?"

Madison's hands stopped moving, but only for a moment, and then she was stretching out the dough and flattening it with a roller. Alex turned his head and watched as she twirled the dough into the air, spinning it against her finger and making it stretch. He wondered where she had learned such a flashy method of cooking. Setting the dough back on the board, she began shaping the crust. Only after she was halfway through did she speak to him.

"No. I appreciate that you gave me the ability to think on my own. I'm just... this feeling in my circuits leaves me uneasy, I guess."

"Worry always makes people uneasy," Alex agreed. "Is the dough ready?"

Madison stepped back and revealed that the dough had been shaped into a perfect circle. Likewise, the ends had been raised ever so slightly to create what would become the crust. It was perfectly symmetrical.

"Yes, it is."

As they spread tomato sauce over the dough and added cheese, meat, and various vegetables, no words were spoken. Nyx came into the kitchen during this time. Her long black hair still glistened with water. She took a seat at the table as Alex placed the pizza inside of the nuclear fission oven. He didn't turn it on. Food cooked instantly, so he would wait until it was time for dinner. The oven would keep it fresh until then.

School would be ending soon. Alex left with Nyx and Madison, traveling to Atreyu Academy, where he waited outside of the school gate. It wasn't long before students started exiting. A few people glanced their way, probably because of Nyx and Madison, but most of the people ignored them. Alice, Ariel, Gabrielle, and Michelle emerged along with Kazekiri, Selene, Ryoko, and Serah about five minutes later.

"Alex!" Gabrielle was the first to notice him, and her pounce was more like a missile attack. Alex stumbled back as she slammed into his chest.

"Gabrielle," Alex grunted. "I'm guessing you had fun at school?"

"You bet! It feels like it's been so long since I last went that I had to make up for lost times!"

As Gabrielle squeezed him until it felt like his ribcage might snap, the others walked over to them.

"I heard you two went to rescue another solar system," said Ryoko, flipping her hair over her shoulder. "Sounds like you've been busy."

Ryoko's dark skin contrasted with her bleach blonde hair, and her narrowed eyes stared at people with a look that made him shiver. Those eyes were like a predator's—except instead of seeking out prey, she sought people to fondle and grope. She wore the traditional school uniform of Atreyu Academy, though her skirt was cut immodestly short.

"Somehow... I'm not surprised you figured out what's going on." Alex sighed as Gabrielle let go of him and stepped back. "And I might still be busy despite being back on Mars."

"That so?" Ryoko narrowed her eyes. "Do tell."

"Don't feel like it."

"Aww! That's not fair!" Ryoko strolled up to him with an added sway to her hips and tried to place her hands on his chest. He grabbed her hands before she could. "What's wrong, Alex? You don't like my touch anymore?"

"It's not that," Alex said. "It's just that I've made some decisions."

"And I can't tease you because of those?"

"That's right."

"Oh, poo." Ryoko backed away before slinking behind Gabrielle, snaking her hands under the other girl's armpits, and grabbing her breasts. "Then I'll just have to grope your fiancé instead."

"Please don't," Alex responded dryly.

"Ryoko! Stop doing that right now!" Kazekiri pointed at the other girl and glared. "That sort of behavior is what breaks the moral backbone of our society!"

Alex frowned as he noticed how Kazekiri's normally shimmering flaxen hair seemed a tad dull, and how there were bags under her dark eyes, and how her shoulders were slumped. She seemed tired. Even her school uniform seemed to denote exhaustion. It was wrinkled and far more slovenly than he imagined the prim and proper Kazekiri would wear her clothing.

"Hey, Kirikiri," Alex said.

"Alex." Kazekiri offered him a polite but distant smile. It was so different from how she had been treating him before he left that Alex was taken aback. "I hope you were able to accomplish what you wanted."

"I did." His frown deepened. "Are you okay?"

"Yes, I am fine. Why do you ask?"

"No reason."

Alex could have brought up his concerns, but they were in front of the campus gate, surrounded by people, and he didn't want to put her on the spot. He also had a lot on his mind. With his worry for Jasmine overriding most of his thoughts, he didn't know how much help he would be to Kazekiri. There was also the fact that she probably wouldn't tell him what was wrong if he asked.

"By the way," he started again, "is that a new necklace?"

There was no mistaking the way that Kazekiri flinched as she raised a hand to the necklace in question. It was more like a choker than a necklace. Wrapping around her throat, made out of some kind of elastic, the object was definitely a choker. There was a small red gem in the middle.

"Oh… yes," Kazekiri said. "I just started wearing it a few weeks ago."

Which meant it was after he'd already left.

"You never struck me as the type of girl who'd wear something like that."

Kazekiri turned her head. "That so? Maybe you just don't know me very well."

"Maybe…"

Alex placed a hand against his chest, which had tightened at her words. The idea that he might not know Kazekiri as well as he thought he did bothered him. It meant they weren't as close as he assumed they were.

"Could you stop squeezing Gabrielle's chest, Ryoko?" asked Selene, bringing attention to the fact that Ryoko was still groping his fiancé.

"I can't help it. They're so squishy," Ryoko said in her defense.

"That isn't a good excuse!"

With her curly brown hair swishing around her cute face, complimenting her dark skin, Selene stood with her hands on her hips, frowning at Ryoko with dark brown eyes.

Selene was Alex's childhood friend. They had known each other since they were little. When his step-mom and father died, they were taken in by Selene's family and raised alongside them for several years, until Alex and Alice moved out. Selene was also the girl that he had confessed to when he was younger, though he'd been rejected.

"It's so disgusting how that girl keeps grabbing Big Sis' chest like that." Ariel curled her lips in distaste.

Michelle twirled a strand of hair between her fingers. "You think so? I think it's kind of hot."

"How messed up are you?"

Alex allowed everyone to talk for a while. As he stood there with Nyx and Madison, Alice walked up to them and eyed the robot maid.

"I didn't know you were with Alex," she said.

"That is because I was not with him until he reactivated me four hours ago," Madison said.

"Do you know where Jasmine is?"

"I do not, but I do know a bit about what happened to her."

Alex could see that Alice was going to ask more questions, so he put a stop to it by raising a hand. "This isn't something we should be talking about here. I can tell you what's going on once we're home."

Alice's lip twitched as though she was a second away from arguing. Then she sighed, muttered a quick "troublesome," and grew silent. Thankful, Alex waited until everyone had said their goodbyes before heading off with his large entourage in tow.

Once they got home, Alex told them all that he had something important to tell them. He had them sit in the living room. Gabrielle and Nyx sat on the couch with him. Alice sat next to Gabrielle. Meanwhile, Ariel and Michelle took the squishy chairs, which he thought looked more like giant balls of red gelatin than actual chairs.

Madison stood by the door.

Alex told them about the most recent developments. He told them that Jasmine had been removed from school because her parents were going to force her into a marriage with a noble named Caelum de Fénelon. He mentioned how he had discovered that Madison had been forcibly deactivated, how the mansion had been abandoned, and how they had no idea where Jasmine was.

"So we don't even know if Jasmine is okay?" Alice asked, clicking her tongue. "Troublesome."

"You've told us what happened to Jasmine," Michelle began, "but what is it that you plan on doing?"

"We're going to rescue her, of course!" Gabrielle said.

"Gabrielle has the right of it." Alex ran a hand through his hair. "The problem is that we can't locate her right now. That's why, Gabrielle, I need your help with something."

"Whatever you need help with, I'll help you." Gabrielle thumped a fist to her chest. "Just leave it to me!"

"Thank you. I'm going to need you to help me boost Madison's ability to receive signals." Alex paused for only a moment to put his thoughts in order. "While she has the ability to locate a person by their IDband for up to about fifty kilometers, I installed a program within Madison that allows her to detect Jasmine's specific IDband for up to four hundred kilometers. I did this in the event that someone tried to kidnap Jasmine, and neither I or Madison were around to stop it. This would allow us to find her so long as she wasn't taken out of Mars City."

Tampering with IDbands was technically illegal without government authorization. Alex had done so knowing full well what would happen if it was ever discovered, but he had deemed Jasmine's safety more important than following the law. Their fates had been tied together because a group of thugs had tried to kidnap her. Such an event could easily be repeated.

I guess that's just another sign that I wasn't cut out to be an officer like my dad.

Alex dispelled the thought before continuing. "The fact that Madison cannot locate Jasmine means that she's no longer within Mars City. I doubt she's even on this planet. Chances are she's on some asteroid somewhere, since the de Fénelon family owns numerous asteroids, including several asteroid belts."

"I'd need to look at Madison's internal components," Gabrielle said, "but I should be able to expand her range to at least five light years if I boost her program using angelisian technology."

"Then let's do that," Alex said, clapping his hands as though the decision was final.

"Okay!" Gabrielle stood up and clenched her left hand into a fist. "I'm gonna get started right now!"

"I'll help." Alex also stood up.

"Hehe, I expected nothing less of you."

"We cannot help you at all," Michelle added, standing as well. "But both of us consider Jasmine a friend, so we'll support you in any way we can."

"Bring her back, ya hear!" Ariel demanded.

"Bro…"

"Don't worry." Alex affectionately ruffled his sister's head. "I'm going to bring her back."

Alice nodded, for once, not muttering troublesome as she stared at him with hope and worry brimming in her eyes. "I'm counting on you."

1

Caelum watched Jasmine through the hologram. The girl had seen better days. Where before she had stood before the viewport, looking out as a queen might stare at her kingdom, now she was lying on the bed. She only moved when she absolutely needed to.

Two days had passed since she had damaged his ribs with her fists, and though the wound had healed, the blow to his pride remained. She had bruised two of his ribs and caused injuries to his lungs. Caelum could not let something like that stand. He wanted nothing more than to show that bitch who was in charge.

I need to be patient.

"Have the drugs taken effect?" he asked the man standing with him.

"Patience," the man said, his voice a surprising baritone. "Jasmine is not ignorant. She knows we're drugging her food and water. That's why she's eating and drinking only as much as she needs to stay alive. Even lying on the bed and moving as little as possible is to slow the drug already in her bloodstream until she can detoxify it."

Jefferson de Truante was an imposing man, though not because of his appearance. He had the same thin body and slender build that most nobles possessed. His slicked back gray hair, while offering him a distinguished demeanor, did not make him seem very intimidating. Even his black business suit didn't help give him this image.

What made Jasmine's father so intimidating was something that couldn't be discerned from the naked eye alone. It was in the way he held himself, in the bone-chilling quality of his gaze, and in how he never smiled. Every time Caelum met with Jefferson de Truante, he could not stop the chill from running up his spine.

"How long do you think it will take?"

"Not much longer." Jefferson de Truante studied the holographic image of his daughter. "We've been monitoring her vital functions, and I was told that the drug will take hold by tomorrow morning. Once that happens, she'll be open to any suggestions we make."

The drug they were using was supposed to be one that would make her mind more malleable to their suggestions. Once her mind became more open, they would suggest that signing the marriage contract was in her best interest.

They wouldn't have resorted to this method normally, but Jasmine had made it clear that she was unwilling to marry him. When Jefferson de Truante told her that she was going to be getting married, not only had she adamantly refused, but she had stated that she was going to marry someone named Alexander.

Caelum scowled at the name. Everyone in the mining industry knew the name Alexander S. Ryker. It was hard not to since quite a few of the machines and androids they used were patented by him. The heavy lifting machinery and drills used in many of his father's mining operations had been created by Alexander. Despite that, the name had never meant much to him...

... until now. Now that name was hindering his family's ultimate goal of seizing more control over the Galactic Defense Force by gaining unrestricted access to the Truante space lanes.

Just you wait, you little brat. Caelum narrowed his eyes as he continued glaring at Jasmine through the hologram. *Very soon, you'll be mine in mind, body, and soul... and then I'll have everything I ever dreamed of.*

2

Gabrielle was able to create a device that they could use to amplify Madison's detection program. She called it Mr. Amplifier, which Alex thought was a silly name, but it was in keeping with Gabrielle's naming scheme. Sadly, none of the names she came up with were ever any good.

The device did not look like much. It was a small tablet about the size of his palm. Angelisian symbols scrolled across the surface. So long as Madison was holding onto it, her detection range extended to five hundred thousand kilometers. Alex hoped it would be enough to detect Jasmine.

He had concocted a plan to locate Jasmine, which was simple, but it should prove effective, if time consuming. Using Azazel's flagship, they would travel to all of the mines that belonged to the de Fénelon family and use Madison's detecting ability. If Jasmine was not there, they would move on to the next one until they found her.

Fortunately, the de Fénelon's were a big family. Their mining operations were common knowledge because so many people worked there. All Alex had to do was hack into Mars' central database, which was connected to the GDF, and download all of the information on the de Fénelon family and their holdings. It told him where all of their mining operations were.

There were only two problems with his plan—two obstacles that he had to remove.

The first was Azazel.

"Of course I will help you, Groom-to-be!"

Fortunately, getting Azazel's help was easy. The moment Alex told Azazel what he wanted help with, that he was going to rescue one of his "future wives"—Gabrielle was actually the one who called Jasmine his future wife—the man had shed tears and agreed to help. He had also spent about fifteen minutes regaling Alex with the tale about how he and his first wife had saved their second wife from a similar predicament.

The second obstacle was going to be a lot harder to solve.

Getting permission to leave the docking station.

Azazel's ship was small, a six passenger vessel that was only used to travel to and from his flagship. Since only six people could go, it meant Alex could only choose one more person to travel with them since the other three spots were being taken by Azazel, Kane, and Abel. He and Madison were definitely going. That meant either Nyx or Gabrielle could come along.

His original thought had been to bring Nyx with him. She was an excellent fighter, well-versed in numerous forms of combat, and more than capable of helping him out. However, Gabrielle had been adamant on going. She claimed it was her duty as his first wife, and that she would not let anyone else rescue her soon-to-be sister.

In the end, he had chosen Gabrielle to come with him.

The vessel that Azazel was using was small and streamlined, with a sharp front that flowed into an organic body of smooth curves instead of hard angles. A pair of fins sat on the back. It didn't look like they did anything. Similarly, the wings jutting from either side near the front appeared to be there more for decoration than function. The entire ship was painted a dark red with blue accents.

Inside the ship was different. It was basically a metal floor with six seats. Two of those seats belonged to the pilot and co-pilot, while the next one was for the navigator. Those stations were taken by Azazel, Kane, and Abel respectively. Meanwhile, Gabrielle sat at the communications station on the left side, while Alex and Nyx sat in the only chairs that were made with ferrying in mind.

"Gabrielle, please patch us through to Commander Karen Kanzaki," Azazel instructed.

"Kay!!"

Gabrielle was quite good at working the communication station, but she had taken apart a lot of ships before, so he wasn't surprised that she knew how they worked. It wasn't long before a holographic screen with Karen's visage appeared before them.

"What is the meaning of this, Azazel?" asked Karen.

"I am requesting permission to leave," Azazel said.

Karen frowned. "Alexander is with you, isn't he?"

Because of the limited adaptability between angelisian and human technology, Karen probably couldn't see anything besides Azazel's face. While Azazel was getting a full view of Karen's body in a holographic 3D image, she was only seeing his face.

"He is," Azazel answered honestly. Alex nodded. Karen could easily find out the truth by checking the surveillance cameras around the spaceport, so there was no point in lying.

"I would like to speak with him."

"Very well. I'm switching perspectives for you."

A moment after Azazel spoke, a screen appeared in front of Alex. It was Karen. Her icy blue eyes, fair skin, and drill-like curls of hair were unmistakable.

"You're going to find Jasmine, aren't you?" Karen asked.

"So you already know what's happening," Alex said. "I should have figured."

But Karen shook her head at his remark. "I do not know all the details, but Caridna informed me that you had asked about Jasmine de Truante's whereabouts, so I did some digging of my own. There's nothing that says what she's doing or where she went, but she was pulled from school by her parents. Sadly, I couldn't find any evidence of her leaving with my surveillance cameras. The de Truante's own a private spaceport on the other side of Mars City."

Alex nodded. "It's probably for the best that you don't ask questions. That way if I get into trouble for what's about to happen, you can claim plausible deniability. Speaking of, is this communication encrypted?"

"I'm using the encryption key that you made me," Karen said.

If she was using the device that he had created for her, then her communication was about as secure as could be. The encryption key was an algorithmic based program that constantly changed the password to her communication station every .5 seconds. The key also used symbols that didn't exist in the human language, therefore no one could break the code unless their hacking program had been specifically made with the intention of decoding his encryption key.

"I won't question what you plan on doing," Karen continued. "However, understand that I won't be able to help you if you get into trouble."

"I know." Alex straightened his back. "But it's not like I'm alone. I have Gabrielle, Azazel, and Azazel's crew behind my back."

"Yes," Karen admitted. The smile on her face seemed a touch bitter. He wondered if perhaps she was envious that he was able to act with this kind of freedom, while she was chained by the bureaucracy and red tape that came from being a police officer. "I suppose that is true. Your vessel is free to launch. Safe travels, Alex."

"Thank you," Alex mumbled as the screen disappeared.

"You okay, Alex?" asked Gabrielle.

"I'm fine," Alex said, sending her a smile from across the shuttle. "I'm just beginning to realize that the world I've stepped into is a lot different than Karen's."

"Do you… regret stepping into that world?"

"No. I don't. You live in that world, after all."

Gabrielle's vibrant smile was all Alex needed to know that he was making the right decision. He might not be following the path of his father, the path that Karen had chosen to follow. He would probably never become a hero like his old man had. However, in the face of that smile, so bright and full of life, Alex concluded that not being like his father wasn't such a bad thing.

3

Jasmine could barely move. Her body felt hot, her mind sluggish, and her thoughts scattered. She understood that this was the drug at work. However, knowing that this sensation had been brought about by a mind-numbing drug didn't really help in this situation. Only one thought kept her from succumbing.

The door to her room opened and someone walked in, the maid who fed her food, perhaps. She could no longer eat on her own, so the maid often force-fed her. Of course, this meant she was getting more of the drug. There was little she could do about that, though.

It wasn't a maid. Jasmine would have groaned as Caelum's face swam into her field of view, but she lacked the strength to do even that much. Behind Caelum was her father, the man who had orchestrated this situation, who was trying to force this marriage on her. She was both afraid of and despised this man.

"How are you feeling, Jasmine?" asked Caelum. "You don't look so well."

Jasmine said nothing.

"You know, all this will end if you just agree to sign the marriage contract," Caelum said.

Jasmine opened her mouth, but no words came out. It wasn't that she couldn't talk. She could if she really wanted to. There was another reason she was pretending to speak.

"What was that?" asked Caelum.

"C… closer," Jasmine said in a weak voice.

Caelum leaned in, further, further, until his ear was literally next to her mouth. He was so close that she could see the pores on his temple.

"What did you say?"

"I said… piss off!"

With a sudden bout of swiftness, Jasmine leaned up and bit Caelum's ear hard. The taste of iron appeared on her tongue as Caelum screamed and yanked his head away from her. The act of jerking his head back caused his ear to tear. He stumbled back and held a hand to his ear. Meanwhile, Jasmine spat out the chunk she had bitten off and glared at him.

"I will… never marry you," she ground out. "I am the Queen of Marriage, and this queen will choose who she wants to be her king."

Caelum's face turned a vile shade of red as his shoulders shook with rage, as he bared his teeth in a snarl. He marched up to her bed and raised his hand. Despite knowing that this was going to hurt in her weakened state, Jasmine did not look away as he tried to bring his hand down.

"No," her father said, catching Caelum by the wrist before he could strike her. "We cannot afford to physically harm her. If you do, they will find out when they perform a physical exam, then the GDF can nullify the marriage."

"Let me go! This bitch deserves it!"

"If you strike her, not even your family name will protect you," her father said. "Since Jasmine is underage, she will have to go through a screening process, and while drugs can be flushed from her system, not even the most advanced healing medicines can keep the GDF from discovering evidence of physical abuse."

Caelum took several deep breaths, shoulders heaving, before he calmed down. Jasmine's father let go of his wrist. Jasmine, who could do nothing but sit there and watch them, remained where she was.

"Consider yourself lucky," Caelum spat. "Once that drug takes effect, you will sign the marriage contract, and you will become my bride. When that happens, I'll make sure you suffer a thousandfold for the insults I've suffered at your hands."

Caelum stormed out of the room, slamming the door shut behind him. Her father remained behind for a while yet. He stared at her with his unwavering gaze that made her think of frozen polar caps, but Jasmine would not let herself be cowed by him. She glared. His entrance was far more quiet than the hot-blooded boy he was following. Only the sound of his cane growing more distant as it tapped against the floor let her know when he left.

Jasmine waited for a full five seconds before allowing herself to fall back on the bed. Sweat covered her body, coating her school uniform to her skin, which was shaking from the intense surge of adrenaline rushing through it. That was not good. When blood pumped through the body faster, it also pumped the drug flowing through her system faster, meaning that she would become more delusional as it took effect.

In hindsight, responding to Caelum like she had was not her best idea. At the same time, she could not let herself appear weak.

She might not be able to escape from this predicament on her own, but she would never let herself show weakness in front of those two.

Now alone in her room, Jasmine's thoughts went back to the one thing that was keeping her from succumbing to the drug.

Alexander... please hurry up and come for me. I don't know how much longer I can last.

4

The de Fénelon family was in charge of twenty-six different mining operations. They ranged to everything from small asteroids to large asteroid belts. Each operation was huge, easily worth hundreds of billions of credits, and some of them were even worth trillions of credits.

The first one that Alex had Azazel travel to was the asteroid belt surrounding Saturn. It was the de Fénelon family's largest operation, therefore the most likely place they would keep her. At least, he would assume so. However, as he stared at the holographic screen, which displayed the mining operation in glorious detail, panning between the many asteroids, surrounded by multiple shuttles and mining machines, he couldn't see anything out of the ordinary.

"Madison? Anything?" he asked.

Madison shook her head. "No. She's not here."

"Then let's move on to the next one."

Alex, Gabrielle, and Madison were on Azazel's flagship, the Dauntless. It was a genesis-class cruiser, which was smaller than the blade-class battleships from Camelot but larger than the destroyer-class cruisers. However, Gabrielle had said that in terms of firepower, the genesis-class was worth at least five blade-classes.

Spanning a length of .5 kilometers, the genesis-class cruiser had the same organic appearance that all angelisian technology had. There were no protruding edges or extensions to be found on the outside, just smooth angles, gentle slopes, and strange hills. It was weird. Alex was used to the harder edges of human vessels. Even the ships from Camelot had the same general hard angles and extending bridges.

The Dauntless' bridge setup was also interesting. The commander's chair was located on a raised platform that overlooked the rest of the bridge. A large viewport filled Alex's vision up front. Down below were the many stations, navigation, fire control, communication, and so on. Alex wondered which seat was the pilot's seat. It seemed odd, but he couldn't figure that one out.

Since they were at Saturn, they decided to expand their search outward from this point. They went to the next closest mining operation. When that turned out to be a bust, they moved onto the next one, and then the next one. After traveling to the tenth asteroid and being unsuccessful, Alex decided that they needed to change their strategy.

"This is taking too long," he muttered, standing beside the command chair with Gabrielle and Madison. Azazel was sitting in the chair. "It took four hours to check all of these places. We don't know what sort of trouble Jasmine is in. We can't afford to take this long."

Azazel crossed his arms and leaned back. "While I do understand what you are saying, it's not like we can do this any other way. We can't use faster than light travel inside of a solar system. It's too small. We'd bypass our target almost the moment we entered. All we can do is travel to each one and check them out."

Hovering in the air above them was a map of the solar system. It showed not only the planets, but also all of the asteroid and asteroid belts. The asteroids owned by the de Fénelon family were marked in blue, while the ones they had already checked were marked in red. There were sixteen more to go, but the rest were out of the way. It would take hours just to reach each one of them.

They didn't have hours.

Alex couldn't explain it, but something in his gut was telling him to hurry, telling him that if they didn't find Jasmine soon, it would be too late. Maybe it was paranoia. Maybe it was instinct. It didn't matter. Even if he was merely being paranoid, he felt it was better to rescue her quickly than leave her to keep suffering alone.

"Is there no way to track her down faster?" Alex asked.

"What if we have this all wrong?" Gabrielle said suddenly. Everyone turned to look in her directions.

Alex blinked. "Excuse me?"

"I was thinking about it this whole time," Gabrielle continued. "We're checking the biggest operations first because it would be easier to hide one person there than at the smaller asteroids, but what if she's not being hidden at any of these places? The de Fénelons are nobles, right? That means they probably have their own private asteroid where they live. She's probably there."

"If she's in a private mansion, or hidden away somewhere, then the chances of us finding her are small," Madison said. "Nobles who live on asteroids often keep the information on the whereabouts of their homes a secret."

"But that doesn't mean we can't triangulate where they might be," Gabrielle said. "Azazel, connect all of the mining operations that the de Fénelon family owns together."

"Hold on for just a moment." Azazel used a keypad on the armrest of his command chair to manipulate the holographic map. "There."

Several lines spread out from each of the asteroids and asteroid belts, moving until they connected with the nearest mining operations to them.

Their solar system had two asteroid belts surrounding it, one just past Mars and another past Pluto called the Kuiper Belt. In between these belts were several single asteroids. Eros. Ceres. Voyager. Eris. Ignis. Astros. Astelos. Then there were the belts surrounding Saturn and Uranus.

As the lines connected the de Fénelons asteroid mining operations together, they created a triangle in the very center of their formation.

"Azazel, zoomed into this spot right here." Gabrielle pointed at the triangle in the center of all those lines.

"Very well."

Azazel manipulated the controls again, and then the holographic map zoomed into that one area, right between the triangles.

"Look at that!" Gabrielle pointed at the spot between the triangles. In the very middle of that triangle was a single, small asteroid. It wasn't large enough to mine. However, that there was an asteroid there at all was suspicious. "See this? I bet you this is where they're hiding!"

"You might be right." Alex smiled. "Good job figuring that out, Gabby!"

"Tee-hee!"

Since they had a new plan and a new destination, Azazel ordered their navigators to head in that direction. It took 2.5 hours to reach the small asteroid. It was smack in the center of all the mining operations, which meant it was further than he would have liked. They were near Uranus, and the center of all these de Fénelon mining operations was inside the first asteroid belt.

The asteroid belt was thick with asteroids. All the asteroids were tightly packed together. The Dauntless was a huge flagship. It was too large to navigate the asteroid belt, so Azazel had them go out in a small frigate that was barely a tenth the size of all those asteroids.

Alex was sitting around a table with Gabrielle, Azazel, Kane, and Abel, while Madison stood behind him. He would have asked the robot maid to join them, but he knew she would refuse. Despite it not being part of her programming, Madison stood by the belief that a maid should always be right behind her master or mistress, in case they needed something from her. She had likely picked it up from a holodocumentary or maybe even an old-fashioned book.

"How should we go about rescuing Jasmine?" asked Azazel.

"We're not going to need any complicated plans," Alex said. "We're going to storm the place, find Jasmine, and get her out. If someone gets in our way, then we beat the crap out of them."

"Won't they have guards?" asked Kane.

"They'll probably have security droids," Alex answered. "Most nobles are allowed to own a security force consisting of droids, but they're allowed no more than one hundred of them. There will probably be more than that, simply because nobles like to think they're above the law, but I doubt they'll be a problem."

"If they have an army of droids, I'll just have to bring out my army!" Gabrielle added.

"Please don't," everyone at the table said.

"Master," Madison said suddenly, "I'm picking up Jasmine's signal."

At her words, Azazel raised a wrist to his mouth. He pressed a button on his vambrace and spoke into it. Alex realized that his armor had communication equipment inside. That was... kind of cool, actually.

"Stella, have we reached our destination?"

"Yes, sir. We've reached the asteroid in question."

"Bring it up on screen."

The center of the table suddenly lit up, and then the holographic image of an asteroid hovered over it. Misshapen and lumpy, the asteroid didn't resemble any specific geometric pattern.

Pockmarks covered the surface as the image slowly rotated. It stopped at one particular section and zoomed in, revealing that there was a blast door located inside one of the craters.

"That's probably a docking bay." Azazel cupped a hand to his chin. "If possible, I would like to avoid entering through the docking bay since it's an obvious entrance. Let's try and find an escape hatch. If these people are nobles, they should have an emergency escape route that we can sneak through."

"Good idea," Alex agreed.

There was, indeed, an escape hatch. It was a small port on the opposite side of the asteroid. Everyone decided that this was how they would be entering.

"Everyone suit up," Azazel said. "Groom-to-Be. Princess Gabrielle. We have prepared atmosphere suits for you."

"Thanks!" Gabrielle said.

"Much appreciated," Alex said.

The atmosphere suits were basically just spacesuits, but they looked different from the ones he was used to. Because human technology was far behind angelisian technology, human suits were large and bulky so as to create and contain its own atmosphere. Oxygen flowed through a tank on the back, while the suit was made purposefully large to help with the circulation of air.

Angelisian suits were skintight. They were a lot like the crisis suits, though they had a bit more wiggle room. A crisis suit was literally like wearing a second skin. These were still like wearing a suit, but it conformed more readily to the body than a human suit.

Of course, like human suits, this one did come with a helmet, though it was shaped like a bullet.

As the ship set down on the asteroid's surface, Alex bent his knees and gritted his teeth as the vibration sent tingles down his spine. It was not a pleasant feeling.

The boarding ramp opened. Azazel led them all out, jumping from the ramp and landing on the ground in a crouch. Alex followed him out with Gabrielle and Madison (who didn't need a suit). His stomach flipped around as he experienced a frightening moment of complete weightlessness, but then the suit's magnetic locks kicked in, and he suddenly found his knees being jarred as he crashed feet first into the ground.

I really don't like this.

Alex almost fell on his knees as a sense of vertigo overcame him. He took a stumbling step forward, righted himself, and then took several slow breaths to calm down. He could do this. He could.

"Follow me." Azazel's voice crackled in his ear. Meanwhile, the ship they had been in lifted back off. It was probably going to hang in orbit until they were ready for pickup.

They moved over to the emergency entrance, which, now that he was standing before it, Alex realized it was a small blast door built into a hill. Next to the blast door was a panel that could probably be used to access the emergency exit from the outside. However, it would probably require a droid to hack.

"I don't see any way to open the door," Azazel said. "Kane, you know what to do."

"Right!"

As Kane walked up to the door, Alex wondered what the man was planning—until a bright greenish silver aura enveloped his body.

"Wait!" Alex shouted. "Don't do that! I can use my—"

But it was too late. With a roar like that of an engine going full throttle, Kane shot a beam of energy from his hand that slammed into the door, blew it wide open, and continued traveling for several meters before blowing up.

"What the hell was that for?!" demanded Alex.

"What?" asked Azazel. "We're just opening the door."

"You didn't have to blow it up! Gabby or I could have easily opened that door!"

"And I have the ability to hack into doors as well," Madison added.

"Oh…" Azazel paused as he absorbed this information. "My bad."

If Alex had not been wearing a helmet, he would have smashed his hand against his face.

There was nothing for it, however. What was done was done. All they could do now was move forward, so Alex rushed ahead of Azazel and turned around to keep him from entering.

"From now on, you are going to obey my commands, got it?"

"You know I cannot do that," Azazel said. "We are soldiers. That would disrupt the—"

"You might be soldiers, but I'm Gabrielle's fiancé. That means I'll eventually be your king. Am I wrong?"

"You are not wrong, but…"

"You will listen to my orders."

Azazel frowned, but then relented. Standing up straighter, he placed his left hand against his breast. "Very well, Groom-to-Be. We will listen to your orders."

"Good. Then let's go."

Sirens began blaring all around them as they raced through a tube-shaped hallway, and Alex resisted the urge to say *"I told you so"* to Azazel, since he knew saying that wouldn't do any good. Damn that Kane and his violent way of doing things. Damn Azazel for ordering it. Now the de Fénelons would definitely know they were here.

The emergency exit led into a really small docking bay with only a single shuttle. From the small size, the wings jutting from either side, and the fact that he could only see two seats in the bulb-like cockpit, it was probably a custom escape model. Nobles used these to run away when the situation got dangerous. Azazel wanted to destroy it, but Alex decided that he and Jasmine would be using that for their escape, since they didn't have a suit for her.

Naturally, the door leading into the next section was locked, but Alex already had a way of getting around that, and it involved a certain robot maid.

"Madison. Open this door please."

"Yes, Master."

Madison raised her hand, and while nothing seemed to happen, Alex knew that she was remotely hacking into the system. It was one of the many features he had given her. After all, if she had to rescue Jasmine, there was no telling when she'd need to hack into a security system.

The door slid open moments later with a gentle hiss.

"Nice! Come on, everyone!"

Alex led the group into another hallway. Their helmets retracted as the air around them pressurized. This room had an atmosphere. There was another door at the end, which was also locked, though Madison opened it easily enough. What lay beyond that door was no station or hidden base. Extravagant marble tiles, beautiful Corinthian columns, and a number of statues lent the entrance hall an opulent air that made his lips curl.

Freaking nobles.

"Madison! Lead the way!" Alex instructed.

"Yes, Master." Madison stepped forward. "Follow me."

They traveled up the entrance hall staircase and into another hallway, but before they could get too far, several droids appeared from in front of and behind them. Oblong heads swiveled around. Red lenses glowed brightly. Spindly arms and hands with five digits held long blaster rifles in their grasp. Their legs moved on completely metal socket joints, which were visible, unlike Madison's. Poorly constructed. That was what Alex thought of them. These things were nothing like Madison.

"Azazel! I want you, Kane, and Abel to hold them off!" Alex ordered.

"Yes, Groom-to-Be!" Azazel pulled his energy sword from his belt, the blade igniting in a flash of incandescent energy. "You heard him, men! Let's show them what soldiers of the Angelisian Army are made of!"

"YEAH!!!" Kane and Abel shouted as they pulled out their weapons, a rifle and a pair of knucklers respectively.

Alex didn't pay attention to the trio as they charged at the droids behind them. He raised a hand and thought of Jasmine, alone and trapped somewhere inside of this mansion, and the warm flood of energy came pouring into him. His body became enveloped in an aura, the Aura of Creation, which he used to create and fire several spheres like they were blaster bolts.

Not all of his spheres struck something, but the ones that did destroyed everything. One robot's head was blown clean off. Another lost chunks of its torso. Still another lost its leg before it was struck again, this time losing a shoulder.

He wasn't the only one attacking. Gabrielle had summoned a rifle of some sort from her D-space, and she was using it to great effect. Bolts of what at first appeared to be lightning slammed into numerous machines, but they didn't go down. Instead, the robots who got hit started shooting at the other robots.

It wasn't long before a large gap was formed in the center of the robots, and as he, Gabrielle, and Madison ran through it.

He turned to his companion. "What kind of weapon is that?"

"It's not a weapon, silly." Gabrielle stored the device back in her D-space. "It's called Mr. Scrambler. It scrambles the operating system of any machine that gets hit with it."

"And that makes them attack each other?"

"I guess… it usually just makes them act weird, but since these are war droids, it might make them attack everything."

"Huh…"

They turned another corner, Madison in the lead. As they reached the end of that hallway, loud shouting echoed from a door several meters away. One of the voices was familiar.

"Mistress is in there," Madison said.

Alex didn't bother seeing if the door would open. He charged his Aura of Creation and destroyed it with a concentrated beam of energy. As the door disintegrated, Alex charged in with Madison and Gabrielle behind him.

What he found on the other side was a large room of decadent taste. Paintings hung from the walls, statues decorated the room, and the red carpet had golden designs swirling over it. Alex had seen Jasmine's room before, back when they were younger, and it had looked nothing like this. He guessed it was because Jasmine, noble though she might have been, was a simple girl at heart.

On the opposite side of the room, two people were sitting on the bed. Jasmine was one of them. She was limply hanging from the grip of a man who Alex had never seen, a blond-haired pretty boy who was holding her against him. His hand was grabbing her chest, while the other held a dueling pistol that was pressed to Jasmine's head, which was lolling about as though the muscles in her neck were non-existent.

"I hope you plan on showing this man what happens when he touches your things."

Don't call Jasmine a thing.

"That was highly inappropriate of you."

"Hmph!"

Despite how callous Asmodeus' words were, Alex would not deny the hot, red anger coursing through his body. Jasmine was being grabbed by who he could only guess was Caelum. He was touching her inappropriately and threatening her with a pistol. Yes, anger did not really begin to cover it. He wanted to tear this guy's limbs off.

"You must be Caelum," Alex said, stepping forward.

"Stay back or I'll kill Jasmine!" Caelum shrieked. "Don't think I won't!"

"If you kill Jasmine, I will kill you," Alex said. It was the first time he had ever threatened to kill someone, but Alex knew that he would do it if Caelum killed Jasmine. "Let her go." Caelum shook his head. Alex felt more fire surge through his blood. "Let. Her. Go."

He took another step forward. Caelum pressed the gun harder into her temple.

"I said stay back! Stay back! Stay back! Stay—!!"

Caelum's head snapped back as Alex flung an energy sphere at him. The gun in his grasp jerked away from Jasmine's head as he fell backward, taking Jasmine, who was still in his grip, with him.

Alex rushed forward, but Madison moved faster, reaching them before Jasmine could fall and pulling her from the man's grip. She held the girl in her arms. Alex thought she looked more like a mother holding her daughter than a maid.

As Alex reached them, he realized what poor shape Jasmine was in. Her body was covered in sweat. Her face was pale. On top of that, Alex could see her veins pulsing beneath her skin, ugly and purple as though they were being clogged. Even worse was how erratic her breathing was.

"They drugged her," Madison said. "It's a mind-altering drug to make her more malleable to their suggestions. She probably resisted until the very end."

Alex moved onto the bed, until he was right next to Jasmine and Madison. Gabrielle said nothing as she followed him. He could feel her presence behind his back, but it was muted. Most of his attention was on Jasmine.

"Hey, Jasmine," he said. "Jasmine, can you hear me?"

Jasmine stirred and slowly opened her eyes, rimmed with dark circles, and stared at him with a nearly incomprehensible look.

"Alex...?" she slurred.

"I'm here," Alex said.

"You're late."

Alex almost smiled. "Sorry."

"I went through a lot... because you took so long to get here."

"I'm sorry."

"Take responsibility."

"Erm... what?"

While it was weak, Jasmine was definitely giving him a determined glare, even though it looked more like a pathetic glance at the moment.

"You will take responsibility for me."

It was amazing how, even like this, in this situation, she could say something like that. Jasmine had been drugged, was currently weaker than a kitten, and couldn't even move, but she was still demanding that he take responsibility for what happened. It was such a Jasemine-ish thing to do.

"Don't worry," Alex said. "I'll definitely take responsibility for you."

Even though she was weaker than Alex had ever seen her, Jasmine managed to smile. "Good."

It seemed just those acts were too much for her. She passed out several seconds later, her eyes closing as her body went limp. If it weren't for her shallow breaths, Alex might have even thought she was dead.

"Let me take her," Alex said. Madison hesitated for a moment, but then she handed the girl over to him. Alex cradled Jasmine in his arms, one under around her shoulder and the other under her knees, and climbed off the bed. He looked around for a moment, thinking about what they needed to do, and then nodded as he organized his thoughts and came up with a plan. "Madison, I want you to find this place's central security system, hack into it, and download every file they have."

"All of it?" asked Madison.

"All of it," Alex said. "Store it in one of your portable memory spaces. We'll need it later."

"Yes, Master."

Madison stared at Jasmine for a second before heading to the door. She paused at the doorway, turned her head back to look at

Jasmine one more time, and then left. Several explosions echoed back to him seconds after that.

While her primary function was to be Jasmine's friend and maid, she also seconded as a bodyguard, so Madison had several anti-personal weapons and knew hand-to-hand combat. No doubt she was tearing through the war droids like they were made of paper.

"Are you ready to leave, Ga... bby?" he paused when he noticed that Gabrielle was staring at Jasmine. "Is something wrong?"

"No." Gabrielle placed a hand to her chest, shook her head, and smiled. "Nothing is wrong. I just felt funny right here... like, my chest felt all tight and stuff."

It sounded like Gabrielle might have been feeling jealous of Jasmine, but he didn't know if that was really the case. She was always so gungho about the thought of him marrying Jasmine and Selene. Could she even get jealous?

"Well, let's move out." Alex made for the door, Jasmine's legs swinging back and forth as her head rested against his chest. "We can't afford to stay here."

"Right!"

Escaping from this place meant backtracking the way they had come. That meant following the path of destruction left by them their first time around. They carefully chose their way around the scattered remains of war droids that littered the floor. It looked like the droids that had been affected by Mr. Scramble had either gone off in search of other prey, or self-destructed after accomplishing their goal. Either way, there was no one to hinder their path.

"Azazel?" Gabrielle spoke into the device on her wrist.

"Yes, Princess Gabrielle?" Azazel's voice came back.

"We've got Jasmine," she said. "We're heading back toward the escape route's docking bay."

There was a short pause. Then...

"Understood. We've already taken care of all the war droids, so we're heading back now as well. I've already contacted Stella. She'll be swinging back around to pick us up."

"You go on ahead without us," Gabrielle said. "Alex, Madison, and I are taking the emergency shuttle out of here. I want you to go on ahead and have your soldiers prepare a healing tank for Jasmine. She's been drugged."

"I understand. We'll go ahead and get everything ready. Be careful."

"Tee-hee! Of course!"

Alex had memorized the route they had taken to reach Jasmine, so he did his best to backtrack, which was harder than it looked since Azazel, Kane, and Abel had clearly gone out of their way to destroy droids everywhere. It didn't matter which hallway he looked down. Everywhere he looked were the remains of droids. Sparking arms lay over there. Dismembered legs sparked to his left. There were heads and the ruined bodies of droids that had avoided outright destruction. This scene of decimation followed them all the way to the entrance hall, where they took the stairs back down.

Someone was waiting for them at the bottom.

He was a tall man. He didn't have broad shoulders or a strong chest. He was thin and walked with a cane. His gray hair was slicked back to show off his cold eyes, and his gaunt, aristocratic face, looked as though it had been hewn from stone. He stood in the middle of the entrance hall, his chilling expression, more emotionless and colder even than Nyx, stared at Alex as he stopped several meters away.

"Alexander S. Ryker," the man said. "I should have expected you to interfere in my affairs."

"Jefferson de Truante." Alex narrowed his eyes as Gabrielle looked between them. "Are you going to stop me?"

Jefferson snorted. "Do not be boorish. I am not a man of violence."

"But you are the kind of man who would drug his own daughter." Jefferson said nothing. "If you aren't going to try and stop us, then move aside."

Jefferson did nothing at first. He stood there, back straight, cane pressed against the floor as he held it in one hand. Eventually, however, he did move, slowly at first, eyes never leaving Alex. It was like he was telling Alex with his eyes that he was always watching. It was creepy, but Jefferson had always been a creepy guy. Alex ignored it.

He and Gabrielle walked past Jefferson, who continued staring at Alex, and even after his back was to the older man, he could still feel Jefferson's gaze on it.

"Do you really think you'll get away with this?" asked Jefferson. "I know that you are the type who acts without thinking, but even you must know that you'll never get away with what you've done this day. Come tomorrow morning, the Galactic Defense Force will come to arrest you. You'll be sent to prison and Jasmine will be back here. Nothing will have changed, not for her, at least."

Alex stopped walking. Gabrielle also stopped. She looked at him, head tilted curiously, but he said nothing to her.

There were so many things he wanted to say, so many things he would have loved to say. He wanted to yell at this sorry excuse for a father. He wanted to rage at him. He wanted to force this man onto his knees and make him acknowledge that he was unworthy to be Jasmine's dad. There were a lot of things that Alex wanted to say and do.

He didn't do any of it.

He merely turned his head, looked Jefferson in the eye, and said, "I think you're underestimating me."

And then he turned his head again and continued walking away. He didn't look back, though he knew that Jefferson was still staring at him. Walking by his side, Gabrielle presented him with a curious look that he returned with a reassuring smile.

"Let's get out of here," he said.

Gabrielle nodded. Her expression went back to her usual smile, the one that reminded Alex of a sun.

"Okay!" she said, and the two of them continued on. They walked through the hall, emerged into the docking bay, and went up to the emergency escape ship.

Looking at it more closely, Alex could see that it was actually a modified version of the A1 Sky Hopper, an atmospheric shuttle used for traveling through domed cities and planets that had an atmosphere. The fuselage sloped from the sharp front, growing bigger in the back, which ended in a pair of fins that jutted from two turbine thrusters. A half-sphere of glasteel covered the cockpit. There were only two seats, meaning that they would be sharing.

Gabrielle opened the cockpit. He had his hands full and couldn't. Fortunately, the gravity here was light, so Alex only had to leap onto the fuselage to reach the cockpit. Neither he nor Gabrielle strapped in as they sat down. Gabrielle would be sharing a seat with Madison, and he had Jasmine resting on his lap. The girl in question murmured something softly as he readjusted her on the seat so she'd be comfortable. Then she pressed her nose against his neck and breathed deeply. He smiled and ran his hands through her golden locks of hair, currently not in her usually twin drills.

"Alex?" Gabrielle said suddenly.

"Yes?" he said.

"Is it bad that I wish I was sitting on your lap instead of Jasmine?"

Alex forced himself not to overreact. "I don't think so. Why do you ask?"

"Because seeing you and Jasmine like this makes my chest feel tight."

"Do you not like it when Jasmine is this close to me?"

"That's not it…" Alex couldn't see her, but he could imagine the way her hair jostled as she shook her head. "I think it's great that you two are so close. I hope you grow even closer. I just… wish I could also be with you like that right now."

Alex was not the best judge of emotions. He didn't think he was dense, but when he was faced with an emotion he didn't understand, or that he couldn't recognize, he ignored it. Even so, Alex was sure that what Gabrielle was feeling was jealousy—a mild form, to be sure, but she was still jealous.

"Are you really certain it's okay for me to take more than one wife?" Alex asked again.

"Of course I'm sure," Gabrielle said with a certainty that couldn't be faked. "I think it's a great idea."

"So long as you're sure," Alex said. It seemed that Gabrielle really was the type who only felt jealousy in mild doses. Perhaps she was simply uncertain of her own feelings because they had yet to do anything as a couple.

Speaking of, I still need to take her out on a date.

He hadn't been able to do it yet because of this incident, but it was a bridge that he would need to cross eventually.

Madison would join up with them a few minutes later, and the four of them would take the emergency escape shuttle and fly their way to the Dauntless.

On a side note, Alex would end up crashing the shuttle when he tried to land it. He had never taken flying lessons, after all.

5

The first thing that needed to be done upon returning to the Dauntless was getting Jasmine into a healing tank.

Medical technology on Angelisia far surpassed what the humans in his solar system had. Their healing tanks were far more advanced, capable of flushing out toxins and healing fatal injuries without leaving a scar. A night in a healing tank would cure Jasmine of any lingering problems. She wouldn't even grow addicted to the drug, which was what would have happened if she'd had it flushed from her system using human technology.

Alex was still seething in rage at knowing that Jefferson had drugged his own daughter—no, that he had drugged Jasmine. The very thought sent red hot anger coursing through his body all over again.

Mind-altering drugs like the one that Jefferson had been giving Jasmine were made to be addictive. The drug would make a person's mind more malleable, more open to suggestion and manipulation, essentially turning them into a puppet. At the same time, it also made them need the drug. They would require more and more of it until they eventually became so addicted that their body couldn't live without it.

"I'm surprised you didn't kill that douche for what he did."

I wanted to…

"But?"

"It wouldn't be right."

No… that's not my reason. The one who deserves to exact revenge on Jefferson isn't me. It's Jasmine.

"Ho ho! Giving the girl her chance for revenge. Good man."

"I must confess, I'm a little disappointed, but I do understand where you're coming from. What that man did was deplorable."

Alex let the two voices talk to each other as he leaned against the wall, closed his eyes, and took several calming breaths. It was getting a little easier to control his urges now that Asmodeus and Sachiel had come to some agreement. He still didn't know why they had started getting along, but he didn't care. It was easier for him. That was what mattered.

By the way, I don't think I ever got your name…

"You'll find out when the time is right."

How cryptic.

"You specialize in cryptic dialogue."

…

Alex sighed as he realized that he wasn't going to get anything out of these two. He wasn't even sure why he had bothered.

The place that he was in was not the medical bay, where Jasmine was currently floating naked in a healing tank, but instead the hallway nearest to it. Gabrielle was with Jasmine. Alex had requested that she stay there. Fortunately, the physician was a woman, so Alex didn't have to worry about a male trying to do something untoward to Jasmine while he wasn't there.

"Are you all right, Master?" a voice said behind him.

Alex turned around. Only one person called him "Master." Madison. The robot maid stood there with her hands clasped, head bowed in polite inquiry, eyes showing concern.

"I'm okay." Alex ran a hand through his hair. "I'm surprised you aren't with Jasmine right now."

"Jasmine is currently healing in a tank," Madison said with a sniff. "There is nothing I can do to help right now."

Alex smiled as he realized how much not being able to help Jasmine was eating at her. "In that case, maybe you can help me."

"Of course, Master. What do you need?"

With his smile growing just a little wider, Alex told Madison of his plan to keep Jefferson from ever touching Jasmine again.

CHAPTER 3

BLACKMAIL FOR A NOBLE CAUSE

Since Alex was busy doing something to help Jasmine with her family, Gabrielle had offered to stay by the girl's side. She knew that Alex wanted to be the first one to greet Jasmine when the girl woke up. However, if he wanted his plan to work, then he couldn't afford to sit and wait. She remembered the old saying about striking while the iron is hot. It was a reference to how people used to create tools by hand. Gabrielle thought it was a cute saying.

In matters like this, speed was of the essence.

The Dauntless had an advanced medical bay, a large room filled with equipment, beds, examination tables, and healing tanks. Being a large vessel with a lot of crew members, the medical bay had ten healing tanks and twenty beds. The beds themselves used a type of memory foam, so patients could sleep comfortably.

Underneath each bed was monitoring equipment that kept constant watch over a person's vitals.

Jasmine was lying on one of the beds. The drugs had already been removed from her body, and there would be no lasting side effects, but she still needed rest to properly recover. According to the doctor, she had been receiving the mind-altering drug for about two days. To top it off, Jasmine had barely eaten anything since being kidnapped by her own father.

It had been about twelve hours since she'd emerged from the healing tank.

Gabrielle had been sitting by the bedside for about an hour now, though she had technically been there for far longer. Having stayed with Jasmine since before she even emerged from the healing tank, she had pretty much been in the medical bay this whole time. She'd just come back from the restroom.

The medical bay was quiet. The physician, a woman named Angelus, was currently out. Gabrielle didn't know where she was. Also, unlike a human medical facility, which had all kinds of machines that booped and beeped and made a variety of noises, the medical equipment in this hospital was silent. Gabrielle liked the human equipment more. Sure, it was outdated and didn't work half as well as angelisian medical equipment, but the noise was a lot more soothing than this eerie silence.

As she stared at Jasmine, Gabrielle thought about what she should say when the blonde woke up. Of course, she would greet her with a smile. That much was obvious. However, there were other things that they needed to talk about.

"She really is pretty," Gabrielle muttered to herself. "I can see why Alex likes her so much."

Jasmine's blonde hair looked almost gold as it spread across the white bed. It wasn't in her usual drill-like curls, so each strand appeared longer than normal. Her hair would reach down to her butt if she was standing. The white smock that she wore also did little to cover her, which meant Gabrielle was aware of the girl's unblemished porcelain skin and large boobs. They weren't as big as hers, but they were still big, and they looked even bigger because she was so short.

Alex liked big boobs. It was only natural that he would like Jasmine.

Gabrielle reached out with a hand and began gently stroking the girls hair. Back when she lived in the palace on Angelisia, she would often do this for her sisters. It comforted her just as much as it did her sisters. She hoped it would help Jasmine.

As she continued to stare at the girl, Gabrielle thought about how she would bring the topic of Jasmine becoming Alex's third wife. It was really important. Jasmine loved Alex, and Gabrielle was sure that Alex loved Jasmine, so they needed to be together. Any outcome besides that was unacceptable. The problem was that she had already tried to convince Jasmine to marry Alex with her, and the girl had thought she was trying to play a trick.

She must have been sitting there longer than she'd thought because a low groan sounded from Jasmine as her eyes fluttered open.

"Jasmine!" Gabrielle leaned forward, though she was careful not to get too close. Alex had once mentioned something about personal space. She didn't know what that was, but she was trying to be conscious of it.

Blinking several times, Jasmine looked around with just her eyes. They seemed a bit unfocused, but Gabrielle thought it was because she had just woken up after having several drugs flushed from her body. There wouldn't be any lasting side effects. Even so, that didn't change the fact that she had been drugged. Short-term problems were to be expected.

Finally, Jasmine's eyes locked onto her. "Trollip? What are you doing here? Where is here? Where's Alexander?"

"Let me answer those one at a time," Gabrielle said. "You're currently in the Dauntless' medical bay—that's Azazel's flagship, in case you were wondering. Alex and I brought you here after saving you from those noble people who were trying to force you into an unwanted marriage. Alex is... busy. He wanted to be here with you, but there's more that he has to do if he wants to keep the same thing from happening to you again. I offered to watch you for him while he was dealing with that."

"I see." Jasmine frowned.

"Are you okay?" asked Gabrielle.

Jasmine looked at her, brows furrowed, and then grunted. "I am fine. I just didn't want your face to be the first thing I saw when I woke up."

That comment stung. Gabrielle felt a strange pain in her chest at the words, which seemed to have been made out of hatred.

"Do you... really dislike me?" she asked. "I thought we were friends."

"I do not hate you," Jasmine admitted, "but I don't like how you hog Alexander all to yourself. I loved him before you and he ever met. I hate that you are closer to him than me."

Gabrielle believed she was beginning to understand Jasmine a bit better. She still remembered the sharp pain she had felt when Alex and Kazekiri went on that date, which had turned out not to be a date at all. This pain that Jasmine felt, which caused the girl to dislike her so much, must have been the same.

In other words, it was jealousy.

"I think I get it," Gabrielle murmured, eyes growing a bit damp. "You love Alexander so much that you don't like it when other people are near him. You want him all to yourself."

"That's right," Jasmine admitted. "I do want him all to myself. I don't want him looking at any other girl. I want him to look only at me, to see only me, and I dislike how he doesn't thanks to you."

She was being awfully honest. Whenever the topic of Alex came up, Jasmine would always laugh her *"Oh ho ho ho ho!"* laugh and say something silly. Then again, she was still groggy from just waking up after being drugged. Maybe that was why she was being so honest. Gabrielle didn't know.

"I understand that you want Alex to pay attention to you. I get that now."

Wanting to be the only one that the person you love looked at, to be the only one that mattered, was natural. Gabrielle sort of understood that now. At the same time, she had a different belief than the people of this solar system, so even though she understood, or perhaps because she understood, she believed even more strongly in her own idea of what it meant to be in a relationship.

"But I also don't want us to fight over Alex. Why do we have to fight over the person we love? I think we can both love him together."

Jasmine sighed as though exhausted. "That's the dumbest thing I've ever heard. It isn't possible."

"It is!" Gabrielle's shout echoed across the medical bay. Jasmine was stunned into silence. "It is possible! Papa is married to my momma, Ariel's momma, and Michelle's momma, and they get along just fine! It works! And we can work, too!"

Gabrielle grabbed Jasmine's hand, the one nearest to her, and held it in both of hers. Jasmine struggled to pull it away, but she was still weak. She didn't have the strength. And even if she was at her best, it wouldn't have mattered because a human could never match the strength of an angelisian, especially not one wearing a crisis suit.

"What are you doing?" Jasmine said. "Let go."

"I love you!" Jasmine froze at her words, and Gabrielle used that moment to continue. "You and Alice and Kazekiri and Selene and Ryoko and Serah... I love all of you. You don't even realize how important you are to me. Before I came here, the only people to keep me company were my robots. I couldn't even see my sisters very often because I was always being forced to make weapons and study up on how to be a proper princess."

Gabrielle didn't like to think about her life before coming to Mars. Outside of the few times where she had been allowed to visit her sisters, or the times she was introduced to foreign dignitaries and potential suitors, she never saw anybody, never spoke with anybody—unless she was causing problems. It had been lonely. She had hated it. Half the reason she kept tearing apart warships was because it at least made people pay more attention to her, Gabrielle, and not the Princess of Angelisia or the genius weapons inventor.

"That's why I know this can work," Gabrielle continued. Jasmine had stopped struggling and was staring at her with round eyes. She pressed onward. "I know this can work because you and I both love Alex, and I love you and Alex, and I want us to always be together."

She understood that her way of thinking was simple. There were a lot of things that Gabrielle didn't understand, that she just couldn't wrap her mind around. It had only been recently that she'd begun experiencing that thing called jealousy, and it was really only thanks to Michelle that she realized what this feeling meant. She would admit, she still didn't fully understand it.

But that didn't matter to her. Gabrielle could do nothing less than give her best with the knowledge she had. Even if she didn't know everything there was to know about relationships, even if she was ignorant about a lot of issues in matters revolving around love, she would continue pushing forward using the knowledge that she did have.

"I don't want to be the reason you can't be together with Alex, but I also don't want you to take Alex from me." Gabrielle tried to will Jasmine to understand with her eyes, tried to express her desire through her hands. She wanted—no, she needed to make this girl understand how she felt. "I know that there might be some bumps along the way. You and I might get jealous of each other from time to time. We might fight. But... but even if we fight sometimes, I think we can make this work. We both love Alex, and I really want... you to become part of my family. I want us to be like sisters."

Throughout her entire tirade, Jasmine had done nothing but stare at her. Gabrielle wanted to hunch her shoulders. The look that Jasmine was giving her made her feel like she had said something she shouldn't have.

"You... you are being serious," Jasmine said at last. "You're not joking."

Gabrielle frowned. "Why would I joke about this?"

"The last time we spoke about this, you said something very similar," Jasmine said. "I thought you were just mocking me."

Her cheeks swelled as Gabrielle pouted. "I would never mock you."

"Yes, I, the Queen of Understanding, am beginning to understand that." Jasmine smiled.

A long silence stretched out between them, awkward and somewhat stifling, at least to Gabrielle. Should she say something else? What should she say? She wanted to convince Jasmine that they could make this work, but she didn't know how to convey that. Gabrielle had never done this before. She wasn't sure how to express herself.

"Let us say that I agreed to share Alex with you," Jasmine said suddenly. "How would that even work?"

"What do you mean?"

"I mean how would that work? We can't both marry him."

"Sure we can."

"Are you making fun of me?"

"No! Why would I do that? I'm being honest."

This was so much harder than Gabrielle thought it would be. She didn't know how to convince Jasmine that they should both marry Alex. It had to be because the people of this solar system had weird ideas about marriage. She wished they would realize why their way of thinking was so dumb. Limiting yourself to one having one husband or wife meant that the other people who loved you couldn't be with you.

Gabrielle was only interested in Alex, but she wasn't the only one who was interested in him. When it came to matters of marriage, the people who weren't interested in another person often married someone who had more than one spouse. That was how it worked for Papa, and that was how it went for Arty's papa.

"Do you really think this can work?" asked Jasmine.

"Of course it can work." Gabrielle was still holding Jasmine's hand. She gave it what she hoped was a comforting squeeze. "I really want you to become a part of my family, and I think it would be fun if we could both love Alex."

"There's just no reasoning with you." Grunting, Jasmine tried to sit up—only to fall back onto the bed. She gave Gabrielle an aggrieved look. "Help me sit up."

Gabrielle didn't understand why Jasmine wanted to do that when she should have been resting, but she decided to concede to the girl's demand. She helped Jasmine sit up. The girl tilted for a moment, one way and then the other, as though she was about to fall, but Gabrielle kept her steady.

Jasmine coughed into her hand, and then she put her hand to her mouth…

"Oh ho ho ho ho!"

And then she laughed. It was weaker than her usual *"oh ho ho ho ho!"*'s, which were often loud enough to be heard across Alex's house, but Gabrielle was pleasantly surprised by the strength it had.

"Very well, Gabrielle Angelise!" Jasmine began. "Your words have moved me, and thus I, the Queen of Magnanimity, will allow you to also marry my Alexander as his second wife."

Gabrielle froze, not out of shock, not entirely, but because she was battling with her first instinct, which was to pounce on this girl and hug her for all she was worth. Alex often complained that her hugs hurt. Alex was strong. He had a very durable body. If her hugs hurt him, she couldn't imagine how they would feel to Jasmine, a regular human.

"Well?" Jasmine crossed her arms and frowned. "Are you not happy that I'm agreeing to this?"

Gabrielle smiled, even as she felt tears stinging her eyes. "I'm very happy. Thank you, Jasmine."

"O-oh ho ho ho! Oh ho ho ho ho! You are very welcome... Ga... Ga... Trollip."

Still overcome with more emotions than she could contain, Gabrielle grabbed Jasmine's shoulders, ignored the startled squawk the other girl released, and pulled her into a hug. She reminded herself to be gentle. Don't use too much of her strength. Jasmine's body was more fragile than an angelisian's. Careful. Careful.

Jasmine didn't struggle in her grip. With her head resting on Gabrielle's chest, she remained unmoving, allowing Gabrielle to enjoy the warmth that came from hugging another person.

"Thank you," Gabrielle said softly. "I really am happy."

"O-oh ho... you're welcome." Jasmine did not move a muscle, but she did talk. It was enough. Gabrielle was content.

1

Alex had decided to be proactive in regards to the problem with Jasmine. Jefferson's last words had all but told Alex that the old fart planned on trying to make him out to be the bad guy. It didn't take a genius to know what that man was going to do. The arrogant coot would use his connections to sic the Galactic Defense Force on him.

That was why Alex had quietly slipped into Mars, using a passenger shuttle under an assumed name, and even went so far as to disguise his appearance with Mr. Disguise. The ring that was Mr. Disguise, which made him appear as someone else, felt odd on his finger, but Alex ignored it as he went through the spaceport's many checkpoints. He didn't know how Mr. Disguise worked, but he got through each checkpoint with ease.

It took about one hour to reach the Mars Police Department's main headquarters. From the outside, the police station looked the same as any other building. It was tall and made from a combination of durasteel and glasteel. Since it held a lot of people and numerous rooms that required high roofs, it was easily one of the tallest skyscrapers that didn't belong to a noble family.

Alex walked into the station, passed several chairs that were lined in aisles with a number of people sitting in them, and up to the front desk. Someone sat there. It was a young woman this time, typing away at her holographic keyboard while listening to something with a pair of headphones. He guessed it was music. It wasn't like he could hear what she was listening to.

"Excuse me," he said, his voice a deep baritone thanks to Mr. Voice Changer—another invention of Gabrielle's. "I would like to speak with Ms. Karen Kanzaki." The woman said nothing. "I would like to speak with Karen Kanzaki." Still nothing. Now wearing a frown, Alex tapped the woman on the head. He ignored her glare and said, "I'm here to see Karen Kanzaki. Could you let her know?"

The woman frowned at him. "Commander Karen is busy right now. I'm sorry, but you'll have to come back some other time."

"If you let her know that Farone's son is here to see her, I'm sure she'll tell you to let me see her."

Despite eying him with an obvious *"I don't believe you"* face, she still opened her commlink and pushed a holographic keypad to contact Karen Kanzaki's commlink.

"Yes?" Karen's voice came through a speaker on the desk.

"Um, yes, someone here claiming to be Faron's son is here to see you. What would you like me to do?"

"... Send him up."

The woman sighed, shut off the communication, and eyed him. "You heard her. Head on up. Do you need someone to show you the way?"

"No, I'm fine. Thank you."

"Uh huh…"

The woman put her headphones back on, but Alex didn't pay attention to her again as he walked up to the elevator on the right and pressed the button to call it down. A soft ping proceeded the doors opening. Alex waited for everyone to get off, and then stepped into the elevator. As the door closed, he leaned against the glasteel wall, stared outside, and went over what he would say to Karen Kanzaki in his head.

The Mars Police Department consisted of ten floors. The first floor was the entrance and registry, where all complaints and reports were filed. It didn't have much else. It was just a waiting room and the file maintenance office. The second, third, and fourth floors were all classrooms. That was where the Mars Police Academy was located. The fifth and sixth was a multi-level training room and forensics lab. The seventh and eighth floors were offices and rooms for officers and active squadrons, and it was also where the locker rooms for fully-trained police officers were located. The tenth floor was the command branch. Commander Karen Kanzaki and Second-in-Command Yuumi had offices on that floor.

Several more people entered as the elevator went up, though few stayed for more than a single floor. Most of them ignored Alex. Those who didn't whispered to themselves. He ignored them.

When the door made it to the tenth floor, Alex stepped off, walked down the narrow hall, which had several lateral passages branching off from it, and arrived at Karen's door. It didn't open for him. He pressed a button on the side, next to a thumbprint scanner, which let her know that he had arrived.

The door slid open seconds later.

Karen Kanzaki's room was Spartan, containing little in the way of decoration. Situated in the center of the room, immediately before him, were two couches sitting around a table. Against the wall to his left, a bookshelf was filled with numerous old-fashioned discs. Beside it, safely locked within a glass case, an ancient record of something called The Beatles hung like a prized possession. On the other side, hanging from frames and sitting on displays, were the various awards that Karen had won.

The woman this room belonged to sat behind a desk, a window at her back, showing an expansive view of Mars City. Blonde hair descended from her head. It was tied back in a ponytail today. What few strands escaped gently framed her face, softening the ice-cold demeanor that she had thanks to her chilling blue eyes and stern appearance.

As Alex entered the room, the door closing behind him, Karen looked up. Her eyes narrowed as he walked up to her. The blue tassels on her shoulders rustled as she straightened her back.

"Alexander?"

Alex stopped, shut off Mr. Disguise, and grinned sheepishly. "I should have realized you'd see through my disguise."

"Nobody else would have dared to use your father's name when trying to speak with me," Karen said. She clasped her hands together on the desk. "You know, I should technically have you arrested right now."

Alex faltered. "Erm, what?"

"I received a communication from Jefferson de Truante several hours ago," she said. "He claims that you broke into the de Fénelon family's private manor, destroyed their security detail, and kidnapped his daughter." She paused, eyed him with a great deal of suspicion, and asked, "It's all true, isn't it?"

He didn't want to admit it, but he was surprised that this had happened so fast. Alex had suspected that Jefferson would try something. However, he had been expecting that something to happen several days from now. The entire reason he'd gone straight to Karen was so he could build a proper defense before Jefferson could make any accusations.

Still, it wasn't like this changed anything.

"Only if you look at it from a certain point of view," Alex answered.

Karen sighed and rubbed her forehead. Guilt hit Alex hard. It seemed that no matter what he did, he was always making trouble for this woman, who had looked after him and Alice when they were children, who had taught him how to look after himself, who had, in truth, done more for him than anyone else. Really, the only reason he and Alice were able to live as they did was because of Karen. He didn't want to give her more trouble.

However…

"I know it seems bad, but I actually believe you'll find that I'm in the right this time."

"This time?" Karen asked.

"Not that I'm not always in the right," Alex said, coughing into his hand and looking away.

Karen snorted. "So… what's your excuse this time?"

Alex walked up to the desk, pulled a small disc from his pant pocket, and set it on the table. With the slightest of frowns, Karen claimed the disc. After studying the device for several seconds, she looked up at Alex, who gave her a grim smile.

"Jefferson claims that I kidnapped Jasmine, but the truth is I rescued her. All of the details are on that disc, but if you want the short of it, then here's my report."

Calming his mind, Alex subtly shifted his stance, sliding his feet shoulder width apart, placing his hands behind his back, and adopting a traditional military briefing stance. It was the kind of stance they made police cadets use at the academy. Even though he was no longer a cadet, this was the most comfortable stance for him to use when giving a debriefing.

"Jasmine's parents told her that she was going to marry Caelum de Fénelon. When she refused, they forced her to drop out of school, took her off Mars, and secreted her away in the de Fénelon family's private asteroid. While she was there, Jefferson de Truante drugged Jasmine's food and water with an illegal mind-altering substance. His goal was to make her more cooperative to his suggestions. He wanted her to marry Caelum because—"

"Because it meant he would gain access to their mining operations," Karen finished.

"Yes."

Karen held both hands up to her face and wedged her nose between them as though trying to stifle a coming headache. She closed her eyes, took a deep breath, held it, and then released it. When she opened her eyes again, Alex felt a shiver run down his spine.

Looking into her eyes is like staring into a mass of razor blades.

"This is going to be a huge scandal if it goes public," she said at last. "Two noble families tried to force the daughter of one into an arranged marriage with mind-altering drugs. I can't imagine how many people are going to be harmed by this knowledge."

The de Truante and de Fénelon families employed a lot of people, and if it became public that they had drugged Jasmine, the outrage from the people would destroy their business. Partner companies would back out for fear of public backlash, people would stop buying from them out of anger, and the GDF would be forced to step in and seize their holdings. It wouldn't just be political suicide. The entire solar system would be affected.

"I know." Alex nodded. "That's why I'm suggesting we don't go public with it."

Karen toyed with the disc, spinning it on its side as if it was a coin. The circuits lit up inside her mind. Alex could practically see the path each electric impulse was taking as she reached a conclusion.

"You want me to blackmail them with this information," she said at last.

"I would do it myself," Alex confessed, "but it would have more impact if Jefferson and Caelum knew that you had proof of their wrongdoings."

"You're asking for a lot." Karen blew out a breath. "It's technically my obligation to report all matters like this to my superiors in the GDF." She eyed the disc again, glaring at it like it was at fault for all this. "However, in light of how many people would be adversely affected by the backlash if something like this became public, I'll do as you ask."

Unspoken was the knowledge that the GDF probably already knew about the de Truante and de Fénelons' illegal activities and were turning a blind eye to their wrongdoings. It was the way of nobles to bribe those in charge of governing into keeping silent, and it was the way of those governing to accept those bribes. Alex and Karen both knew this, though they said nothing.

"Thank you," Alex said. "I'll leave that in your hands. I also have several copies in case you ever need it again."

"You mean in case Jefferson uses his connections to somehow erase it," Karen retorted. "Don't worry. I'll keep this with me and make several copies myself."

Alex nodded in gratitude, knowing that he could trust Karen with this. Even if they'd had their differences recently, Karen wasn't the type who would let something like this go; she had the people's best interests at heart. Their goals in this matter coincided.

"Alex?" Karen began again. "I have another question for you, one unrelated to our current discussion."

Relaxing his shoulders and stance now that the hard part was out of the way, he asked, "What's up?"

"Have you heard anything from Kazekiri?" Karen asked.

Alex shook his head. "I haven't. Why?"

Hesitating for just a moment, Karen eventually said, "Kazekiri recently dropped out of our advancement program, the one where she works part-time in filing and maintenance. She said it was because she wanted to focus on her studies, but…"

"That does seem strange," Alex murmured.

Kazekiri was always working hard toward her goal of becoming an officer. He remembered her telling him about her past, about how her parents had been terrible people, and how she wanted to become an officer so others wouldn't have to go through what she did. Everything she did was done to further that goal. Her elective classes at school were police-oriented. She was taking hand-to-hand combat, forensics, police investigations, and numerous other courses designed to help her become an officer. The idea of Kazekiri suddenly dropping out of a program that would give her a straight shot into the Mars Police Academy was just bizarre.

"Gabrielle also said she's been acting kind of weird at school," Alex admitted. "I'll talk to her when I get the chance."

"I'd appreciate that. I would do it myself, but I can't look into it because people would accuse me of having a conflict of interest."

"Don't worry. I understand." Alex smiled at her. "Kazekiri is important to me. If something is going on, you can bet I'll get to the bottom of it."

"I know you will. Just try not to blow anything up when you do," Karen said, sending him a stare that seeped equal amounts of amusement and exasperation.

Alex flinched. "Ouch. That's harsh."

"The truth sometimes hurts."

The words were accompanied by Karen's sage-like nod.

2

There was a bit more that Alex needed to discuss with Karen, but he left the Police Department about fifteen minutes after concluding their conversation. He planned to eventually head back to the Dauntless. However, before he could leave, he wanted to make sure that his sister, Nyx, Ariel, and Michelle were doing well, which was why he took a shuttle to the Outer District.

Fortune smiled on him. His house was still in one piece. As he walked through the front door, took off his shoes, and called out his traditional *"I'm home!"*, the sound of rushing feet hit his ears seconds before the living room door opened.

Alice was the one who came out first, followed by Ariel and Michelle. Nyx came out last. She paused when she spotted him, but then she moved fully into the hallway and stood behind the others.

"You're back." Alice looked behind him as though searching for something. She clenched her fists so tightly that the knuckles turned white.

"Jasmine is still on the Dauntless," Alex said, knowing exactly who she was looking for. He didn't tell her that her friend was having drugs flushed out of her system. If Jasmine wanted to, then fine, but worrying his sister when she was already fretting over this wouldn't help. He gave her a reassuring smile instead. "You don't have to worry."

"What makes you think I was looking for Jasmine? I wasn't interested in knowing that," Alice said, looking away.

"That so? Then I guess you won't be joining me when I go back up there?"

"I never said that."

Alex chuckled at how obvious Alice was. Her left foot was tapping against the floor and her arms were crossed as though defensive, but the way she glanced at him, the telling look in her eye, pretty much told him everything he needed to know. The moment he said he was going back to the Dauntless, she would subtly demand to go with him. He wouldn't be surprised if she claimed that it would be more troublesome to not make sure Jasmine was okay than to stay at home.

Really, my sister is so adorable when she gets like that.

"I'm pleased to hear that your mission was a success," Michelle said.

"Yeah, it was surprisingly easy to accomplish with Azazel's help," Alex admitted.

"Well, Azazel is Father's best general," Ariel stated. "That was the reason he was brought on as Big Sis's bodyguard."

Alex nodded. He hadn't really thought much of Azazel at first. Sure, the guy had kicked his butt when they first met, but he had also bawled like a child during Alex's speech, kept getting lost when given simple tasks, and didn't seem to know his left from his right. That said, when the cards were on the table, Azazel and his two men, Kane and Abel, decimated an entire security detail, around three hundred wardroids, practically on their own.

"Anyway, Jasmine and Gabby are still on the Dauntless," Alex said. "I'm gonna call Azazel and have him send a shuttle to pick me up so I can go back there tomorrow, but I wanted to ask if you four were interested in coming with me?"

When he received three affirmatives and one troublesome, Alex went down to the lab and opened a direct line of communication to Azazel, requesting that he send a shuttle to pick them up. Thanks to the political situation with Jefferson trying to frame him, he couldn't do anything publicly yet. He had to wait for confirmation that he could travel freely from Karen. She had assured him that a response should be forthcoming tomorrow, so he just had to hunker down and wait.

"Thanks for all you help, Azazel."

"I am happy to be of service, Groom-to-Be." Azazel tilted his head before rubbing his chin. "Before I end our communication, would you like me to fetch Princess Gabrielle and Jasmine?"

Alex thought about it for a second, but he soon shook his head. "No, I think it will be better if I wait until tomorrow to speak with them. If we talk right now, I wouldn't be able to offer them any good news."

"A prudent decision. I'll see you on the morrow."

"Yeah. See you."

The communication line shut off, the holographic screen going blank. Alex turned, prepared to leave, but then he paused as he remembered something else that he said he would do. There was one other person he wanted to speak with that day.

He turned back around and opened another line of communication. It took a lot longer than he expected for the other person to answer. When they did, a grainier holographic screen appeared.

Disheveled flaxen hair framed a pretty face, though said face was currently marred by bags under slightly red eyes. Her posture was slouched. It was like she was carrying a great weight on her shoulders. Yet as she stared at him, blinking like she couldn't figure out who she was staring at, her expression cleared and became more cognizant, sharper, and more embarrassed.

"A-Alex?!" she suddenly squeaked as she realized who he was. "W-what are you calling me for?!"

"I'm calling to check up on you," Alex said. "I got back from Camelot yesterday, but because of some issues that came up while I was gone, I wasn't able to really speak with you. I wanted to see how you were doing."

"Oh." As though she was just realizing that she looked like a mess, Kazekiri combed a finger through her hair in a vain attempt to fix it. "I'm doing fine. I've just been keeping myself busy."

Alex wanted to play it cool, to converse about nonsensical subjects that would put Kazekiri at ease and smoothly insert the subject of her dropping the police advancement program. He didn't want to frighten her off. He needed to be subtle about this.

"Is that so? Are you so busy that you needed to stop working for the police?"

It was too bad that subtlety had never been his strong point.

"H-how did you find out about that?!" Kazekiri's face grew pale as the blood drained from it. Her eyes had become two bulging spheres that looked ready to pop from their sockets. He couldn't see her hands, but he bet they were trembling.

"How could I not find out about that?" Alex asked in return. "Why did you quit? I thought you wanted to be a police officer. Wasn't that your dream?"

Biting her lip, Kazekiri turned her head away from him, looking at something slightly off screen and to the left, or perhaps she wasn't looking at anything. He couldn't rightly tell. That said, he did notice how her hand went to the new choker wrapped around her throat. It looked familiar. He could have sworn he'd seen something similar before, but the memory of just where he had seen it eluded him.

"It's... there's no particular reason. I simply decided to focus more on my studies. It's becoming a lot harder to keep my grades up while working a part-time job."

Bullshit.

She was lying. She had to be. Kazekiri had been one of the most exemplary students in school. Even before he had graduated from Primary, her grades had consistently been within the top ninetieth percentile for the entire school. He couldn't imagine her grades ever dropping either.

He didn't call her out on it, though, because even he had enough tact to know that not saying anything was the better option until he had a more clear picture. Alex wanted to help her. He didn't want to scare her off.

"I do hear that your last two years in Primary can be rough," he said instead.

Kazekiri's tired smile seemed at least somewhat amused. "Coming from someone who took the accelerated course, I'm not sure that's saying much."

"I guess not."

Alex spoke with Kazekiri some more, mostly asking if anything interesting had happened while he was gone, and also informing her about what happened to Jasmine. He didn't tell her everything, not about the drugs or the kidnapping. That was still Jasmine's story to tell. However, he did tell her about how Jasmine's father had tried to force her into a loveless marriage.

"That sounds horrible. I'm sorry I couldn't help you," Kazekiri apologized. "Had I known, I would have done something."

"You don't have to apologize." Alex shook his head. "Everything turned out alright."

"Well, I'm glad things worked out at least."

A loud thumping noise made Kazekiri turn her head. A muffled voice came over the speaker. Alex strained his ears, but he couldn't hear what was being said. He only heard Kazekiri's response.

"I-I'm getting off," she stuttered. She turned back to Alex, her face drawn and almost ghostly white. She offered him the most fake smile he'd seen from her and said, "I'm sorry, Alex. I wish we could talk more, but I really have to get going. Have a good night."

"What? Night? Wait, Kazekiri! I—"

The holographic screen faded. Alex bit his lip as he stared at the spot where the screen had been.

"What was that about?" he asked.

Naturally, the empty lab, filled with nothing but his and Gabrielle's inventions, did not answer him. The only sound was the whirring and beeping of machinery. Alex sighed and left the room, traveled up the stairs to the second floor, and went into the restroom.

While he sometimes called it the restroom, it was actually a changing/shower combination room. The changing room was composed of tiles. There was a sink along one wall, a clothing rack to fold and hang up clothes and towels, and a toilet. No one was inside, thank Mars, and so Alex was able to do his nightly routine without accidentally walking in on someone naked.

After finishing up in the restroom, Alex went to his bedroom to get some sleep. However, just as he was getting ready to lie in bed, a soft beep alerted him to someone at the door. A holographic screen appeared before him. It was Nyx. She stood before the door, a long nightgown covering her body. Blinking, Alex climbed off the bed, padded to the door, and opened it with the push of a button.

"Nyx," Alex said as the door slid open. "Is something wrong?"

Nyx shook her head. "I want to sleep with you."

"Oh?" Alex hesitated for just a second as he wondered if letting her stay with him would be okay, but then he remembered that he had already committed himself to this and stepped aside. "Come on in."

Giving him a nod, Nyx stepped inside. Alex closed the door. As he turned around, it was to find that Nyx was already crawling onto the bed. She was on her hands and knees, her feet sticking off the edge and her butt in the air. Turning her head, she looked at him, frowning as though wondering why he wasn't already in the bed with her.

With a small sigh, Alex wandered over to the bed as Nyx crawled underneath the covers. He followed her. As the memory foam conformed to his body, Nyx scooted over to him, where she proceeded to burrow herself between his arm and torso. A jolt ran through his body as one of her hands pressed against his chest. He wasn't wearing a shirt, so her soft fingers were like electrodes sending shocks through his skin.

"You've become awfully affectionate," Alex muttered.

Nyx didn't answer right away, but her fingers did scratch at his chest. "Do you not like this?"

"Erm…"

"I… like this." Nyx pressed her face into his shoulder. "This feeling, this warmth. I've never felt it until I met you."

"There really was no one else who gave you this feeling?"

Nyx shook her head. "The only person I was close to was Rhea, and she wasn't warm like you. She was cold. Always cold." Her fingers grasped at his chest as though she were trying to grab a shirt that wasn't there. "You're the only person I've met who gave off this warmth. You make me want... a life other than that of an assassin."

I see...

Nyx was an assassin, a weapon created through nanotechnology. Her life up to this point had been one of killing. She traveled from one side of this galaxy to the other, accepting assassination contracts for criminals and killing without mercy. It was no wonder she hadn't experienced any kind of warmth. Hers had been a life of nothing but the icy coldness of death.

Turning onto his side, facing Nyx, Alex reached out and pulled her into him. He tucked her head underneath his chin, wrapped his arms tightly around her small body as if shielding her from the world, and slowly entwined their legs together. He felt a few small jolts of electricity as they came into such intimate contact. He tried to ignore the way his pajama pants tightened. Now was so not the time to let his arousal get the better of him.

"I want to give you a life outside of being an assassin," Alex mumbled, closing his eyes. "I hope that you'll always consider this place your home from now on."

Nyx hugged him back. Her voice was partially muffled by his chest. "That sounds nice. I would like that."

"I'm glad."

A moment of silence passed. Then...

"By the way..."

"Yes?"

"You're poking me."

"… S-sorry," Alex mumbled, very glad that Nyx couldn't see how red his face had become.

3

The next morning, Alex received a communication from Karen. Her message was simple and to the point; she had succeeded in "convincing" Jefferson de Truante to not only drop the charges that he was trying to press, but also to let Jasmine go. He was impressed. Karen certainly worked fast. Alex had not been expecting her to reach a solid conclusion to this matter for at least a few days. Then again, the evidence that Alex had given her about the de Truante's and de Fénelon's illegal activities was pretty damning.

There were a lot of strict laws regarding children, particularly in regards to matters like abuse. Parents who were caught physically abusing their children suffered harsh punishments. They would be fined, lose the rights to raise their child, and spend a minimum of five years in prison.

It was even worse if it was discovered that they had drugged their child. What Jefferson had done to Jasmine wasn't just deplorable. Drugging a child was met with the harshest punishment. A life sentence. Not even a noble could escape from this, though considering the incredible power that Jefferson wielded, he might be able to escape life in prison. That said, his reputation would be ruined forever. His business would crumble, his empire would vanish, and he would be left with nothing.

While nobles liked to pretend they were above the law, they were just as accountable to follow it as anyone else. Most nobles didn't like that. In fact, many of the more heinous crimes were often committed by a noble. Slave trading. Drug dealing. Smuggling illegal weapons and contraband. Alex's father had been well-known for breaking up several powerful noble families who'd been involved in the smuggling of Redline and the slave market.

After taking a quick shower that morning, Alex wandered down to the lab and opened a line of communication with the Dauntless. It took a moment for the communication to go through. When it did, the person who appeared before him was none other than Azazel.

"Groom-to-Be," Azazel said. "You are calling awfully early. Does this mean there's been a change in the situation? Shall I prepare a shuttle to transport you to the Dauntless?"

"There has been a change in our situation," Alex began, "but not in the way you're thinking. I received a message early this morning from Karen. She's already settled matters with Jefferson. I guess he didn't expect her to have any evidence to prosecute him with. Anyway, I'd like you to escort Gabrielle and Jasmine back to Mars. There are still some matters that I need to discuss with them, so the sooner they get back, the better."

Azazel bobbed his head. "Very well. I believe they are still asleep, but I'll have them ferried down to Mars within the next hour. I'll send a message through your IDband. It can accept angelisian communications, correct?"

"Yes."

"Then that's what we'll do."

"Nice. Thank you, Azazel."

"You are welcome."

When the holographic screen vanished, Alex left the lab and entered the kitchen. He paused in the doorway. Nyx was awake and seated at the table. She swung her legs back and forth. Alex hid his snort behind a cough. The knowledge that Nyx, a deadly assassin capable of transmuting objects with little effort through alchemy, was too short to reach the floor, amused him a great deal.

He would never say that out loud, though.

"Morning, Nyx. Sleep well?" Alex walked over to the fridge and began gathering ingredients. He was going to make banana pancakes this morning.

"Good morning." Nyx's soft voice reached his ears as he set a container of eggs on the counter. "I slept well until you left."

"That so? Sorry about that." Alex moved over to the pantry, grabbed ten bananas, and walked back to the counter. "I received a message from Karen, so I wanted to let Azazel know that it's safe to send Jasmine and Gabrielle back to Mars. We'll be picking them up after breakfast."

"Understood."

Alex split the bananas in half, placed them into a blender—a regular blender that actually worked—and then cracked a dozen eggs and also put them into the blender as well. He closed the capsule and pressed a button. The blending process was nearly silent. Alex turned on the stove, which also seconded as a skillet, next. As the flat black surface turned a vibrant red, the blender stopped, and he took the container out of the capsule and began pouring the contents directly onto the skillet.

The pancakes cooked to perfection quickly.

"Nyx," Alex called as he placed the pancakes on a tray, "could you please go and wake the others?"

"Okay."

Nyx hopped off the chair and left the kitchen. Meanwhile, Alex set the tray on the table, grabbed plates and utensils, and quickly set everything up for breakfast. Barely a minute had passed before Alice walked in with Ariel, Michelle, and Nyx in tow. He would've been surprised since she was often the last one to enter, but he guessed she was anxious to see Jasmine again.

In fact, that was the first thing she asked him about.

"I found out from Karen that Jasmine can return back to Mars," Alex said. "She and Gabby are coming back. We're going to pick them up at the spaceport."

"Really?" Alice perked up.

"Yes."

"Then I'll get to see Jasmine soon!" Alice cheered before she realized what she was doing. She paused midway through her cheer, looked at everyone else, noticed the smiles that he and Michelle were wearing, blushed when Ariel snorted with repressed amusement, and then coughed into her hand and sat back down. "I mean, it'll be good to see her soon. She's troublesome, but she's still my friend."

"You don't need to pretend everything is too much trouble to bother with," Alex said as he sat down between Alice and Nyx. "It's okay to get excited, you know?"

"Whatever."

"What time are we going to the spaceport?" asked Michelle. Beside her, Ariel had stabbed her pancakes with her fork and was now eyeing the object like it was offensive. She took a bite. Her eyes brightened before she began eating the food in earnest.

Alex smiled at her before turning his attention to her sister. "We're heading there within the hour. Azazel didn't specify a time, but he said it would be this morning. I think it's better to wait there so we can greet them when they arrive."

"I agree," Michelle said.

Getting everyone ready wasn't much of a chore. Once breakfast was finished, Ariel and Michelle went and changed into their regular clothes. Alex had to admit that Ariel looked awfully cute in her jean shorts and tank top. Meanwhile, Michelle presented a far more mature aura. Her delicate skirt swished as she walked, and her black shirt had ruffles along the hem and a small dip in the front.

"You two look cute," Alex said.

"R-really?" Ariel looked down as she used her left foot to draw circles on the floor. "Y-your compliments don't mean anything to me, idiot... b-but t-thank you."

"Are you embarrassed?" Michelle smiled at her sister as she twirled a strand of hair between her fingers. "How cute."

"Shut up you!"

"Alice!" Alex called after he and Nyx finished putting on their boots. Ariel and Michelle were slipping into a pair of sandals. "You coming?!"

"H-hang on!" Alice shouted. Loud thumping echoed from upstairs. The sound of footsteps. Alice emerged seconds later, rushing down the stairs. "Sorry. I couldn't figure out what to wear."

"You mean all of your clothes were dirty and you had trouble finding a clean pair, right?" Alex gave his sister a knowing look, to which she clicked her tongue and looked away, avoiding eye contact with him. He rubbed his jaw. "I'll do the laundry later. For now, let's just head over to the spaceport."

Because the spaceport was in the Outer District, technically, it didn't take as long to get there. They took a shuttle and arrived with time to spare.

Since it was so early, the spaceport wasn't that busy. Of course, saying it wasn't busy was like comparing ratchets to screwdrivers. The space inside still had dozens of people walking to and fro. A couple of men in suits spoke as they walked past Alex and the others. One of them men turned and eyed the girls in his group before they went out of sight. Alex scowled. He didn't like the look in that man's eyes.

Disgusting pig.

"It's not like you're any better."

Shut up.

"Hm hm hm. So angry."

"Please do not antagonize Alexander. You remember our agreement, do you not?"

"Fine. Fine. You're such a spoilsport."

Alex pressed a hand to his face as the voices died off. Taking several deep breaths, he did his best to push back his annoyance, both at the man who had been ogling the girls with him and at the voices inside of his head. Listening to them always caused his head to ache. He believed it had to do with how they were inside of him —not that he knew for sure. It wasn't like psychology or biology were his strongest subjects.

"Let's wait off to the side," Alex said.

The spaceport was just a large terminal with several hallways that led into any number of different docking bays. Each docking bay was numbered one through forty-one. They were signified by large durasteel doors. The one that Gabrielle and Jasmine would be coming through was probably docking bay forty-one, which had been quarantined specifically for angelisian use.

"I think I see them!" Ariel shouted as she suddenly rushed forward. Alex turned to find a large figure with a head of dirty, snow-colored hair lumbering toward them. That was definitely Azazel. If the height wasn't enough to tell, the armor certainly was. As the crowd parted to reveal Jasmine, Gabrielle, and Madison, Ariel nearly tackled her sister in a hug. "Big Sis!"

Gabrielle laughed as she hugged her sister back. "It's good to see you, Ariel! I hope you've been staying out of trouble."

Ariel scowled as she pulled back. "Of course I have. I'm not you."

"Tee-hee! I guess not." Gabrielle rubbed the back of her head.

"Honorable Sister," Michelle greeted with a lot more poise than Ariel. "I'm pleased to see you safe and unharmed."

"Me too!" Gabrielle admitted, giving them the peace sign.

While Gabrielle was being greeted by her siblings, Alice had marched up to Jasmine and, before the girl could do anything, pulled her into a hug. The stunned look on Jasmine's face, complete with bulging eyes and open mouth, made Alex snicker. It was always amusing when Jasmine became surprised. Her reactions were the greatest.

"O-oh ho! Alice? What are you doing?"

"Idiot," Alice muttered as she hugged Jasmine even tighter. "How could you worry me like that?"

The words made Jasmine relax her shoulders and hug Alice back. "Oh ho ho. I'm sorry. As the Queen of Apologizing, I can do nothing except express my regret over worrying you. I did not mean to."

"It's fine. Just don't do it again," Alice said.

"I promise."

Alex and Nyx stood back, letting everyone else have their time to greet each other. This was an important moment for them, a touching moment that he should not interrupt.

As they watched the proceedings, him with a soft smile and Nyx with a blank look, Madison walked up to them.

"Master?"

"Hm?"

When Alex turned his head to look at the maid/android/bodyguard, Madison clasped her hands together and bowed. It was a low bow at the waist. Alex was startled because Madison normally only curtsied.

"Thank you very much for rescuing Jasmine."

Alex tilted his head. "I'm not sure why you're thanking me for doing what I want to do, but you're welcome."

"It seems you have accomplished your goal, Groom-to-Be," Azazel said, suddenly right next to them. Alex nearly jumped in shock. For such a large man, he could sure move quietly when he wanted to, and how the heck did he move so silently wearing all that armor?

"Not yet." Alex frowned as the two groups finished greeting each other. "There's still something that I need to do."

He needed to have a talk with Jasmine. That could wait, though. She had just returned to Mars. He would give her some time to settle down and relax with Alice and the others before talking to her.

Azazel said his farewells to them and returned to the Dauntless, while Alex took everyone outside and had them hop onto a shuttle that took them to a stop near their home. During the ride there, Jasmine kept frowning at him. He thought it might have been due to how Nyx and Gabrielle had claimed the spots next to him, or how Gabrielle had clung to his arm and Nyx held his hand, but every time he looked her way, she would blush bright red and pretend she hadn't been looking.

How odd... she's normally more—well, not more subtle, but she usually doesn't act so demurely around me.

It was still Wednesday. Alice, Ariel, Gabrielle, Jasmine, and Michelle should have been in class, but Alex decided to give them the day off. Their friend had just been through a harrowing experience. They should be there to support her. He would need to speak with Mrs. Tepes about re-enrolling Jasmine anyway, since she was no longer within the school register. That reminded him, he would need to call her and set up an appointment for tomorrow. Great. It was one more thing to add to the list.

While everyone else settled in on the couch to watch a holodrama, Alex went up to his room, sat down on his desk, and sent a message to Mrs. Tepes. In it, he asked if she could set up an appointment so he could re-enroll Jasmine after certain matters were taken care of. He received a response back barely a minute after he hit the send key. Her reply was short: *"Come to my office after you've filed Jasmine's new citizen registration."*

He stared at the message for a moment before clicking his tongue.

Karen must have contacted her.

It wasn't surprising, really. Karen and Mrs. Tepes were sisters. Mrs. Tepes had married Karen's older brother. Speaking of, he had never met Karen's brother, had he? That was weird. Karen used to come over to his place so often, and Mrs. Tepes was on his father's team in the special forces. One would think they would have met at some point. How odd.

A soft ping alerted him to someone at his door, and if that wasn't enough, another holographic screen appeared in front of him. It was useful how this always popped up, but kind of annoying. The person at the door was Gabrielle. Alex wasn't too surprised, though he was sure she'd have been caught up in watching *Titan Girl* with Alice and the others. She was every bit the fan that his sister was.

Alex stood up from his seat and opened the door. Gabrielle's beaming face was so close that he almost jerked back in surprise. She was leaning over and giving him an expression so bright that it was more blinding than if he'd been staring at the sun.

"Gabby, what's up?"

"Tee-hee. I wanted to spend some time with you, so here I am!" She stepped inside as Alex took a step back. "Everyone else is watching some kind holodrama."

"Not *Titan Girl*?"

Gabrielle shook her head. "Jasmine chose what to watch. It's like a documentary of some kind. Something about maids."

"Ah, yeah, I almost forgot that Jasmine likes to watch that stuff."

When she was younger, Jasmine would often come over and watch shows involving maids. They were documentaries that taught people about how maids worked and maid ethics. After he built Madison and Jasmine had begun dressing her in maid outfits, he'd merely assumed it was a hobby. It had only been recently that Alex discovered that Jasmine actually ran her own maid café. Knowing this now, it was understandable that she would want to learn more about maidome.

"Did you have something specific you wanted to talk about?" asked Alex.

Gabrielle sat down on his bed and grinned. "No. I just wanted to be with you."

Alex tried not to let the words get to him, but he could still feel his face heating up. Gabrielle said these things so easily, and she was so honest and upfront that it was hard for a guy like him to keep his composure.

Still, this was a good opportunity. He'd wanted to speak with Gabrielle sooner rather than later.

"Then this is a good opportunity."

"A what?" Gabrielle tilted her head.

"Could you... close your eyes for me?" Alex asked.

"Okay." Gabrielle didn't seem to know why he wanted her to close her eyes, but she did anyway, As her eyelids slowly fluttered shut, Alex took a deep breath and moved until he was standing right in front of her.

He began to lean down.

"Don't open your eyes until I say so."

"Okay."

Alex gulped as he stared at her soft, pink lips, so close, and coming closer as he continued to move his head forward. His heart was a wardrum in his chest. It kept beating and beating and beating, as though it was trying to beat its way out. What if Gabrielle didn't like this? What if she didn't want to kiss him? They were stupid concerns. He wasn't even sure Gabrielle knew what a kiss was, but in that case, wasn't he taking advantage of her naivety?

He had thought long and hard about his first kiss with Gabrielle. His initial idea had been to kiss her after their first date, but then a thought had occurred to him. Wasn't that what everyone else did? Also, Gabrielle didn't seem to understand relationship dynamics, so a kiss after their first date wouldn't have the same meaning. In which case, Alex wanted to let her know, right here, right now, how he felt through his actions instead of just his words.

Before Alex could lose his nerve, he leaned down the rest of the way. Their lips touched. It was only for a brief moment before he pulled back, but in that moment, Alex couldn't help but feel amazed. Were all lips soft like Gabrielle's? It felt like someone had slid chiffon over his mouth.

"A-Alex?"

When Alex opened the eyes that he had unknowingly closed, it was to discover a blushing Gabrielle staring at him with wide eyes and trembling lips. His own face began heating up as she continued gazing at him.

"Uh… s-sorry," he apologized. "That must have been… pretty sudden for you."

"No… it's okay." Gabrielle placed a hand to her lips. Her cheeks turned a deeper shade of scarlet. "That was a kiss, right?"

Alex looked away. "Yes."

"Hehe, I knew that." Giggling, Gabrielle looked down at her toes. She lifted her legs and wiggled her toes around. "I was wondering if we would ever kiss."

"Erm… it wasn't bad, was it?"

"Of course not!" Gabrielle looked back at him. "I really liked it!"

"R-really?"

"Yes!" Gabrielle nodded. "In fact, I want to kiss you again!"

This girl was going to be the death of him. Who said stuff like this so bluntly? She had all the subtlety of a space barge plowing into Earth's atmosphere.

Still... if she can be this bold, I should be, too.

Alex sat down on the bed next to Gabrielle, who turned her entire body to face him. As he reached out and cupped a hand to her face, he leaned forward. Gabrielle mimicked his actions. Slowly. Slowly. They came ever closer to each other.

When their lips touched again, a jolt traveled through his body. It felt like his mouth had been hit by an electric discharge. Beyond the shock, however, was the soft warmth of Gabrielle's lips. He slid his hand from her cheek to her neck. He moved his other hand as well, placing it on the soft curvature of her hip.

As their kiss continued, Alex became bolder—far bolder than he'd have expected from himself. It was almost like something was controlling his actions. He slid his arm around her back and pulled Gabrielle to him until her legs were lying on his lap, and then he proceeded to stroke her thighs. Gabrielle released several noises that were somehow both cute and sexy. They made his blood burn.

He moved the hand from her thighs to her stomach. Her skin was so soft. He couldn't even describe its delicate softness. She wasn't wearing a crisis suit either, so he had direct access to her stomach, and the feeling of her muscles coiling under his touch compelled him to keep going. He rubbed his hand across her stomach before slowly moving up.

When Gabrielle opened her mouth to release a cute moan, Alex slipped his tongue inside of her mouth. Gabrielle jerked for a second, but then she calmed down, her body relaxed. She returned his gesture. Her small tongue slipped out of her mouth and pushed against his.

The feeling of friction as they stirred up the saliva in Gabrielle's mouth drove Alex into delirium. He pushed Gabrielle onto the bed and straddled her waist, continuing the kiss. Now that she was on the bed, he was able to grab the hem of her shirt and lift it over her chest. Gabrielle apparently didn't believe in bras still. Her breasts sprang free with a bounce.

Alex swirled his finger around her breast with his left hand, using the other to keep him up, lest he fall over. He let his fingers dance along her skin. They created goosebumps that made Gabrielle squirm beneath him. Then he placed his hand over her breast and fondled it.

Gabrielle's chest was huge. He didn't know what her cup size was, but she was way bigger than anyone else he knew, save for maybe Kazekiri. Her breasts were capped with light pink nipples that seemed to beckon him. As he began tweaking her nipple with his fingers, Gabrielle's cries, muffled by his mouth, became louder. Her nipple stiffened into a point.

"That feels so good," Gabrielle mumbled as Alex began kissing her neck. "It feels so much better when you touch me than when I touch myself!"

Alex had no idea what she was talking about, but he was barely paying any more attention. He was getting lost—lost in her scent, in the taste of her skin, in the feel of her large breasts and the stiffness of her nipples. Some part of him knew that he should stop. He could hear that part screaming at him. However, that part was being smothered by the passionate haze that had been thrown over his mind. It was like his mind had been blanketed in a fog.

He took Gabrielle's nipple into his mouth, swirled his tongue around it, and as Gabrielle cried out and pulled his head further into her chest, a voice spoke from behind them.

"Hey, bro! Are you planning on making us… huh?"

Alex stopped cold. Gabrielle, her breathing still heavy, didn't seem to realize that they were no longer alone. She complained, asking him, "Why did you stop?" but he barely heard her. Slowly, oh so slowly as though he was a droid and his neck hadn't been oiled in centuries, Alex turned his head.

"Alice…"

Indeed, Alice stood behind him, body halfway through the door, eyes rather round as she stared at him. Her body quivered. It was like she was trying to decide whether she should stay or run. She looked from him to Gabrielle, still on the bed, her shirt pulled up to expose her breasts. There was no way she could mistake what was happening here.

I should have never keyed her into my lock.

He'd keyed her so she could enter his room in case of emergencies, but it seemed like that idea had now backfired.

"Erm… aren't you going to tell me this isn't what it looks like?" Alice asked.

Alex somehow found the strength to shake his head. "I don't think that's gonna work here."

"Right." Alice took a step backward. "I'll just… leave you two alone now. Um, try not to get her pregnant."

"I wouldn't do that!" Alex snapped, but the door closed behind Alice as he was saying that, so he didn't know if she even heard him. He sighed, rolled onto his back, and laid beside Gabrielle, whose mountainous boobs were still exposed.

"Alex?" Gabrielle asked.

"Yes?"

"Are we not going to keep kissing?"

"Not right now."

"Oh… that's sad. I really like kissing."

He chuckled, somehow not embarrassed by what had transpired. "Me too."

"I especially like it when you kiss my breasts. It felt really good."

"I'm… not sure what I should say to that."

"Can we kiss again sometime?"

"I'm sure there will be many kisses in our future."

"Hehe, I'm happy to hear that." Still on her back, Gabrielle lifted her right hand into the air and peered at it. "I only recently learned about kissing thanks to Michelle, but it's a lot nicer than I thought it would be."

"Hmm…"

Alex did feel a bit guilty now that he had confirmation that she really didn't know much about kissing, but she said she liked it, so he didn't feel too bad. That said, he did feel like he'd let himself go way too far. Now that he was thinking clearly, his actions when he was kissing Gabrielle had been nothing like him. It was as if someone inside of him had taken over...

Someone inside of him...

Hey, Asmodeus.

"What do you want, brat?"

You didn't take control of my body, did you?

"Are you stupid? Of course not. I made an agreement with your dumber half that I wouldn't try anything right now."

Alex knew nothing of this agreement, but he was sure she wouldn't tell him even if he asked, so he didn't bother.

"I can confirm that she did nothing."

"Sorry, brat, but that was all you."

Damn...

"Alex?" Gabrielle said after several minutes of silence.

"Sorry." He shook his head to clear out his errant thoughts. "I was thinking about something."

"What were you thinking about?"

"I was thinking about something that I wanted to ask you." Alex turned over on his side and looked Gabrielle in the eyes. "Gabby, how would you like to go on a date with me this weekend?"

Gabrielle's response was to tilt her head in curiosity.

CHAPTER 4

DATE AND DISASTER

Gabrielle had been smiling ever since she woke up this morning. She hadn't been able to stop, not in the bath, not during breakfast, not during the walk to school, and not at school. Even now, sitting at her desk in the third row, the smile hadn't left her face.

Most of the students had already arrived at class, gathered in their groups, and were chatting amongst themselves. Gabrielle's long ears wiggled as she listened in on some of the conversations. A lot of the things people talked about were everyday stuff, what she thought was everyday stuff, like school and games and boys or girls. The boys liked talking about the girls they liked, and the girls did the same to the boys. Gabrielle understood. She liked talking about Alex.

Ryoko and Serah were there as well. They had already greeted Gabrielle by grabbing her boobs and thighs. It was the standard way they said hi. Gabrielle thought about greeting Alex like that, but he didn't have boobs, so she wasn't sure it would work the same way.

Selene and Kazekiri aren't here...

It was a little odd for those two, who always arrived earlier than most of the other students in their class, to show up so late. Selene would often wait for Gabrielle by the front gate. Meanwhile, Kazekiri arrived at class before anyone else did. That she wasn't here made Gabrielle wonder if something had happened to her. Maybe she wasn't feeling sick?

Should I visit her?

She immediately liked her own idea. However, the more she thought about it, the more she realized the great flaw in her plan. She didn't know where Kazekiri lived. It wasn't possible to visit someone if she didn't even know where their place of residence was located.

"Hey, Gabrielle!" Ryoko suddenly said.

"Huh?" Gabrielle snapped out of her trance and looked at the dark-skinned girl. "Yes? What is it?"

"Is it true that Jasmine was kidnapped?"

"Where did you hear about that?"

Ryoko shrugged as Serah butted in, saying, "That's the rumor that's been going around. People are saying that she was kidnapped and forced to become some disgusting pig's sex slave."

It was kind of surprising that a rumor like this had spread. Gabrielle remembered hearing Alex and Alice once talk about the Atreyu Academy rumor mill, which was basically a bunch of girls who loved to gossip, but she wouldn't have expected them to be so close to the truth. According to Alex, the rumor mill usually created far-fetched rumors that could never be possible in real life. Thinking on it, maybe the reason this rumor was so accurate was because it generally didn't happen? There was some food for thought.

"I don't know anything about Jasmine becoming a sex slave." Gabrielle shrugged. "But she was kidnapped by her papa."

"Really?!" Ryoko and Serah shouted at the same time, leaning forward until their noses were almost touching her.

"Yes." Nodding once, Gabrielle crossed her arms. "But I can't tell you what happened. Sorry."

"What?!" Serah complained.

"Why not?" asked Ryoko.

"Because Alex said it wouldn't be a good idea."

That wasn't the only reason she couldn't say anything, but it was the only one she could give. Gabrielle cupped her chin. There were a lot of politics involved in this matter, and even though she didn't like politics, she understood what sort of ramifications they could expect should Jasmine's papa decide to push things. If anyone found out what had actually happened, Jasmine's papa would retaliate. It would bring a lot more trouble than it was worth. Gabrielle understood that much at least.

"Alex can be such a spoilsport," Ryoko muttered.

"I don't suppose I could convince you to disobey him, can I?" asked Serah.

"Nope. Sorry."

"Thought not."

While Ryoko and Serah tried to convince her that she should tell them what happened to Jasmine, Gabrielle looked toward the door as it slid open. Selene walked in. Her curly brown hair was frazzled. There were small bags under her eyes. Her shoulders were hunched. As she stepped further into the room, Gabrielle stood up and walked over to the girl.

"Selene, are you okay? You look tired."

"I'm fine." Selene offered Gabrielle a smile, but it was mixed with exhaustion. "My sister's boyfriend is currently staying at our place. It's caused a bit of trouble between my sister and our parents. They were up all last night arguing, so I couldn't get any sleep."

"Why were they upset by your sister's boyfriend staying over?" asked Gabrielle.

Selene frowned at her for several seconds, long enough to make Gabrielle wonder if something was wrong. Then Selene pulled back, sighed, and rubbed her forehead.

"I forgot who I was talking to."

"Huh?"

"It's nothing." Selene waved off Gabrielle's questioning voice. "Anyway, here on Mars, it's unusual for a couple to live together unless they're married."

"Like Alex and I!"

Selene paused before a strange smile came over her face. "Yes, I suppose it's like you and Alex."

"Hehehehe…"

"You know, I just noticed it now," Ryoko began, studying Gabrielle like she was a puzzle. She sat in her seat and tapped a soft rhythm against her desk. Meanwhile, she was using the other hand to support her head, elbow on the surface. "You seem to be in an awfully good mood. Did something good happen?"

Rubbing the back of her head, the smile still not leaving her face, Gabrielle said, "Am I that obvious?"

"Yes," all three of them answered.

"Tee-hee."

"So, what's going on?" asked Ryoko. "Don't tell me you have a date with Alex or something."

"How did you know?!" Gabrielle said. "Are you psychic?"

"So, wait. You really are going on a date?" Ryoko removed her elbow from the table and leaned back, body slumping against the back of the bench. "This isn't a joke, is it?"

"Why would it be a joke?" Gabrielle asked. "Alex asked me to go on a date with him this weekend. I don't know what we're doing, but we plan on going out together this Saturday."

Selene, Serah, and Ryoko all looked at Gabrielle with wide eyes and dropped jaws. None of them spoke. They just stared at Gabrielle like she had said something unbelievable.

"Do you know where he plans on taking you?" asked Selene.

"No." Gabrielle shook her head. "I don't know where he plans on taking me, or what we're going to do, but I don't really think it matters. As long as he and I have fun together, I don't care what we do."

Gabrielle still didn't know much about this dating thing, but she had spoken with Michelle about it several days after her sisters had first arrived, and so she at least knew the gist of it. Men and women went out and had fun together. That was basically what it amounted to.

But before her friends could question her further, which was what Gabrielle assumed they wanted to do, the doors slid open again and their teacher walked into the room. Grayish hair. Crows feet around obsidian eyes. He walked up to the front of the classroom, greeted everyone, and began lecturing them on the virtues of keeping their grades up.

Gabrielle didn't pay much attention. She had been absent the previous two days, so she hadn't caught up on all of her work, but it shouldn't take too much time or effort to get herself caught up. Outside of history and language, the homework in Atreyu Academy was very easy. As the day continued on, Gabrielle noticed something that caused a small sliver of worry to tighten her chest.

Kazekiri had never shown up.

1

While Alice, Ariel, Gabrielle, and Michelle went to school, Jasmine did not. She was no longer a student. Her father had pulled her from school, filing the application that had forced her to drop out. That meant she couldn't go to school unless her father signed another application that allowed her to attend again, but the chances of that happening were slim.

Alex knew all this, which was why, when Jasmine had told him that she would rather not walk to school with the others, he had complied. He also had some things that he wanted to talk to her about. Since he hadn't gotten a chance to speak with her about them last night, now would the perfect time. They would have errands to run after this anyway.

Jasmine and Nyx were sitting on the large couch when he arrived home. He didn't know what they were watching, but it appeared to be a type of holo-documentary, or perhaps a holo-drama, detailing the Unification Wars that united the many different planets in this solar system. Madison was standing behind them.

"Oh ho ho ho ho! Alexander, you have returned." Jasmine turned away from the screen to face him.

"Yep," Alex said. "And I need to speak with you. Do you mind if we talk in my room?"

"I-in your room?" Jasmine squeaked. "Oh ho! Oh ho ho ho ho! Very well, Alexander. I, the Queen of Conversation, shall grace your room with my presence." She stood up from the couch and placed her hands on her hips, giving Alex an imperious grin like she was the one telling him that she wanted to talk, and not the other way around. "Please lead the way."

"Come on." He withheld a chuckle. "Nyx, we'll be back down in a minute."

"Okay," Nyx said, not taking her eyes off the holo-documentary that was playing on the holovid.

"Oh, and Madison?"

The realistic robot maid stopped walking toward them. "Yes, Master?"

"You don't need to be here for this. I'd like to speak with Jasmine alone."

Madison struggled. Alex actually witnessed the maid scrunching up her face as her processors struggled with her desire to follow his orders and her wish to be by Jasmine. It was actually kind of cute, and it made him glad that he had built her.

"Yes... Master. I shall stay down here and await yours and Mistress' return."

"Thank you."

Alex led Jasmine up to his room and shut the door behind him. Jasmine looked around the room, studying the shelves, which were not covered in books but inventions. She wandered along the walls, looking at everything with glimmering eyes that could barely contain their fascination. This was the first time that she had been in his room, to the best of his knowledge. It was a small wonder she was so interested in looking around.

"Sit down over here," Alex said, sitting on his bed and patting the spot beside him.

"Oh ho!" Jasmine blushed. "O-okay."

Jasmine sat next to him on the bed, clenching the sheets as though she was afraid. He didn't think that was the problem, though. She was looking around, as though purposefully avoiding his gaze, perhaps out of a sense of embarrassment, or maybe nervousness. It was sometimes hard to tell with Jasmine. She always acted so confident.

Coughing into her hand, Jasmine turned to him and tried to present a strong front. "So, Alexander, what did you wish to speak with me, the Queen of Conversation, about?"

Alex tried not to smile at the very Jasmine-ish line, but what he wanted to talk about wasn't something that he could just laugh off.

"You know that I had Karen Kanzaki talk your father into not coming after you, right? She's basically blackmailing him with the evidence of his wrongdoings." Alex looked down at his hands. "While that worked and Jefferson decided not to pursue you further, he also did something else to further disassociate you and him."

"What did Father do?"

Alex took a deep breath. "He disowned and disinherited you."

The words had an immediate effect. Jasmine stilled, her entire body going stiff. Her hands, which had been clenching the sheet of his bed, suddenly went slack as if the bones and muscles in her hands had become jello.

Disowning someone was basically saying that a person was no longer recognized as a member of the family, and disinheriting someone was striking them from a person's will so that specific someone could not gain the family inheritance once the family head passed away. By doing this, Jefferson was essentially denying his daughter's existence.

"Oh ho… Oh ho ho… I see. So, Father has decided that I am no longer fit to be his daughter." Jasmine stared at the floor. She wiggled her toes, digging them into the carpet before relaxing them. "I suppose I should have seen this coming. I don't think he ever really saw me as his child, not like he did Jameson. I was just a tool to him. He would marry me off to some rich nobleman's son and gain whatever advantage was to be had from the arrangement."

If this had been anyone else, Alex would have done everything he could to reassure her that this wasn't the case, but he couldn't do that, not to Jasmine. What she said was true. The only time her father asked for her presence was during important political functions. He would dress Jasmine up, parade her in front of various nobles, and see which ones were interested in marrying her.

Alex had seen the list of Jasmine's potential suitors. It was quite long.

"Do you think it's because of your real mother?" asked Alex hesitantly. He wasn't sure bringing up Jasmine's mother was the right thing to do, but all she did was smile and shrug.

"I do not know, though it might be. However, I do not think that is the case. The only one who really cared about my lineage was Reina de Truante."

Reina de Truante was Jameson's mother and Jasmine's step-mother. Jasmine's real mother was a commoner, a woman of no real standing in high society who Jefferson had bedded at some point. Alex didn't know the whole story. What he did know was that Jasmine's mother had died during childbirth, and Jefferson had taken the girl in.

He had not done so out of any sense of kindness or moral obligation, but because his reputation would have been ruined if he didn't take Jasmine in. He signed the papers stating that she was his daughter, paid the doctors who birthed her some hush money so no one would find out about his infidelity, and then he left Jasmine to her own devices. He hired her tutors who taught her how to become a proper noblewoman, but he had no hand in raising her himself.

Jasmine only saw her father when he wanted to show her off, and that hadn't happened until she turned twelve. Before then, she was lucky if she saw him once a year.

Jasmine brought her hands onto her lap, clutching at the fabric of her pink blouse, which she must have borrowed from Alice. Tears began spilling from her eyes as her lips trembled. Her arms and shoulders were shaking.

"I always knew that Father saw me as nothing more than a tool to further his career and connections," Jasmine whispered. "But I always thought that if I did well enough, if I proved how useful I could be outside of my use as a pawn for marriage, he would come to see me as his daughter." She laughed, but it sounded nothing like her normal laugh. This was a hollow sound. "I suppose that was just wishful thinking, wasn't it?"

There wasn't anything Alex could say that would make Jasmine feel better. What did someone say to a person who had just been disowned by their own father, who had, after years of trying to earn her parents approval, suddenly realized that nothing she did would ever give her what she wanted? Nothing. No one could say anything to that.

However, just because he didn't know what to say that didn't mean he would do nothing.

"Jasmine…"

When Jasmine looked up and turned to him, Alex placed his hands on her shoulders and fell over onto the bed. Jasmine squawked as they landed on the mattress, on their sides, with a thump. They bounced once before stilling.

"Alexander, what are you... oh."

Jasmine stopped talking as Alex pulled her into a hug. He wrapped his arms around her body and held her. It was strange to think about, but this was actually the first time he'd ever hugged Jasmine of his own volition. He marveled at how much smaller she was than him. Her body was warm and fit comfortably within his arms. Alex wished he had done this sooner.

"I'm sorry," he said. "It was never my intention to hurt you with this knowledge."

Jasmine sniffled and shook her head, her nose rubbing against his chest. "I know you didn't. You don't need to apologize." She paused. "Though I... do not know what I should do from here on out. I am no longer of the de Truante family. What am I supposed to do?"

"That's why I wanted to discuss this with you." Still lying on his side, Alex moved back slightly so he could look into Jasmine's eyes. Large and blue, they were a lot more open and vulnerable than he was used to seeing. They were also rimmed with red from crying. "Now that Jefferson has disowned you, you're no longer a member of the de Truante family, which means you are free to take on someone else's last name."

He paused to let that sink in. Jasmine's nose wrinkled slightly as she began slowly connecting the dots. She looked cute when she was thinking.

"Gabrielle said she talked to you about, um, about how the rest of the galaxy allows polygamy."

"S-she did," Jasmine stuttered, her face suddenly turning pink.

Alex grabbed Jasmine's hand and brought it closer to him, ignoring her squeak as he rubbed her ring finger. Her hands were small, like her, and they were also soft, but he could feel the callouses gained from training and exercise. It made him happy to know that she had continued with her training.

"Eventually…" Alex began, doing his best not to lose his cool. Now was not the time for him to be embarrassed. "Eventually, I plan on putting a ring on this finger, which is why I was wondering if… ahem… I mean, that's why I was hoping you would be willing to take on my family's name."

Jasmine's breathing stilled. She sucked in a deep breath and remained unmoving. Alex waited as the seconds ticked by, listening to the loud thumping of his own heart, and tried not to let her know how unnerving her stare was. He had all but admitted that he was going to take her hand in marriage if she accepted him. That was a huge step. It wasn't just that he was talking about marriage. Jasmine would become his third wife after Gabrielle and Nyx.

In many ways, this was as much a declaration that he was casting off the laws of this solar system and accepting the laws that the rest of the galaxy adhered to. He still didn't feel right about it. His heart told him that this was for the best. It told him that he could make Jasmine happy if he did this. However, his head was telling him that he was making the dumbest decision of his life.

Then there was the guilt. Alex was asking Jasmine to marry him when he was already going to marry Gabrielle and Nyx. He would not want the person he married to have another spouse, but here he was, asking Jasmine to do just that. He felt like he had sunk to a new low.

"You'll get over it."

Not now, Asmodeus.

"Yes," Jasmine mumbled.

"Yes?"

"Yes." Her lips curving into the first smile he'd seen since this conversation had started, Jasmine reached out with her free hand and cupped his cheek. She let him continue holding her other hand. "Yes, I would love to take on your family name. Yes, I would love to marry you. Oh ho. However, I am the Queen of Matrimony, so I expect you to ask me that question again properly."

By properly, he took that to mean she wanted him to ask for her hand in marriage again when he had a ring. Considering his unreasonable demand, her request was more than reasonable.

"I'll make sure to find the best ring for this finger," he said, taking hold of Jasmine's ring finger and wiggling it back and forth. Jasmine giggled. It was so unlike anything else he'd heard from her. It was girlish and sweet, completely different from her normal rich girl laugh. This sounded more natural, more genuine. It made his heart light.

"As the Queen of Rings, I shall be waiting for that day."

They sat up. Alex grabbed both of Jasmine's hands as he stared into her eyes. They were still rimmed with tears, the redness still present, but she was smiling again. However, much as Alex wanted to remain like this, they still had some tasks to complete.

"For now, we should file out the paperwork to have you adopt the Ryker name," Alex said. "We can travel to the police station after that and verify that everything is correct. They'll also have to change your IDband, unless you want them to update this one."

Wiping the last vestige of tears from her eyes, Jasmine stood up, took in a deep breath, and then adopted her traditional rich girl stance. It was the one where she spread her feet shoulder width apart, placed her left hand on her hip, and her right hand near her mouth as she thrust out her chest and drew her head back. Alex couldn't keep the smile off his face. That stance meant she was more or less back to her normal self.

"Oh ho ho ho ho! As the Queen of IDbands, I think it would be best to merely update this one. After all, this is the one with all of the unique and useful programs that you made for me. It would be ridiculous to get a new IDband and have you reinstall every single program."

"I guess that's true." Alex stood up and stretched his arms. "By the way, I think calling yourself the Queen of IDbands sounds kind of silly."

"O-oh ho! It does?" Jasmine cheeks turned a vibrant shade of red as the hand near her mouth dropped to her side.

"Yeah, it does."

"H-how vexing."

2

Two days passed by quickly. It almost seemed like a blur.

The first thing that Alex did was file the paperwork for Jasmine's name to be changed from de Truante to Ryker. Of course, that came with the added issue of having to explain the nature of their relationship. He had put third wife on her papers, which, in hindsight, had been a bad idea. Karen had called him up to her office, lectured him for an hour, and then asked him to change it.

He had changed it.

To third spouse.

It had taken nearly an hour of arguing with Karen to make her understand that he planned on marrying Jasmine after he became the Emperor of the Galaxy. The laws of their solar system wouldn't apply to him when that happened. Despite his explanation being perfectly logical, Karen had told him that he was an idiot, and that until he became Emperor of the Galaxy, he would follow their laws and that if he kept pushing the issue, she would kick his ass all the way to the Sun.

Alex had changed her relationship status from third spouse to adopted sister.

Because Jasmine already had an IDband and was already a Mars Citizen, all Alex had to do was take her in to get the IDband updated.

Of course, because of all the illegal programs installed on her IDband, Alex had to wipe it clean. Jasmine had squawked at him and demanded to know what he was doing. When he told her that they would find the extra programs installed, and that he would re-add them once her IDband was updated, she had said that she might as well get a new IDband at this point.

In the end, Jasmine didn't get a new IDband, and Alex ended up re-adding all of the programs that he'd installed, plus a few extra programs that he thought would help keep her safe.

There was one issue that came up when Alex mentioned to Jasmine that he was re-enrolling her at Atreyu Academy.

"Oh ho ho ho ho!" Jasmine's laugh echoed around the living room. "While I do appreciate that you wish to re-enroll me at Atreyu Academy, as the Queen of Academics, I do not believe it is necessary for me to attend school anymore."

They were sitting on the couch in the living room, three steaming cups of caffa sitting on the glasteel coffee table. Only he, Jasmine, Nyx, and Madison were present. Everyone else was attending school. It had been his intention to set up a meeting with Mrs. Tepes today, but when he told Jasmine what he was doing, she had told him not to bother. Now they were sitting there. He was trying to convince her that she needed to attend school, but she was adamantly against it.

Nyx had not spoken up at all while he and Jasmine argued. Sitting on the couch next to him, she lifted the cup of caffa to her lips, blew on it several times, and then took a slow sip. She smiled and set the cup back down. Because she was so short, her feet didn't reach the floor. Likewise, Madison was present as well, but she was in the kitchen.

"Look, Jasmine, you need to go to school, at least until you graduate from Primary," Alex said. "It's required by law."

"Nyx isn't going to school," Jasmine pointed out.

"Nyx is also almost nineteen years old."

Jasmine opened her mouth, but then she snapped it closed. She stared at him for a full ten seconds before looking at Nyx, who was shorter than her, had smaller breasts than her, and whose feet didn't reach the floor when she was sitting down.

"You are nineteen?"

Nyx had just been about to take another sip of caffa when she paused, turned to look at Jasmine, and then set the cup on her lap. Her fingers gently moved against the cup as though letting them adjust to the heat.

"According to your solar system's calendar, I will be nineteen one week from now."

Jasmine looked like she had swallowed something foul. Her nose wrinkled, and her face became scrunched. She turned to Alex, her blue eyes larger than normal, almost as if she was trying to manipulate him by looking really cute.

"You know, my sister once tried that with me," Alex said. "It didn't work with her, and as pretty as you are, it's not going to work with you."

"O-oh ho ho ho ho! I have no idea what you mean, Alexander! I am the Queen of Understanding! I would never try something as underhanded as trying to manipulate you with my beauty! Oh ho ho ho ho!"

Jasmine had stood up as she started her mini-monologue. She had even adopted the traditional rich girl pose that she usually took when mini-monologuing. Alex shared a look with Nyx as Jasmine continued to laugh. Call him crazy, but he didn't believe her.

"Jasmine," he said as the girl calmed down and stopped laughing.

"Yes, Alexander?"

"Why don't you want to attend school?" he asked. "All of your friends are there, my sister is there, and I know you worked really hard to keep your grades in the top ninetieth percentile of the school. With all the effort you put in, not attending anymore would be a waste."

Jasmine sat back down on the couch and grabbed the teacup, which she took a slow sip of, sighing afterward as she set the cup back down. It was a delaying tactic. Alex sometimes did this when he wasn't sure what to say. Jasmine had actually picked this minor quirk up from prolonged exposure to his own habits.

Alex waited patiently for Jasmine to talk. When she did, it was much slower than usual. He had the distinct sense that she was thinking about her answer more than she normally would.

"I only have two real goals in life," she began as she traced the edge of her cup with an index finger.

"One of them is to make your mother's maid café a success, right?" Alex asked.

Jasmine smiled. "Yes, that's right. I want to make my mother's, my real mother's, maid café famous, so famous that I can create a chain of maid cafés across the entire solar system... and maybe even the entire galaxy."

Alex nodded, having remembered her telling him that one of the times he'd visited her café. If he was not mistaken, he'd been with Kazekiri that time. He recalled that Kazekiri had been paying off her brother's debt by agreeing to work there part-time. She had been forced into a maid costume and was told to serve him.

"What's the other goal?" asked Alex. Jasmine didn't answer. Ten seconds passed. Twenty. The only sound in the room was Nyx as she sipped her caffa. Jasmine still didn't answer. "Jasmine?"

"Oh ho ho ho ho!" Jasmine stood up so swiftly that Alex almost jerked backwards and fell off the couch. As she continued to laugh, Jasmine said, "I thought that would be obvious, Alexander! Am I not the Queen of Matrimony? There is only one other goal that I have ever wanted, and that is to become your wife! Oh ho ho ho ho!"

Nyx looked at Jasmine as the girl continued to laugh, then looked at Alex, who noticed and shrugged as if to say that he wasn't sure what this was all about either, and then she went back to her caffa. She took another sip, glanced at Jasmine again, and apparently decided to ignore the other girl. Alex thought it was a good idea.

In the end, Alex decided to re-enroll Jasmine in Atreyu Academy. She would be starting next Monday. Jasmine had complained to him for a bit, but fortunately, Alex had a secret weapon.

"Jasmine." Alex placed his hands on her cheeks and leaned down until their foreheads and noses were touching. He caressed her cheekbones with his thumb, slowly drawing circles against her skin. "I know you don't want to go, and I do understand your reasons, but please do this for me. I'm not asking you to attend University, but I want my wife to be well-educated, and after all the time you spent attending school, after all the work you put in, it would be a shame not to complete your last two years of Primary and graduate with your friends."

"O-oh ho... D-do you really think so?" Jasmine's eyes shook like she was trying to look away but couldn't. Her pale cheeks were a startling shade of scarlet. "If... if you want me to show everyone why I am the Queen of School that badly, then I guess I could attend school."

For just a moment, Alex thought of leaning in to kiss her. She was so close, and as he stared at her soft, glossy pink lips, the desire to kiss her increased. Alex even imagined what it would be like. He would place his mouth over hers, softly at first, but with increasing passion, and then he would take her lower lip between his teeth and gently nibble on it. And then...

With a deep breath, Alex let go of her face and took several steps back, shaking his head. Jasmine was not Gabrielle. He couldn't treat them the same. Also, unlike Gabrielle, who was happy just kissing whenever, he knew that Jasmine would not appreciate it. She was a romantic at heart. She would want to go on a date first, and then share a kiss after its conclusion.

Alex smiled. "Thank you."

"O-oh ho ho! Oh ho ho ho ho ho! You are welcome, Alexander."

As Jasmine threw her head back and laughed, a plan was forming in his head, of taking Jasmine on a date, of letting her have fun and be herself, and of coming home later that night and sharing a kiss before they fell asleep in each other's arms. That was the plan, at least. Whether or not it would happen was another matter altogether.

First, he had to plan a successful date with Gabrielle.

Alex didn't think he'd ever been more excited or nervous at the same time.

3

11:00am. Saturday. The day when he and Gabrielle would go on their first date. Alex had already planned out what they were doing. Gabrielle had mentioned that she'd never seen any aquatic life before when they were watching a holo-documentary about the oceans on Earth, so he'd ordered tickets to the aquarium that opened up a few months ago. According to an ad he saw, the aquarium boasted over one thousand different types of sea creatures, including whales and dolphins.

He was actually pretty excited himself. He'd never seen animals that lived in the water in real life either.

Alex was standing by the door, waiting for Gabrielle to get ready. Alice, Jasmine, Madison and Michelle were with Gabrielle. Purportedly, they were helping the alien princess get ready for their date, but they had told him that twenty minutes ago and still weren't out. He was beginning to wonder if they were really helping her get ready.

"You will treat my sister right," Ariel said. She was standing next to him, arms crossed, glaring at nothing. "If you don't, I'll pound your face in."

"Don't worry," Alex assured her. "I'll treat Gabrielle like a princess."

Ariel snorted at the joke. He tried not to grin.

He wasn't sure why Ariel and Nyx had decided not to enter the room with the other girls, though he guessed it was because neither of them were interested in fashion. Nyx was an assassin. Ariel was kind of a tomboy. A lot of the things that the girls he knew took interest in, like makeup, shopping, and gossip, she was not interested in.

A tug at Alex's sleeve made him turn his head. It was Nyx. She was holding the sleeve of his collared shirt and looking up at him. Her apollonian gaze remained unchanging, but he detected a soft gleam within them.

"What's up, Nyx? Is something wrong?"

"I want to go on a date as well."

"Wha…" Beside them, Ariel blushed.

Alex wanted to say he was surprised that Nyx was being this forward, but with everything that had happened in the last few months, with all of the revelations he had, he didn't think he could be surprised anymore.

"I'll take you on a date sometime next week. How does that sound?"

Nyx nodded. "I'd like to attend a festival."

"A festival, huh…"

Mars City didn't have many festivals, maybe one or two a year, but there were a number of other domes that did. Mars Homespring Resort had a festival almost every night. It wouldn't be too expensive to take a short trip there, spend the night, and then come back the next morning. The only concern he had was money. He was severely lacking in funds thanks to Karen fining him for, ironically, saving Nyx from the police.

"I'll see what I can do," Alex said. Nyx accepted this with a nod and let go of his sleeve.

It wasn't until ten minutes later that Alice and Michelle finally came back downstairs. Judging from the satisfied smile on Michelle's face, he assumed they were done. Even Alice was wearing a smile. She almost never smiled.

"Ahem." Michelle coughed into her hand. "May I present to you, my honorable sister, Gabrielle Angelise."

Alex and everyone else looked up as she descended down the stairs. Silver hair had been twisted into artful braids that allowed all to gaze upon her slender neck and shoulders. Each braid bounced with a strange buoyancy as she walked. Her outfit was simple, but somehow, the light pink shirt that hung around her shoulders and the blue skirt that swished as she walked made her seem more elegant than normal, more mature. Maybe it had something to do with those strapon heels, which emphasized her lovely calves and cute feet. Perhaps it was just the combination of her wings and shimmering silver hair. Alex couldn't say what, exactly, enthralled him so much. He only knew that as she stopped in front of him, he found it hard to remember to breathe.

He grunted when Alice elbowed him in the side. "Aren't you going to compliment her, troublesome big brother?"

"Erm…" That's right. Alex had forgotten that complimenting a girl was an important ritual when on a date. The problem was that he couldn't think of what to say. "You are, uh, you look really nice."

"Really?" Gabrielle's eyes gained an extra level of vibrancy.

Alex nodded. "I always thought you were pretty, but you look even more beautiful than usual."

"Eh ehehehe." Gabrielle rubbed the back of her neck and grinned. "I feel kind of embarrassed getting complimented like that."

"Oh ho ho ho ho!" Jasmine threw her head back and smiled. "She looks this amazing because I, the Queen of Style, am the one who chose her outfit and did her hair."

"Correction," Madison said. "I am the one who did her hair."

"Erm… yes, that's true." Jasmine coughed into her hand before starting over. "Oh ho ho ho ho! It's only natural that she would look amazing! I chose the outfit and Madison did her hair. Oh ho ho ho ho!"

"Actually, I believe I was the one who chose her outfit," Michelle chimed in.

Jasmine blushed and scowled at the same time. "Well, I was the one who helped her in it!"

"That is true."

"Oh ho ho ho ho! Then it is only thanks to my efforts. All in a day's work for one who is known far and wide as the Queen of Clothes Changing!"

"Right…"

Alex's lips involuntarily twitched into a smile. He didn't know if they were doing this on purpose or not, but the strange comedy routine had done an amazing job of soothing his nerves. His heartbeat slowed to a more regular rhythm; the panic filling his mind calmed; he felt like he could do this.

Michelle shook her head, then walked up to Alex. Before he could say anything, she leaned into him and slipped something inside of his pocket. He didn't know what it was, but it was smooth and round.

"It's a good luck charm." She stepped back and winked.

"Oh. Um, thank you." Alex didn't know what she had put in his pocket, but it was very thoughtful of her to give him something for luck. "You ready, Gabby?" Alex held out his hand.

Gabrielle beamed as she took his hand. "Yes!"

"We'll see you all later." Alex waved at the group as he and Gabrielle prepared to leave. "Try not to break anything, okay?"

"Don't say something so troublesome, Big Bro." Alice glared at him. "We aren't you."

And with that rosey response, Alex and Gabrielle gave their final goodbyes and left for their date.

4

Ariel watched as Alex and Gabrielle walked down the street, ignoring the loud thumping that came from behind her—it was probably Michelle being stupid—until the two of them had disappeared. Then she turned away from the window.

While she was happy to know that her sister was going on a date with the person she loved, her chest ached. She reached up and rubbed her chest. Ariel couldn't fathom why seeing those two act so intimate with each other would invoke such a reaction, unless…

No. There's no way. Alex is a great guy, but I'm not interested in him like that.

At least, Ariel did not think she loved Alex.

"I won't let you do what you want with them! I'm not going to let you lay one fucking hand on them, and I sure as hell won't let some pompous ass who thinks he can just claim them both touch them either! Ariel and Michelle will make their own damn choice! They'll decide who they want to marry! Not you!"

Ariel's heartbeat quickened as she remembered Alex's passionate speech to her father.

"You're the one who's being cruel! Marriage isn't something you do just because! It's a precious bond between people who love each other!"

She remembered the anger in his voice as he defended her and Michelle.

"I will protect them, and if they decided they wanted to marry me, then I would, but I won't make that choice for them. I'll let them make their own choices."

More than anything else, Ariel remembered how Alex had said he would give them a choice, how he refused to let their choice be taken from them. Her heartbeat became a rampaging wardrum just remembering how ardently he had fought for her and her sister's sake.

I could marry him if I wanted to.

If she told Gabrielle that she was in love with Alex, she knew that her sister, unendingly kind and silly, would be overjoyed with the idea. She wouldn't think twice about letting her and Michelle marry Alex.

But she was hesitant. Ariel didn't know what she wanted, much less if the erratic beating of her heart was a sign of love or something else.

More loud thumping echoed behind her, what sounded like a dozen feet running down the stairs. Ariel did her best to ignore it. Her sister could be such a pain sometimes. However, the thumping soon stopped, and her sister's voice spoke up behind her.

"Ariel, why aren't you getting in disguise?"

"Huh? What are you—"

Ariel turned around—and froze.

Her sister smiled as she twirled her gray mustache between her fingers. She was no longer wearing normal clothes. Her blue skirt and velcro shirt reminded Ariel of this police holo-drama she had watched a few days ago. Michelle was even wearing the black heels.

She wasn't the only person dressed up. Jasmine had opted to wear a red cheongsam and black wig; Alice was dressed as a butler; Madison wore bandages over her chest, black pants, wooden sandals, and had slung a bokuto across her shoulder; and Nyx was dressed in the dark brown vest and pants of a grease monkey.

"What... what is this?" Ariel asked before the cold realization set in and she slowly deadpanned. "You four are planning to follow them."

"I am just ensuring their safety," Madison said.

Jasmine threw her head back and laughed. "Oh ho ho ho ho! I am merely looking out for my best interests."

"I'm only interested in seeing how their date goes," Michelle assured, still twirling her mustache.

Alice scowled. "I have to make sure nothing troublesome happens."

"There is a lot riding on this date," Michelle added. "We have to ensure that it's a successful one."

"Indeed." Jasmine nodded. "My future as Alexander's second wife depends on it."

"Third wife," Nyx corrected.

"Second!" Jasmine glared.

"..."

"Come, comrades!" Michelle shouted as she led the way outside. "Let us follow them!"

"AYE!" everyone but Ariel shouted back.

Ariel stared after the group as they began marching down the street. She sighed several seconds later and ran upstairs to grab a costume.

Someone has to keep those four out of trouble, she decided before glaring at the only costume remaining. A black nun's habit. *Who the hell chose these costumes?*

5

Alex and Gabrielle were sitting on the shuttle that was taking them into Mars City. They had already experienced much of the city together, but today, they were on a date, and he was taking her to the aquarium. Before that, however, Alex planned on taking her to get some lunch. It was noon anyway.

"Where are we going first?" asked Gabrielle. They were sitting in the back of the shuttle to avoid other people. She was hugging his arm to her chest as she leaned against him. The smile that she had been wearing since the day he asked her out still hadn't left.

Alex grinned. "First we're going to grab a bite to eat."

After the shuttle dropped them off, Alex led a curious Gabrielle to their destination. She didn't know anything about what he had planned today. Alex had been keeping his plans close to his crisis suit so as to surprise Gabrielle.

"Isn't this one of those maid cafés?" asked Gabrielle as they reached their first destination.

The building they stood before sat on one of many hubs in the entertainment district. It had three-stories. Rather than the gleam of durasteel, it was made of bricks, not necessarily a rarity, but it was an unusual material for buildings in this day and age. There were several glasteel windows, through which he and Gabrielle could see patrons sitting down as women dressed in skintight outfits flitted between tables. A sign above the door said *Mars Kitten Café*.

"Come on." Alex began walking, and Gabrielle, connected to him by the arm, went inside with him.

True to its name, the women who worked there were dressed in a skintight version of a pilot's suit. A cat tail stuck out of a small hole in their backsides, and two triangular ears sat on their heads. While the tails waved behind them, their ears periodically twitched like real cat ears. As they entered the café, a woman wearing the same skintight clothes and cat appendages smiled at them.

"Welcome home, Master."

"Clarissa," Alex greeted. "How have you been?"

The woman named Clarissa blinked several times before her eyes lit up. "Master Alex! It's so good to see you! And this must be Gabrielle." Clarissa clasped her hands together and bowed before them. "It's a pleasure to make your acquaintance. All of us have been wanting to meet you, especially the mistress."

"Mistress?" Gabrielle asked.

"Let me show you to a table." Clarissa turned around and gestured for them to follow her. The two of them trailed after the woman as she flitted through tables and chairs, directing them to a table. "I'll go and fetch the mistress. She'll be so excited to finally meet your girlfriend!"

"I'm sure she will," Alex groaned as Clarissa left.

Gabrielle looked from Clarissa as she disappeared to him. "Who's this mistress?"

"She's talking about my grandmother."

"Grandmother?" Gabrielle's eyes suddenly began shining. "I'm going to meet your grandmother?"

"I figured it was about time I introduced my family to my fiancé."

Gabrielle blushed and bashfully rubbed her head. "Ehehehehe, I love hearing you call me your fiancé."

"Fiancé, huh?" said a voice. Alex and Gabrielle turned their heads and looked at the voice's owner. It was an older woman with gray in her hair and wrinkles around her eyes and mouth. Despite her age, she stood with her back straight, projecting an aura of youth and vitality of someone half her age. Unlike the girls who worked in space suits, she was wearing a traditional black and white maid uniform... with kitty ears and a tail. "So, this is Gabrielle Angelise, huh? The daughter of King Lucifer?"

"Granny Mor—Erm." Alex ceased talking when the woman glared at him. Knowing better than to finish his sentence, he started over. "I mean, Auntie Morella, this is Gabrielle Angelise. Gabrielle, this is Auntie Morella. She's Alice's grandmother."

"It's very nice to meet you!" Gabrielle stumbled to her feet and bowed. "I'm really pleased to make your acquaintance! I am Alex's fiancé!"

Alex raised an eyebrow at the very un-Gabrielle-like action. She'd never really been the type to bow like that, and he'd never seen her stumble over anything either. If he didn't know any better, he would have said that she was nervous, but that couldn't be possible. Gabrielle never got nervous.

... Right?

Auntie Morella studied Gabrielle with a critical eye. "So this is what an angelisian looks like. I see it now. Yes... the resemblance is uncanny..."

"Have you met an angelisian before?" asked Alex.

Auntie Morella merely smiled at his question, walked toward them with incalculable grace, pulled out one of the two empty chairs, and sat down at their table. Gabrielle looked almost stiff as the woman sat there. Her shoulders trembled, and a cold sweat had broken out on her forehead.

Maybe she really is nervous.

"Well," Auntie Morella began, "since I finally have you here, I suppose this is the part where I get to ask all kinds of questions about you and your relationship with my grandson." She eyed him and smirked. "Of course, I would have been able to ask these questions much sooner if my grandson had brought you to me before now."

Alex wasn't blushing at the admonishment. He wasn't. The heat on his cheeks was merely because of the temperature outside.

"I would have introduced her sooner," he muttered, looking away. "But a lot's happened."

"Oh, I know," Auntie Morella said. "Trust me, I've been paying attention to everything you've done, including your escapades in Camelot."

It somehow didn't surprise him that she knew he'd left the galaxy, though just how she knew he'd gone to Camelot was another matter entirely. He didn't know much about her network of informants. However, they surely didn't extend beyond this solar system.

"Nick knows as well," she added. Alex just sighed.

"Um, um, excuse me?" Gabrielle raised a shaking hand. "But, um, do you mind if I ask why you aren't living with Alex and Alice?"

"It was a decision that Alex made himself." Crossing her arms, Auntie Morella gave him a look before turning back to Gabrielle. "When Alex and Alice's parents died, neither I nor Nick were in a position to take care of them. Both of us were grieving, and we were going through our divorce. They lived with the Metronomes for a time, but Alex eventually decided that he wanted to live independently. I guess since Nick and I were so busy back then, Alex decided he didn't want to rely on us."

"Oh, I see," Gabrielle said, shoulders slumping ever so slightly.

A cat waitress came by and asked what they wanted to order. Gabrielle decided on omarice, while Alex went with a ham and cheese sandwich. Auntie Morella did not order anything to eat and merely had her maids make her a caffa.

Alex tapped his left foot against the ground, a habit that he could have sworn he had kicked. His palms were sweaty, his heart was a bit jittery. He felt like breathing incorrectly might bring his grandmother's attention on him. Being in Auntie Morella's presence, and with Gabrielle at that, was making him wish he had chosen a different café.

Well, it's too late to turn back now.

"I hope you don't mind if I ask you a question," Auntie Morella said to Gabrielle.

Gabrielle squeaked, straightened her back, and feigned the confidence that normally came to her naturally. "I don't mind."

Smiling in that devious way that only an old lady could, Auntie Morella asked, "How much do you like Alex? What is it that you wish from this relationship?"

The maid who had taken their order came back with a cup of caffa, which she set in front of Auntie Morella. Perhaps because this place was a maid café, both the cup and the small plate it was sitting on were made of the finest china, a pure porcelain cup with swirling blue designs. The brown liquid within had steam wafting from its surface.

"How much do I like Alex?" Gabrielle paused as she took that question in. One of her hands went to her chest, and then she closed her eyes and smiled. "I love Alex more than anyone else in the galaxy. He means everything to me. I want to marry Alex and one day start a family with him."

Thump-thump.

Alex could swear his heart was going to explode out of his chest if Gabrielle kept talking like that. He already knew that she loved him, of course, but hearing her talk like that, with such a heartfelt tone of voice, made him feel like he was melting.

"I see." Auntie Morella stared at her, then glanced his way. "It looks like Alex was quite lucky when he found you."

"I don't need you telling me that," Alex mumbled.

They didn't speak for much longer. Auntie Morella was still the owner of this establishment, and there were still a lot of customers, so she left them soon after finishing her caffa.

"She seems like a nice lady," Gabrielle said.

"Yeah." Alex nodded. "She is pretty nice, though I'm kinda shocked she didn't pick our brains out."

"Why would she pick out our brains?"

"… Nevermind." Shaking off his small moment of shock, Alex decided that it was time to ask a question that he had been hoping to ask for a while now. "Do you think you could tell me more about angelisians? I only know what you and Eostre have told me about the Aura of Creation."

Gabrielle perked up. "Did you say Eostre?"

"Erm… yes. Do you know her?"

"Eostre is the name of Ariel's mama," Gabrielle said.

Alex froze for a moment, but he quickly calmed down. There was no way the Eostre that he knew could be the same one that had birthed Ariel. That was way too coincidental. While this wasn't a common name where they lived, he was sure there were plenty of people in the galaxy at large who had this name.

"Anyway, I don't know a whole lot about your society or anything like that," Alex said. "I was hoping you could fill in the blanks for me."

The maid arrived again, this time balancing two plates on her arms. She set their meals down in front of them, omarice for Gabrielle and a ham and cheese sandwich for him. Before leaving, the maid told them to let her know if they needed anything else. They thanked her and began eating.

"This is really good!" Gabrielle exclaimed as she cut another slice with her fork, stabbed it, and stuck the speared food into her mouth. She moaned in delight. "I've never tried this stuff before, but Ryoko and Serah always said it was to die for. I can understand why."

"They make good food here," Alex said after swallowing a bite of his sandwich. "Anyway, about angelisians…"

"Right." Gabrielle took another bite of her food, then set her fork down and gave him most of her attention. "I suppose the first thing you should know is that angelisians are divided into castes based on things like power, ability, and blood purity. The three castes are Alpha, Delta, and Beta. Papa and I are Alphas. Our blood purity and power are the strongest, which you can tell by our silver hair. Mama is also an Alpha. Ariel and Michelle are both Deltas because they're only half-angelisian. Azazel is a Beta, if you want to know, though his first wife is an Alpha."

"Then I would be a Delta as well, right?" asked Alex.

"Hmmm… I think so." Gabrielle tilted her head. "It's hard to say. The silver in your hair tells me that whoever your angelisian parent was had to be an Alpha. I don't know what your other half is, but if your mama or papa was an Alpha, then you might also be an Alpha if the power you have locked away exceeds a certain level."

Alex didn't understand what she meant by levels, though he guessed angelisians had a way of measuring power, but he knew that his father was an angelisian. Now that some of his memories had been unlocked, he remembered that his father had long ears like Gabrielle's and silver hair. He also had wings. However, he normally hid those using a device that made them invisible.

As he thought about his father, Alex remembered something else about himself that he wanted to ask someone. He took another bite of his sandwich. Should he tell Gabrielle about Asmodeus? Would she even know what Asmodeus was? He remembered her mentioning daemons before, so she might, but...

"Have you ever heard the name Asmodeus?" asked Alex.

Gabrielle chewed her omarice with a thoughtful frown. Alex tried not to let his nervousness show, but his leg was thumping something fierce underneath the table. He placed his hand on it as if to stop it from moving. That didn't work. His leg continued to bounce.

After she finished swallowing her food, Gabrielle took a sip of water, let out a tiny burp, and then said, "That name doesn't ring any bells."

"I see." Alex hesitated again. "What can you tell me about daemons?"

"Hmm..." Crossing her arms, Gabrielle made several thinking noises, which were awfully cute. "I can't tell you much since I don't know too much about them. A really long time ago... like, a really, really long time ago, the daemons were the sworn enemies of us angelisians. I hear we fought them a lot. From what I understand, they were the only people in the entire galaxy who could fight on par with us. However, during the Unification War, Papa destroyed several of their planets and forced them into submission."

"What about their powers?" Alex asked. "Do you know what kind of powers they have?"

Gabrielle shook her head. "Sorry. I only know a little about that. Let's see…" Her cheek twitched several times as she scratched it, as though doing so might somehow help her recall what she knew. "I know that daemons are different from angelisians. Angelisians receive their power through genetics, but daemons receive their power through incarnations."

"Incarnations?" Alex frowned at the unfamiliar term. "What's that?"

"I don't know. That's the extent of my knowledge." Gabrielle offered an apologetic smile. "Sorry I can't be of more help."

"No, it's okay." Alex reached over the table and placed his hands over hers. They were soft and warm. "You've given me a lot more information than I used to have. Thank you."

Gabrielle blushed. "Tee-hee! You're welcome!"

6

Just outside of the maid café, several individuals were watching Alex and Gabrielle enjoy their meal. They hid behind a tree, peering out from either side. Alice, Jasmine, Michelle, Madison, and Nyx were practically on top of each other as they hid, though if someone were to ask Ariel, she would have said that their choice of hiding spot wasn't very good. They were drawing a crowd.

Then again, it could have been the costumes.

"It looks like they are having fun," Michelle said.

"Oh ho ho ho ho! I'm so jealous—I mean, I'm so happy they are enjoying their time together. Oh ho ho ho ho!"

"Your rich girl is showing."

"What do you mean by that?!"

"Ha... would you two keep it down. You're being troublesome," Alice muttered, only to yelp when Jasmine accidentally elbowed her on the cranium. "Ouch! Watch what you're doing!"

"S-sorry, Alice."

"Please forgive my mistress, Alice. She did not injure you on purpose."

"Yeah, whatever."

"..." Unlike the others, Nyx silently stared through the glasteel window at Alex and Gabrielle. Ariel wondered if the girl was even aware of how her nails were turning into claws.

That must be alchemy...

Ariel had seen alchemy several times. Michelle's mother specialized in it, but her alchemy was different. For one thing, Michelle's mom had to create a transmutation circle. She couldn't just transmute things at will like Nyx could. Supposedly, this ability came from the fact that Nyx's body was made up entirely of nanomachines.

As she turned her attention back to Alex and her big sister, something else caught her eye, a person who appeared to be doing the same thing they were. Spying. It was a young man with blond hair. The shape of his face and color of his eyes reminded her of Jasmine. He stood in front of the glasteel window and was glaring jealously into it.

"Hey," Ariel said, "isn't that your brother, Jasmine?"

Jasmine frowned, looked at her, looked at where she was looking, and then squawked. "It is! That's my brother—I mean, that's my former brother! What is he doing here?! Don't tell me he's here to ruin Alexander and the troll—I mean, Gabrielle's date!"

Before anyone could stop her, Jasmine growled, stomped out from behind the tree, and marched over to her brother. She stopped barely half a meter away. Placing her hands on her hips, she leaned forward and glared at him.

"Oh ho ho ho ho! What are you doing here, Jameson?"

Jameson turned his head. He scowled when he saw her.

"Jasmine… what are you doing here?"

"Oh ho ho ho ho ho! Do not question the Queen of Questions. I just asked you that question!" She pointed an accusing finger at him. "You're here to spy on Alexander and Gabrielle, aren't you?! Don't deny it! I know you've had your eye on her for awhile now!"

"So what if I am?! I am the King of Romantic Warfare! Spying is my right!"

"I won't let you!"

Jasmine and Jameson leapt away from each other, but only so they could adopt a fighting stance. The world around them slowed. Time seemed to stand still. Then, on some unseen signal, the two charged forward and began what was quite possibly the most one-sided brawl that Ariel had ever seen.

Jasmine thrashed Jameson. She slammed a palm strike into the underside of Jameson's chin, then whacked him in the gut with two fists, sending him stumbling backward, leaning over and curling his hands around his stomach. Blood ran down the boy's mouth as he glared at her.

"I see that peasant really has been teaching you how to fight like a barbarian." Jameson's scowl looked rather petulant, like a child who had just realize he was outmatched. "That's fine. If you want to act like a barbarian, then I've found some friends who can oblige you!"

He pushed a button on his IDband, and six people appeared before them so suddenly it was like they had teleported there. The group that now stood between Jasmine and Jameson looked like thugs. They wore dark suits and sunglasses. The one in the front looked vaguely familiar. He had spiky blond hair, dark skin, and slightly pointed ears.

"Meet my new bodyguards, the Black Panthers!" Jameson giggled as he pointed at Jasmine. "Take care of the girl! I do not care what you do with her!"

The man in the lead cracked his knuckles. "With pleasure, boss!"

As the men began advancing on her, slowly as if they were savoring the moment, Jasmine huffed and settled herself back into her combat stance. "If you think a bunch of low-life grunts can defeat me, the Queen of Combat, then you have another thing coming! Oh ho ho ho ho!"

Ariel was conflicted as she watched the proceedings. On the one hand, she really didn't want to get involved. On the other, Jasmine was her friend and even if she looked confident in her abilities, it was still six on one.

There was also the fact that they were gathering a crowd, with over two dozen people having stopped in the middle of the walkway to watch the proceedings. Ariel didn't understand why these idiots were just watching. They should have called the police or something, but no, some of them were even taking pictures.

"Guess I got no choice," she muttered. However, before she could do anything, someone else stepped in.

Nyx slammed her hands onto the ground, and suddenly, six hands emerged from the walkway. They appeared behind the group of thugs. The brutes in suits barely had time to scream like ninnies before the hands grabbed them and hurled them through the air. Ariel and the others could do nothing but watch as the six people slowly disappeared in twinkles of light.

"W-what the hell was that?!" Jameson asked in shock.

He wouldn't get an answer, not in the form of words, but Nyx marched forward to stand beside Jasmine. She had already transmuted two of her armbands into swords. The pretty assassin stood in front of the former rich girl, her curved blades gleaming ominously in the light.

"If you wish to hurt Jasmine, you will have to go through me," she said emotionlessly.

"N-Nyx, what are you doing here? Why are you helping this begotten former sister of mine?!"

Nyx didn't answer in the form of words. She merely slid her feet apart and readied her blades. Jameson took several steps back before, like a frightened animal, he bolted away from the group, shoving his way through the crowd. Sadly, Nyx was not willing to let him go so easily.

"I will not let you hurt my friends or ruin Alex and Princess Gabrielle's date," she said in her toneless voice as she gave chase, leaping over the crowd of pedestrians.

"Well," Ariel said as Alice, Michelle, and Madison walked out from behind the tree, "this is turning into a precarious situation."

"I'll say," Alice muttered. "We just lost Alex and Gabrielle. Talk about troublesome."

"Wait. What?" Michelle asked. "Where did they go?!"

"Master is now two point six kilometers that way." Madison pointed off in the opposite direction that Nyx had begun chasing Jameson.

"Oh ho ho ho ho! Then let us make haste and catch up with them!" Jasmine said. Sadly, before they could go anywhere, several cop shuttles appeared above them.

"All of you remain where you are! We've received reports from several people who have claimed there's a girl disturbing the peace with her violent behavior! We'd like all of you to remain here for questioning! Try to escape and you will be arrested!"

Jasmine froze, Michelle frowned, Alice muttered, and Madison asked her mistress, "Shall I open fire?" While all this was going on, Ariel sighed and clasped her hands together.

"God give me strength," she prayed.

"Preach it, sister!" a random passerby encouraged her.

CHAPTER 5

KAZEKIRI

The recently opened aquarium was located on the far eastern side of the entertainment district. Unlike most buildings, which were either small structures that sat on hubs or large skyscrapers, the aquarium was like a hub unto itself. It was far wider than any skyscraper, but it was also taller than most of the buildings around it. At an estimate, Alex would have said it was one hundred stories tall.

Reaching the building required them to board a shuttle that took them to a docking bay inside of the aquarium itself. When Alex and Gabrielle arrived, there was already a huge waiting line. Alex had bought tickets in advance, but even the line to get onto the shuttle was long. Other people must have had the same idea as him.

Since it looked like they would be waiting, Alex bought them a pair of ice cream cones from a nearby stand. His was plain vanilla, but Gabrielle had chosen a strawberry-banana swirl. It looked like red and yellow ice cream mixed together in a spiral pattern. With an excitement that couldn't be denied, Gabrielle bit into her ice cream. She immediately regretted it.

"Ack! That's cold!" She took another bite. "But it's so good!" Another bite. "But it's so cold, too!"

Alex snorted as he ate his ice cream at a more measured pace. He had no desire to get a brain freeze, thank you very much. While they ate, the line slowly moved as people were herded onto the shuttles.

"That was delicious!" Gabrielle said with a sigh of content after she finished her ice cream, cone and all.

He chuckled. "I'm glad you liked it. By the way, you have some ice cream on your cheek." When Gabrielle just blinked at him, Alex reached up, cupped her face, and wiped the ice cream away with his thumb. He licked it off his finger. "Got it."

"Thank you," Gabrielle said.

"You're welcome."

They soon reached the end of the line, were herded onto a shuttle, and found a place near the front to sit down. All of the shuttle benches were two to a seat, so he and Gabrielle were able to sit together, just them. Gabrielle used that opportunity to cuddle up. Alex didn't resist.

"I just realized," Alex said as the shuttle lifted off. He barely felt it. "It's only been less than half a year since you and I first met, but it feels a lot longer."

"Has it really only been half a year?" Gabrielle mulled that over with a thoughtful frown. "How weird. I could have sworn it was longer, too. I feel like you and I have known each other forever."

"I know what you mean."

So much had changed since Gabrielle had come into his life. Thinking on it, outside of getting kicked out of the Mars Police Academy, most of the changes that came about were directly because of her presence. It was thanks to Gabrielle that he now understood he was loved, thanks to her that he had a girlfriend, thanks to her that he had rebelled against the police, and thanks to her that he was getting engaged to multiple women. Really, if it wasn't for her, Alex didn't know where he'd be.

I'd probably still be moping about getting kicked out of the police forces.

Four or maybe five months ago, or perhaps a little over, Alex had come across Gabrielle in a small alley. After learning that she had nowhere to go, he had offered her a place to stay. Since then, they had been attacked by bodyguards, marriage candidates, assassins, and a host of other extra-terrestrial problems. He'd been so busy dealing with all the issues that came with Gabrielle that he hadn't had time to be mopey or depressed. Thinking about it like that, he really did have to thank her.

"Hey, Alex?"

"Huh? Yes?"

Gabrielle looked at him, once again, with cheeks a startling pink. Her hands were in her lap. He looked down. She was twiddling her fingers. Huh. He didn't think he'd ever seen her do something like that. It was such a self-conscious gesture.

"I wanted to thank you for everything you've done for me," she said, glancing at him only to look away again. "I also wanted to apologize. I know I caused you a lot of problems."

"What brought this on?" asked Alex.

"I just... I realize that I've caused you a lot of problems." Gabrielle continued twiddling her fingers in her lap. She was biting her lip. "I don't even just mean my marriage candidates. I know that I've been pushing beliefs that you don't understand onto you, and I know it can't be easy for you to accept them, but you have anyway." Finally, she looked at him, and for the first time, Alex saw something in her eyes that he'd never seen before. "I want you to know that I am more grateful to you than you will ever know. I love you. I love you so much that thinking about how much I love you makes my chest hurt. When you're sad or angry or in pain, it hurts me. And I know that you've been suffering a lot thanks to me. That's why I want you to know that whenever you're feeling aroused, you can come to me and I'll help."

Alex had never realized that Gabrielle's feelings for him were this deep; he knew she loved him, of course. However, the extent of her feelings, their depths, their strength, he had underestimated how powerful they were.

It made warmth engulf his chest, made him want to cry and laugh at the same time. He was overcome with an emotion that he couldn't place. No, he was overcome with too many emotions, so many that he couldn't tell what he was feeling. All he knew was that Gabrielle's words meant the world to him—the galaxy even.

"Thank you," Alex said. "I really... hearing you say that means so much to me. I..." he trailed off, his brow furrowing, expression twitching in perplexity as the rest of her words penetrated his mind. That last part, in particular, stood out. "Wait. What did you mean by when I'm feeling... aroused? How did you even know about that?!"

"I mean that you were aroused whenever we bathed or slept together, right?" Gabrielle tilted her head. "I didn't know what that meant at first. Actually, it was only thanks to Ryoko that I became aware that a boy having an erection means he's feeling sexually aroused. I'm sorry. Had I known, I would have helped you sooner."

"W-what do you mean by that?" Alex was afraid to ask, but he asked anyway.

"Angelisian bodies are quite sturdy," Gabrielle lectured. "We have to be, to control the power we have. Nyx told me that you were afraid of losing control and doing perverted things to people without meaning to, but if you and I had sex whenever you felt aroused, you wouldn't need to worry anymore."

Their conversation was way too private to be having on a shuttle—Alex could practically feel the disapproving eyes on them —but he no longer had a choice now that she had said something. That meant he could only do one thing.

He leaned in and whispered in her ear. "How do you know about sex?"

"What are you talking about?" asked Gabrielle, her voice not lowering in volume. "Everyone knows what sex is. It's when a man sticks his—"

"That's enough." Alex covered her mouth to keep her from saying anymore. "Let's not talk about this in public anymore."

"Mfay," Gabrielle said, voice muffled by his hands. Alex took his hands from Gabrielle's mouth and sighed. It looked like he was saved— "Does that mean we should continue our conversation about sex after our date?"

Nevermind. It looked like he had spoken too soon.

1

After the shuttle set down inside of a docking bay, everyone disembarked. Several employees wearing bright red vests directed traffic through a door, telling people to get in single file, not to push, and move slowly. Alex and Gabrielle followed the advice. Holding hands, they stepped through the door and into a hallway that left them breathless.

"Wow…" Gabrielle muttered. "I've never seen anything like this before."

"Me neither," Alex agreed.

The hallway was rounded except for the floor. While the floor was made of durasteel, the walls were made of glasteel, which allowed them to see the world beyond. Aquatic life of all kinds swam through water, kept at bay by the glasteel shaped like a tube. Some were small, able to fit on his palm. Others, however, were massive. Even as he and Gabrielle walked along with everyone else, a gigantic shadow appeared above them. It was a giant creature of some kind, gray, with a white belly and rows of sharp teeth. Alex had no idea what it was called.

As they left the hall, the area around them widened, the walls straightened, and the material changed from glasteel to durasteel. He and Gabrielle walked through the seemingly unending series of connecting passages. Each passage had a series of tanks, which showed off different types of fish. A holographic screen in front of each tank told them details about the fishes they were looking at.

"Check it out, Alex!" Gabrielle pressed her face against one particular tank. "Look at it's face! It's all blown up!"

Alex looked at the fish that she was staring at, which reminded him of a balloon with spikes. He then looked at the holographic display and read the contents out loud.

"Pufferfish can inflate into a ball shape to evade predators. Also known as blowfish, these clumsy swimmers fill their elastic stomachs with huge amounts of water (and sometimes air) and blow themselves up to several times their normal size.

"Some species also have spines on their skin to ward off predators. Even if a predator gobbles up a puffer before it inflates, it won't enjoy the snack. Most pufferfish contain a toxic substance that makes them foul tasting and potentially deadly to other fish. The toxin is deadly to humans. There is enough poison in one pufferfish to kill thirty adult humans, and there is no known antidote."

Alex finished reading the small segment and looked back at the pufferfish. Gabrielle was giggling as she poked at the glass. The pufferfish seemed to respond to what she was doing, for every time Gabrielle's finger touched the glasteel screen, it would swell up to about four times its previous size.

"It seems even things like this cute fish can be deadly," Gabrielle murmured. Alex paused. He looked at Gabrielle again. Her eyes were slightly clouded, and her shoulders were slumped. It was like she was carrying a great weight.

"Are you okay?" asked Alex.

Gabrielle's smile was surprisingly sullen. She rarely ever looked mopey like that.

"I was just remembering the past." Gabrielle stopped poking the glass and now had her hand pressed against it, palm flat, fingers splayed. She stared at the pufferfish as it stared back with its swelled body. "Before I ran away, the Angelisian Military had me make weapons for them. I was always good at building weapons because weapons are generally more complicated than regular appliances. When I was younger, I didn't really know any better and kept making weapons for them because I loved to invent things."

It was a small thing, but as she continued staring into the glasteel display, her lips began trembling. Her fingers curled in on themselves, though they didn't form a fist. She closed her eyes and took several deep breaths. When she opened them again, she turned her head to stare into his eyes, and smiled.

Alex couldn't remember a time when her smile looked so depressing.

"It wasn't until I created the pulse cannon that I realized what the military was doing with my inventions," she finished.

"Pulse cannon?"

"The pulse cannon is a weapon that takes energy from a pulse generator, which is used on all angelisian vessels, condenses it into a beam, and fires it through a warp gate."

Pulse generators created a power known as pulse energy. While that didn't sound powerful, pulse energy was based on the cosmic energy that had created the very universe. It was loosely based on the Big Bang Theory, which proposed that the universe sprang into existence as a singularity, a zone which defied humanity's current understanding of physics.

Singularities are thought to exist at the core of black holes, which are areas of intense gravitational pressure. The pressure is said to be so intense that finite matter actually gets squished into infinite density, and these zones of infinite density are called singularities. The Big Bang Theory states that the universe began as a singularity, though this has never been proven. Actually, Gabrielle's own dimensional technology somewhat disproves this theory, since the Big Bang Theory doesn't include the existence of alternate dimensions.

And, of course, angelisians did not call it the Big Bang Theory. That was a concept created by the humans of this solar system. Gabrielle called it the Concept of Creation, or the Creational Theory of Everything.

"That must be a powerful cannon," Alex said.

Still wearing that mirthless smile filled with sorrow, Gabrielle leaned forward and pressed her forehead to the glasteel. "It is very powerful. It was so powerful that many people gave the pulse cannon another name."

Alex was almost afraid to ask. "What name is that?"

"Planet buster," Gabrielle said with a tone of finality and infinite sadness.

2

Out of all the people who had come with her, only Alice managed to escape from police questioning after only fifteen minutes. Jasmine had been contained because she'd been blamed for beating on those thugs after Nyx ran off, Michelle had been confined because she tried to help Jasmine escape by summoning plants, and Madison had remained where she was because "she wouldn't leave without her mistress."

Nyx had probably caught up to Jameson by now. It was anyone's guess when she would show up.

It had taken longer than she'd hoped, but Ariel and Alice had finally made it to the ticket station for the aquarium. Their plan was to get tickets, head inside, and watch Alex and Gabrielle to make sure their date was a success. Ariel wanted her sister's first date to go perfectly, even if the idea made her chest feel like it was being constricted by an angelisian anaconda.

Unfortunately, when they went up to the ticket booth, Ariel found out that all of the tickets were already sold out. They had apparently been sold out for hours now. Alex and Gabrielle had probably only been able to get inside because Alex had bought tickets in advance. And as if matters weren't bad enough…

"Look, I can't let you in without a ticket."

Now she was arguing with the guy who scanned their IDbands.

"But I have to get in there!" Ariel shouted at the man. "My sister is on a date with a perverted beast!"

"Really? That's nice," the man said, his voice even more bland than his appearance. "But it's unfortunate. I can't let in anyone who doesn't have a ticket."

"Let's just go home," Alice said. "This situation has become troublesome enough already."

"But what if someone ruins their date?" Ariel sucked in a deep breath, drew herself up to her full 147 centimeters in height, and thrust out her nonexistent chest. "Could you really live with yourself if your inability to let me pass ruined their date? Could you live with that on your conscience?"

"Hmmm, let me think about that," the man said, and then he thought about it, for like, .2 seconds. "Yes. Yes, I could."

"Ariel," Alice tried to get her attention, "let's just go. I'm sure they'll be fine."

"You heartless fiend!" Ariel shouted as she clasped her hands in prayer. "Oh, Lord! Please strike down this heretic!"

"Look here, Sister, quit making a scene! It doesn't matter how much you want to, I'm not letting you in." The guard crossed his arms and glared at her.

"Oh, Lord!" Ariel continued as she swiped her finger through the air. "Send me a divine beast, so that I might exact holy retribution on this heathen standing before me!"

"RAAAGGGGG!!!!"

Appearing before the crowd of people within a flash of light and a roar was Kong, the giant monkey that Ariel had befriended and turned into a pet some years ago. He towered over everyone there. He beat his fists against his chest. While the crowd began to panic, running every which way as they screamed in shock and fear, the man who had refused to let her in, stood underneath the massive ape, his knees shaking as the scent of urine filled the air.

"Kong! I choose you! Headbutt now!"

With another roar, Kong headbutted the man.

It was super effective.

3

Seeing such a destitute expression on Gabrielle's face made Alex's stomach clench and his heart ache. He never wanted to see a look like this on her. Ever.

To get his mind off the memories, Alex took her to the dolphin exhibition. It was a decently-sized stadium with a large body of water in the center. A bridge ran through the pool's center, upon which a woman dressed in a wetsuit stood, gesturing with her hands and using a whistle to make the dolphins do tricks.

He and Gabrielle were sitting in the second row from the bottom. They had a nearly perfect view. Alex smiled as, whenever the dolphins would leap into the air or perform flips, Gabrielle would laugh and clap her hands. It did his heart good to see the previous sadness wiped away. He was fortunate that Gabrielle was the kind of person who almost always remained positive.

"Someone gag me. This date is so boring."

Alex twitched.

"Be silent. We agreed not to talk while they were going out."

"Hmph! I'm not interrupting them. I just wish they would start fucking instead of dancing around with all this cutesy romantic crap!"

"Sex should only come after a bond has been formed."

"They've already bonded, or did you not see what I saw during the first time they kissed?"

"No, I saw it, but that is that and this is this."

"Prude."

"Slut."

Shut up!

Alex resisted the sigh threatening to escape. Asmodeus and Sachiel had been silent for the most part recently, but sometimes, they would just crop up out of nowhere. He didn't know what to do about them. However, he didn't think there was anything he actually could do, not until the seals were gone, and some part of him, some small part that he couldn't ignore, was afraid of having the memories those seals were blocking come back.

"Alex?" Gabrielle's warm hands clasped his, snapping him back to reality. "Are you okay? You were spacing out?"

"I'm fine," Alex said. "I was just thinking about my sealed memories."

"Are you worried?"

"Yeah, I guess so."

"Don't be." Gabrielle pulled his hands and held them to her chest. "When you decide to get the rest of your memories back, I'll stay by your side the whole time. We all will!"

"Thanks, Gabby," Alex whispered.

After the dolphin show, Alex and Gabrielle wandered through the aquarium some more. They checked out the exhibits, watched some interesting holo-documentaries on aquatic life, and were given a "river tour" where they rode on a boat through a manmade river meant to simulate rivers found within the Amazon rainforest on Earth. They spent upwards of four hours there, and by the time they left the aquarium, it was already noon. The simulated sunlight was starting to fade.

"What should we do now?" asked Gabrielle as they walked along one of many walkways in the entertainment district.

Alex thought about it for a second. "Why don't we grab some dinner, and then go to Metronome's Sweetshop and get dessert?"

"That's a great idea!" Gabrielle clapped her hands. "I can tell Selene about how amazing our date was!"

Alex only blushed a little as they used one of the warp points to reach a hub that had several restaurants. The one they had decided on specialized in Italian food.

He had no idea how authentic the food was, but he had to admit that their ravioli was astounding, truly an incredible dish bursting with flavor. Sadly, the restaurant kicked him and Gabrielle out after he'd begun analysing the ingredients and cooking methods they had used. The jerks.

Since they had been kicked out, Alex and Gabrielle headed over to the *Metronome's Sweet Shop*. It was a small venue made of plasteel. With a glowing sign over the door and windows that allowed a glimpse inside, it looked a lot like the retro diners on Earth.

The door jingled as he and Gabrielle entered. Because it was so late, there weren't that many people present, but Selene was still there. She wore an apron over her regular clothes. Her curly brown hair had been pulled into a bun. She turned around as they entered, a smile on her lips.

"Hello! Welcome to—oh! Alex. Gabrielle. What are you two doing here? I thought you had a date?"

"We did!" Gabrielle ran up to Selene and hugged her. The dark-skinned girl laughed as she hugged the princess back. "We're almost finished with our date, so we decided to visit you!"

"Is that so?" Selene asked as Alex wandered into the shop a lot more slowly. "I'm guessing you had fun?"

"We had an amazing time!"

"That's good. Why don't you two sit down, and you can tell me all about it?"

They did just that, though Alex didn't actually talk and let Gabrielle do all the talking for them. He figured this was more of a girl thing anyway. He sat next to Gabrielle as she gesticulated, using wild and emotive gestures to describe how their date went, highlighting specific points with a fist thrust. Selene wore an indulgent smile as she nodded at all of his girlfriend/fiancé's points. She'd occasionally glance in his direction, but otherwise kept her attention on Gabrielle.

Alex used this time to relax. This date had been harder on him than he'd expected. He'd had a great time. Going out with Gabrielle had been fun and exciting.

The problem was his own emotions, feelings, and lust. Even though he'd accepted that what he felt wasn't bad, he still didn't want to take things too far. He wanted to take things slowly. He wanted to do this right.

He also had Jasmine and Nyx to consider. How should he deal with those two? The same way he did Gabrielle? That wouldn't work. They weren't Gabrielle, so treating them the same was a disaster waiting to happen. More than that, it was rude to them and to Gabrielle.

As he was thinking and Gabrielle was chatting up a storm, the doors to the backroom opened and two people walked out. One of them, a woman, Alex recognized easily enough. Melanie looked a lot like her younger sister. Her brown hair was shorter, her skin was a bit lighter, but she looked very much like an older Selene. Alex also knew the other person. He had messy black hair, brown eyes, and wore fashionable clothing. His face looked more gaunt than Alex remembered, but it hadn't been that long since they last met.

Keiichi. Kazekiri's older brother.

"Alex?" Melanie looked at him. "What are you doing here so late?" She spied Gabrielle and suddenly smiled. "Is this a date?"

"Yes, it is!" Gabrielle beamed before he could say anything. "Alex and I just went on our first date! I was telling Selene all about it!"

"Bastard!" Keiichi growled and, before anyone else could say anything, he stormed up to their table, grabbed Alex by the shirt, and hauled him to his feet. "You bastard!"

"What are you doing, Keiichi?!" Melanie screamed while Gabrielle and Selene shot to their feet.

"Taking a girl on a date while Kazekiri is suffering! Who the hell do you think you are?!"

Alex twitched as he fought against reflexes honed from sparring with Nyx. He had almost reached up and broken this guy's arms, but he didn't know what was happening, so he didn't want to do that.

"W-what are you talking about?" asked Alex.

"Kazekiri loves you!" Keiichi's shout stunned everyone into silence. "She writes about you in her diary everyday! She loves you so much, it isn't even funny! And now she's suffering because our father returned, but rather than helping her out, you're here going on dates! What the fuck is wrong with you?!"

Alex froze. He'd never heard about any of this! And didn't Kazekiri have a boyfriend? She'd told Gabrielle, Ryoko, and Selene that she was already dating someone. She had even confirmed it when he mentioned her boyfriend. Did that mean she had been lying? Why?

However, beyond his shock at Keiichi stating that Kazekiri loved him, another part of Keiichi's yelling speech took root in his mind.

"What did you mean when you said she was suffering?" asked Alex.

"You mean you don't know?" asked Keiichi, letting go of Alex and taking several stumbling steps back. He clenched his hands into fists as Alex straightened up.

"If I knew what was going on, I wouldn't have asked you," Alex said. "So why don't you tell me what's happening."

With a frown and a sigh, Keiichi's already slumped shoulders sagged further down as he explained how their father had somehow found them, how his sister had been enslaved, how he had managed to escape before their father could put a slave collar on him, and how he couldn't do anything about it because the slave collar attached to Kazekiri's neck kept her from run away. By the time he was done, Alex was already making the call to Karen Kanzaki.

4

Karen was at home when the call came in through her personal IDband. She was sitting on her couch, a glass of brandy in hand. The holovid was on. It was playing some police holo-drama about a member of the space forces, but she wasn't really paying attention. She took a swig of her alcohol, sighed, and wondered how everything had become so utterly messed up.

It's all that Gabrielle's fault.

She knew that she was drunk if she was having these thoughts, not that she didn't agree with them, because she agreed with them so hard it wasn't even funny. Karen just didn't allow herself to think like that when she was sober.

She also knew that Alex had been causing problems before Gabrielle showed up. It was just that the number of problems that cropped up before she had appeared and after she had appeared was exponentially larger. More property had gotten destroyed, those marriage candidates had caused all kinds of trouble, and now Alex

was getting himself into galactic trouble, and she could no longer keep an eye on him.

Years ago, Karen had promised on Farone's grave that she would do everything within her power to protect Alex, and yet, the more time that passed, the more she realized that Alexander S. Ryker was... different. He didn't have Farone's calm cunning, his ability to think analytically. Alex jumped into every situation headfirst, used inventions that never worked, caused more property damage than anyone she had ever met, and spoke out against a superior when he believed they were wrong. Not only that, he had even directly confronted the police when they had gone after Nyx. Really, the only thing Alex shared with his father was Farone's stubbornness.

It was during her contemplations that her IDband began vibrating. Withholding a sigh, she looked at the communication ID. She scrambled to press the accept button when she saw who was calling.

"Alex?"

"Karen, I'm sorry for calling you so late."

"Don't worry about it," Karen replied. "Though I am curious to know why you're calling so late. You haven't destroyed any property, have you?"

"No."

"Has one of your inventions blown up?"

"Of course not!"

"Then one of Gabrielle's marriage candidates has arrived and is destroying part of the city?"

"Why are you assuming that the worst case scenario is happening?!"

"Because the worst case scenario always happens whenever you are involved." Karen almost laughed into her drink when Alex shouted something over the communication. "If this isn't about some trouble that you or one of Gabrielle's marriage candidates have caused, then what is this about?"

"You wouldn't happen to know anything about slave collars, would you? Specifically how to deactivate them without killing the one wearing them?"

Karen stilled. "You want to know about slave collars?"

Slave collars were basically devices put on slaves that kept them obedient. If the person wearing the slave collar disobeyed the handler, the one who's genetic code was implanted into the collar, the slave, would experience intense pain. If the slave tried to escape, the collar was designed to kill them once they ran a certain distance away. It would also kill them if anyone tried to tamper with it.

"Yes, I do."

"Is someone you know wearing a slave collar?"

"... Yes."

"You're trying to take it off?"

"Yes."

Karen took several deep breaths to calm down. She tapped her finger against her chair and thought about what to do. Of course, she could try and force Alex to tell her who was wearing a slave collar, but he probably wouldn't reveal that unless she really pushed. Also, if he was asking this, then he already planned on doing something himself. It was technically illegal, but Alex had already made her aware that he was willing to play the "Emperor of the Galaxy" card if he thought it necessary.

"There is a way to break a slave collar without killing the person it's attached to. All slave collars work on a frequency. If you can find the frequency, then you can override the master control for the collar and deactivate it manually."

"Can I scramble it by creating an override frequency?" asked Alex.

"No. If you did that, then the slave collar is designed to kill the one wearing it. You have to find the exact frequency, override the master control, and manually shut off the collar."

Slave collars were a huge problem for the GPF. If shutting them off was as simple as creating an override frequency, they wouldn't have so much trouble dealing with slavers. Half the reason slavers got away with slave trading was because of those blasted collars.

"I see. I understand. Thank you very much."

"Sure."

The comm went dead. Karen stared at her IDband for several seconds longer, and then she looked away and slowly brought the glass of brandy to her lips. She took a small sip. The alcohol had a nice, slow burn as it flowed down her throat. It helped clear her thoughts a little. She had a feeling that this alcohol was going to be needed later tonight.

Don't do anything reckless, Alex...

She paused.

That would have been a good time to tell him that all of the people living in his house were arrested today. Another pause. She shrugged. *Oh, well. I can tell him tomorrow.*

5

Alex and Gabrielle were huddled together beside Kazekiri's house. It looked like a normal enough house. It had two-stories. It didn't have a fence, but it was built into a well-known hub in the residential district. The house was squished between two other houses that looked exactly the same, large blocks of durasteel with a few windows but nothing that really made them distinct.

They weren't alone.

"Why aren't you two going in to rescue Kazekiri?" asked Keiichi.

"Because we don't have the frequency yet," Alex answered.

Gabrielle nodded. "Karen already mentioned it: Unless we can find the frequency the slave collar is using and override the master control, we can't do anything."

"How long is that gonna take?" asked Keiichi.

"We don't know," Alex and Gabrielle said at the same time.

"Shut up and let us work," Alex added.

Keiichi slumped to the ground and crossed his arms. "Fine. Whatever. Just know that I'm blaming you if something happens to her."

Neither Alex nor Gabrielle listened to him, busy as they were twisting dials and typing symbols into the device sitting beside their feet. It was a simple device. It looked like a sphere standing on eight spindly legs. He and Gabrielle had literally made it several minutes ago and brought it here. Gabrielle called it Mr. Frequency, but Alex called it the Frequency Decoder.

Both he and Gabrielle paid careful attention to the wavelengths that appeared on the holographic display hovering over Mr. Frequency aka the Frequency Decoder. There were numerous wavelength frequencies that were constantly fluctuating. All of these frequencies were caused by devices like IDbands, Holovids, and various commlinks and commlink channels. They were looking for one specific frequency, which, due to the nature of the frequency, should be different from the ones caused by other devices.

"Alex, expand our search radius."

"Right."

Alex cranked back on a dial, expanding the number of frequencies they could see.

"Hold it here," Gabrielle instructed. Alex stopped expanding their range, and then waited as Gabrielle typed into the console. Soon, one frequency after another began disappearing, one by one, until there were only about ten left. "Close our radius... more... more... more... stop!" Alex stopped. Two more disappeared. Four more. Nine more. There was only one frequency left. "This is it!"

"Are you sure?" asked Keiichi. "If you're wrong, then my sister is going to die."

"Of course I'm sure. I would never put my friend's life in danger by getting it wrong." Gabrielle puffed out her cheeks. "That's the one."

Keiichi stood up. "Then let's go."

"Sorry," Alex said as Gabrielle summoned Mr. Rope from her dimensional space and promptly used it to tie Keiichi up, "but we don't know what the situation is like. You'd only be in the way, so you're staying here."

Before Keiichi could begin screaming at them, Alex shoved a ball gag into his mouth. The man released several muffled shouts. He flopped against the ground. He eventually stopped when he ran out of energy, but all that meant was he had switched from flopping to glaring at him and Gabrielle.

"You ready?" asked Gabrielle as Alex stood up.

"I am." Alex took a breath as he psyched himself up. "Let's go."

"Okay!"

They made their way to Kazekiri's house, their steps somehow sounding ominous in the mostly dark night. There wasn't much in the way of light. A few street lamps illuminated some of the hub, but most of the area was pitch-black.

"By the way, Alex…"

"Yes?"

"Isn't that ball gag my sister's? How did you get it?"

"…"

Alex didn't say anything. He was glad this place was so dark. It meant she couldn't see him blush.

6

Kazekiri stood before the heater, watching the soup as it came to a boil. She stirred occasionally, but that was the only movement she really made.

"Hey!" A shout came from the living room. "Aren't you finished yet?! Why the fuck are you so slow?!"

Kazekiri tried not to flinch at her father's harsh shouting. His words were being slurred, and the grating harshness of his anger made Kazekiri tremble. No matter how much she tried to stand up to him, no matter how much she wanted to stand up to him, she couldn't.

She could still remember when he had appeared before her as if by magic, just showing up one day out of the blue. He had begun making demands the moment she had arrived home. Kazekiri had immediately felt the terror that she had known long ago, back when her parents were still together, back when they were always arguing, back when they were always fighting, back when her father would...

"What the fuck?! What's taking you so long, you fucking cunt! Hurry up and bring my food!"

A shock ran through her body as the slave collar he'd forced on her activated. Kazekiri's body shook as she collapsed to the floor, her body jerking as her muscles spasmed. She didn't cry out. She bit her lip so hard that the taste of liquid iron filled her mouth. Curling into a ball, Kazekiri could do nothing but wait for the pain to subside, and then she had to wait even longer before her body was capable of moving.

She eventually brought a bowl of soup and a bottle of ale, which she carried on a tray, into the living room. Her father was there. His spacer suit was unzipped, revealing the large gut that was sagging over his waist. He was lounging on the couch in the most lackadaisical manner possible, sprawled completely out as he watched some kind of space drama on the holovid.

The moment she entered the room, Kazekiri froze as she became the unwilling recipient of her father's leer. She tried not to show the terror filling her heart, tried to pretend that she did not fear this man, but it was so hard. Every step she took caused her chest to hammer against her ribcage. It was like her heart wanted to leap out of her body and run away in fear.

She set the tray on the table in front of him and stood back up, turning around. Her goal was to leave before he could say anything. If she could just not be in his presence, then she would be okay. So long as she wasn't near him, couldn't see him, then she would be okay.

"Where do you think yer going?" asked her father. Kazekiri froze. "Sit yer ass down. Yer going to feed me."

Kazekiri's mind went blank, body locking in place. She didn't want to feed him. She didn't want to go near him. If she went near him, then he would... he would...

"Well?" Her father demanded. "Do you want me to use the collar again?"

"N-no..." Kazekiri choked out, tears leaking from her eyes as she turned around and resigned herself to her fate. "I-I'll feed you."

The lecherous smile on her father's face told her all she needed to know. "Good. Now, come here and use those pretty hands of yers to—"

He never got to finish that sentence. Both he and Kazekiri screamed as the ceiling suddenly exploded, sending dust and debris flying everywhere. While her father was smacked in the face with a chunk of plasteel that sent him sprawling off the couch, Kazekiri's police training kicked in, and she hurriedly found cover behind one of the chairs.

As the dust began to settle, a voice spoke up.

"I'm thinking maybe we should have just used the door," said a male.

"But if we did that, our entrance wouldn't have been as cool," said a female.

Both voices were familiar, and they caused Kazekiri to feel a mix of hope and terror. It couldn't be. There was no way they would be here. With her fists clenched, with emotions of hope warring with despair, Kazekiri peeked out from behind the couch and stared at the two people standing in the middle of her now ruined living room.

The first person her eyes landed on was a male. His black hair was messy and swept back, but his bangs were silver, and they hid bright blue eyes behind them. He wore black pants and a white shirt underneath a dark gray hoodie with fur lining the hood. His black boots were covered in dirt, but he clicked his tongue and tapped them on the floor, making their shine return. It was Alexander S. Ryker.

Standing next to Alex was a girl with long, silver hair that went down past her butt. Her blue skirt swished around her thighs, and her pink shirt was slightly wrinkled, likely from the fall. Her skin was strangely glossy. It was like she had a layer of film over it. She wore a pair of strap-on sandals that fit her small feet perfectly. Gabrielle Angelise looked around before spotting her.

"There she is!" She pointed.

Alex turned in Kazekiri's direction and his eyes lit up, but they quickly dimmed into a frown when he saw her. "Kazekiri... what happened to you?"

She looked away. She didn't know what he was doing here, but she didn't know what to say to him anymore. She didn't want him looking at her either.

I must look disgusting.

"Who the fuck are you two?!" Her father suddenly growled as he stood up from his seat and glared at them. "I don't know who you think you are, barging into my house like that, but I won't... put up... with..." he trailed off as his eyes landed on Gabrielle. Kazekiri felt an intense surge of hatred as he leered at the innocent silver-haired girl.

Kazekiri shrieked when Alex suddenly kicked her dad in the face. His head snapped back as he was launched into the air, over the couch, and landed on the other side with a thud.

"W-what are you doing, Alex?!" Kazekiri shouted as she stood up.

"It's not what I'm doing!" Alex suddenly whirled around and pointed at her. "What are you doing?! Why are you letting this man run roughshod over you?!"

Kazekiri took a step back at the finger pointing at her, at the eyes that were accusing her of something she couldn't understand. "W-what are you...?"

"Where's the strong woman who wanted to become a police officer and put people like that man in prison?! What happened to her, huh?! The Kazekiri I know would have never allowed this man to come near her, much less let him put that slave collar on her."

Why? Why? Kazekiri clenched her fists, which shook as she glared at Alex with tears in her eyes.

"What do you know?!" she shouted back. "Do you think I haven't tried to defy him?! I have! But I can't! He's... he's..."

"He's a loser," Alex said, his voice suddenly calm. "That man is nothing but a weak, pathetic loser who can't do anything for himself. He has nothing over you."

"You don't understand!" Kazekiri cried in frustration. "I can't do anything against him! Even if I wanted to, this slave collar means I can't do anything against him!"

"Um, I hate to interrupt, but the slave collar doesn't work anymore," Gabrielle interrupted.

Kazekiri faltered. "W-what did you say?"

"The slave collar." Gabrielle tapped her neck, indicating the choker around Kazekiri's throat. "Mr. Frequency has already overrode the master control and deactivated it."

As Gabrielle spoke, Kazekiri's father was clambering to his feet. He swayed drunkenly and placed a hand on his jaw. It was red and bruised, and it would probably swell up tomorrow.

"That thing on your neck has no power over you anymore," Alex said. "Are you going to keep using an excuse to follow this pig's orders? Are you going to keep letting yourself be shackled by what happened when you were younger? You told me that you were going to become a police officer so you could stop people from treating others like he treated you. How can you help others if you can't even help yourself?"

The words struck her hard. It was true. Her reasons for being a cop was to prevent what happened to her from happening to others. So, then, why was she letting her father control her like this?

He's bigger than me...

When she was younger, her father had seemed like a goliath. Whenever he came into her bedroom at night, he seemed so big, so intimidating. When he had appeared before her, even though he no longer looked the same size, to Kazekiri, her father had seemed so much larger and more powerful than her. It was just like when she had been a little girl.

"You little... shit." Her father glared as he stumbled forward. Alex's kick must have hit harder than she thought. Her father was walking like a drunkard, but he could also just be really drunk. He had been drinking all day.

"I... I don't know if I can..." Kazekiri admitted.

"You can!" Gabrielle said, startling her. "You can! Alex and I both know you can!"

Alex nodded. "I wouldn't admire you so much if I didn't think you were strong enough to overcome this." Swiping a hand through the air, Alex summoned a pair of handcuffs from somewhere and tossed them to Kazekiri, who caught them out of instinct. "You know what to do when someone breaks the law, right?"

Kazekiri stared at the handcuffs, and then looked at her father, who had now grabbed the master control for the slave collar she was wearing. Her hand shook. Could she really do this? She tried to still her shaking hands. She took a deep breath, looked back at Alex, and then looked at her father again.

"Don't even think about it," he said, holding up the master control. "You know what'll happen if you try anything, don't you?"

She hesitated, but then she looked back at Alex, whose eyes stared at her with a confident gleam, as though he knew what she would do, as though he was placing his faith in her. Kazekiri took a deep breath. Then she hardened her resolve, turned toward her father, and began marching up to him.

"You have the right to remain silent…"

"Don't do this," her father warned.

"Anything you say may be used against you in a court of law…"

Her father pressed the button. Kazekiri didn't stop walking. She also felt no pain. Her father's eyes bulged from their sockets. The look was so comical that, had the situation been different, she might have laughed.

"You have the right to consult an attorney before speaking to the police…"

"Stop! Don't think you can do this to me!"

Spittle flew from the man's mouth as he shouted at her, but Kazekiri continued moving forward, and when her father raised a fist and swung it at her, she ducked underneath it, grabbed him by the arm, and used his own weight against him. She threw him over her shoulder. He landed on his back with a harsh crack, the air expelling from his lungs in a single *woosh!* Then she flipped him onto his back, pulled his hands together, and clipped the handcuffs around his wrists.

"And to have an attorney present during questioning now or in the future." Kazekiri paused, then added, "it doesn't change the fact that you are still under arrest."

7

Alex called the cops after Kazekiri placed her father under arrest. They arrived within five minutes.

"You can't do this to me!" her father shouted as a pair of police dragged him to a police shuttle. "I'm her father! That cunt is my daughter! I can do whatever I want to her! She's mine! I gave birth to her!!"

Did he really just say that?

"He doesn't seem very bright."

"It makes me wonder how someone as amazing as Kazekiri could be born from someone like that."

I can't believe I am saying this, but I agree with both of you.

Alex watched as Kazekiri's father was shoved into the police shuttle. The door closed, but even though they were now muffled,

his incoherent screams and unintelligible curse still reached him, Kazekiri, and Gabrielle.

They were standing off to the side, the three of them. Gabrielle was busy making adjustments to Mr. Frequency. He wasn't sure what she was doing, but from the muttering she gave off, he assumed she was adjusting the wavelength detector to make it more accurate. While Gabrielle was crouched over Mr. Frequency with a tablet, which was connected to Mr. Frequency via a cable, Kazekiri was speaking to Karen Kanzaki, who stood by another police shuttle alongside her second in command, Yumi.

Alex didn't know what they were saying. Standard procedure was to question the victim, but from the way Karen had her hands on Kazekiri's shoulders, and from the glances they sent his way, he assumed the conversation had changed to a different line of questioning.

"How is it looking?" asked Alex.

"I think I can increase the power and precision of Mr. Frequency if I change the output on the operating system." Gabrielle's tongue was poking out from between her lips. It was a habit that she did whenever she was working on something that required more effort than normal. "It's gonna take some work, though. Alex, would you mind changing the operating system for me? You're better at that than I am."

"Sure." Alex nodded. "I'll do that when we get home."

Kazekiri and Karen finished their conversation and walked over to where he and Gabrielle were standing. While his friend shuffled back and forth, twiddled her thumbs, and refused to meet his gaze, Karen was staring at him with a mixed expression. However, eventually, she just sighed.

"Thank you, Alex," she said at last. "I appreciate how you helped Kazekiri."

Alex shrugged. "I didn't do much. Kazekiri's the one who found the strength to stand up to her father."

"I... don't know if I could have done it without you," Kazekiri mumbled, though she still refused to look at him.

Gabrielle returned Mr. Frequency to her D-space and stood up. She walked over to Kazekiri and smiled.

"Are you okay now?"

Kazekiri looked at her and nodded. "I am. Thank you for coming to help me."

"Tee-hee! You're welcome!"

"What's going to happen now?" asked Alex.

"We're taking Mr. Kimihito into custody," Karen began. "He'll be charged with sexual assault of a minor, enslaving a minor, abuse of a minor, and several accounts of battery and assault. I'm not sure how he got out of prison on Earth, but with all of the evidence we have against him, he's going to the deepest levels of the Mars Penitentiary for life."

The Mars Penitentiary was the most secure prison on Mars. Located underneath the planet's surface, it was not only nearly impossible to break out of—nearly because Alex had broken out of it—but it was the harshest prison in the solar system. If he was being sent into the lowest levels of that prison, where some of the solar system's worst criminals lived, he probably wouldn't last for more than a month.

"Thank you again for this, Commander Karen." Kazekiri bowed to the commander, who smiled and waved her off.

"I'm not sure why you're thanking me. You did an excellent job there. I'm very proud of you."

"Th-thank you." Kazekiri's cheeks lit up something fierce as she looked down at her sandals.

"Now then, Alex." Karen turned to him. "I don't know how to tell you this, so I'm just going to come out and say it. All of the people living with you are currently being held in custody at the police station for minor infractions. We can't arrest them because they're minors, so I'm going to need you to come down to the station with me and file out some paperwork—as well as pay a fine for their release."

"Um, what?" was the only thing Alex could say as his mind tried, and failed, to compute what she had said.

It seemed his night still wasn't finished.

8

"Your skin is so smooth, Kazekiri!" Gabrielle complimented as she scrubbed her friend's back.

"Oh, thank you."

They were in the shower room at Alex's house. Since her roof was currently destroyed, they had offered her a place to stay, and Alex had mentioned that he didn't want her to live alone. The thought warmed her chest.

Alex was currently at the police station, filing paperwork and paying fines to release the others who lived with him, those being Alice, Ariel, Jasmine, Michelle, Madison, and Nyx. Kazekiri hadn't realized there were so many people living with Alex, and all of them were women to boot! It really was quite shocking.

Kazekiri felt like she should have been furious at Alex, but she wasn't. It was probably because he had rescued her. That must be it. Alex had come to her when she had given up hope, bolstered and supported her, and helped her overcome the fear that she had of her father. In light of everything he had done, she couldn't get upset at him for living with a bunch of girls.

Besides, it's not like they're a part of his harem or anything.

Gabrielle hummed as she knelt behind Kazekiri, scrubbing her back with a loofa. Kazekiri tucked her hair over her shoulder so it wouldn't get in Gabrielle's way.

Kazekiri had never done something like this before. It was oddly comforting. She couldn't really explain it, but Gabrielle's hands as they scrubbed her back made her feel secure somehow. Sadly, thinking about Gabrielle's hands made her wonder how it would feel if Alex was scrubbing her back, and then she turned bright red.

"Are you okay?" asked Gabrielle. "Your face is burning up. The water isn't too hot, is it?"

"I-I'm fine." Kazekiri shook her head to dispel those thoughts. They were bad. She shouldn't be thinking about them. She was going to become a corrupting influence on the moral backbone of society! "I was just thinking about something and got distracted."

"Were you thinking about Alex?"

"Wha—no!" Kazekiri said hotly as she tried to ignore the heat on her cheeks. It was just the temperature in the shower room. It was too hot! "I was thinking about other things."

"Oh. Okay. I'm sorry. I thought you were thinking about Alex."

"No... I'm sorry for shouting. I was thinking about Alex." Kazekiri found herself unable to lie to this girl, who had come to her rescue, helped her out, and was giving her so much moral and emotional support.

"I heard from your brother that you don't actually have a boyfriend." Kazekiri froze as Gabrielle switched from washing her back to her hair. "He said that you love Alex, that you write about him in your diary all the time."

Kazekiri could feel her body burning as she struggled to come up with a suitable response, but she couldn't think of anything. If she said that she did love Alex, Gabrielle might get upset, and if she said that she didn't, she would not only be lying, but she would be contradicting her brother's words, which were the truth.

The part of her that wanted to be a police officer couldn't lie, especially not to her friend.

"Y-yes, I do love Alex," Kazekiri admitted. "I'm sorry, Gabrielle. I know you and he love each—"

"That's great!" Gabrielle's excited squeal interrupted her. Kazekiri couldn't give a response, partly because she was stunned by the loud voice ringing in her ears, but also because Gabrielle was now hugging her. Strong but soft arms wrapped around her midsection as a joyous Gabrielle laughed.

"W-what?"

Kazekiri didn't know what was going on. Why was Gabrielle so happy? She had just admitted that she was in love with Gabrielle's boyfriend!

"Gabrielle, why aren't you... shouldn't you be angry?"

Gabrielle didn't stop hugging Kazekiri, and in fact, she had started rubbing their cheeks together. It was an electric feeling. Kazekiri couldn't explain it, but she felt both mortified and warm, like her body was being wrapped in a blanket.

"Why would I be angry?" asked Gabrielle. "I love you, Kazekiri! And if you love Alex, it means you can marry him too, and if you get married to Alex with me, then you can become my sister!"

"Erm... I don't understand," Kazekiri confessed.

Gabrielle laughed. "Don't worry. I'll explain everything to you later."

"Uh, okay."

Since Gabrielle had finished cleaning her, they switched places, and Kazekiri became the one who cleaned Gabrielle. Once again, Kazekiri was stunned by how utterly at peace she was with this whole situation. Here she was, naked in a shower room with another girl, cleaning Gabrielle's back and hair, and she didn't even mind. But it was even more than that. She was actively enjoying their time together.

After cleaning off, they got into the bath and lounged there. Once more, Gabrielle had hugged Kazekiri as though they were best friends. She didn't know how long they stayed in there, but she felt mildly flushed when they emerged, dried off, and got dressed.

"That was fun!" Gabrielle said.

"It was kind of fun," Kazekiri admitted reluctantly.

"We should do it again."

Kazekiri hesitated. "I... guess that wouldn't be so bad."

"We should have Alex join us next time!"

"L-let's not."

If Kazekiri weren't already aware of Gabrielle's naivety, she would have lectured the girl on proper female behavior. Sadly, she knew that Gabrielle wasn't even thinking sexual thoughts. She literally just thought it would be nice if Alex joined them.

As they traveled down the stairs, the sound of voices reached them.

"I can't believe it took you so long to get to us, you troublesome brother."

"Oh ho ho ho! Alexander, as the Queen of Gratitude, I kindly thank you for getting me out of that uncouth predicament."

"Hmph! I guess you're not so bad for a perverted beast."

"Oh, my. Ariel, are you not being honest with yourself again? How childish. Why can't you be more... mature?"

"That joke is getting so old, Sis!"

"Now, now." Alex's voice rang above everyone else's. Kazekiri's heart stopped beating, but then it began beating again even faster as she and Gabrielle emerged down the stairs. Alex came into view as he continued lecturing the girls standing around near the entrance. "You girls shouldn't fight right now, especially because I'm still disappointed by all of you. Honestly, what were you thinking?"

It was almost funny how all four girls wilted under his gaze. Alice looked away as though unable to maintain eye contact, Michelle looked down and twirled her hair, Ariel blushed as she began stuttering excuses, and Jasmine's nervous laughter filled the air. The only two who didn't talk were Nyx and a woman wearing a maid outfit. They remained silent. Nyx's expression was blank and while the maid had raised a hand like she wanted to stop them, she didn't say anything.

"We're sorry," all four girls said.

Alex sighed. "I hope you know that I plan on punishing all of you."

"What?!" they shouted, but Alex was no longer paying attention to them.

Nyx had grabbed his sleeve and was tugging on it. Kazekiri couldn't possibly figure out what the look on her face meant, but when Alex looked at her, his expression cleared and he placed a hand against her cheek. It was such an intimate gesture that Kazekiri felt her cheeks warm from just watching them.

"Even you are going to be punished for this," Alex said. "I don't like Jameson, but you can't do... what you did to him."

Nyx looked down as though disappointed.

"Alex!" Gabrielle bounded down the last few steps and rushed over to him. Alex laughed as he caught her and twirled around.

Kazekiri's chest constricted as she watched them. She felt like an intruder.

"Gabby," Alex greeted before noticing her. Kazekiri stiffened when his eyes landed on her. "Kiri-kiri. Come on over."

"O-okay."

Kazekiri took the last few steps down the stairs, wandered over to him, and stopped about half a meter away. She clasped her hands together and twiddled her fingers. She didn't know what to say. Opening and closing her mouth several times as she tried and failed to talk, Kazekiri eventually settled for looking away.

Alex smiled. "I'm going to make dinner in just a bit. Why don't you join the others in the living room?"

"Um…" Kazekiri had no idea what she should do, so she just nodded along with him.

Alex went into the kitchen as Gabrielle led Kazekiri by the hand into the living room with everyone else—everyone except Nyx, she noticed. The group sat down in the living room, which was far larger than it looked like it should be. Alice sprawled out, while Jasmine sat like a prim and proper woman. Ariel sat on the floor, hands behind her back and legs spread out to form a V. Unlike Ariel, Michelle sat on the other couch alongside Gabrielle, who had Kazekiri sit right next to her.

Kazekiri soon learned that Nyx was in the dining room when Alex came in and told them that dinner was ready. Alex had made marinated chicken baked in various herbs. She had known that Alex could cook, but she hadn't expected something so delicious. It let her know that she didn't know him nearly as well as she thought she did.

Dinner was far more lively here than it was at her place. Keiichi was usually out on dates, so she often ate alone. Eating with so many people, all of whom were talking and arguing, was a novel experience. Gabrielle kept chatting with her. Even though Kazekiri didn't speak a whole lot, just having someone to speak with, who actively wanted to speak with her, was a blessing in and of itself.

She didn't know how long she would stay with them. Karen had said that it wouldn't be a good idea for her to live alone, and had further imposed upon Alex by stating that Kazekiri was his responsibility. She did feel a little bad about that, but Alex and Gabrielle had both smiled and said they'd be happy to have her.

I think I can get used to this, Kazekiri thought as she smiled at the banter taking place between Alex, Alice, and Jasmine. However, a thought soon occured to her.

"Alex?" she said.

Alex stopped trying to convince his sister to eat her vegetables and looked at her. "Yes?"

"Where is my brother?"

"Um…"

The startled glance that Alex and Gabrielle shared made Kazekiri wonder what she was missing.

7

Keiichi was still lying on the street behind the house, still tied up by Gabrielle's invention. He had long since stopped trying to break free. He didn't have the strength to even try anymore, though he had at least managed to remove the ball gag. He was lucky that Alex didn't really know how to put it on properly. As he lay there, he called for help, hoping that someone would find him.

"Hello!!! Somebody! Anybody! HELP!!!"

Sadly, there was not a soul to be found on the dark and empty street.

EPILOGUE

NYX'S SURPRISE BIRTHDAY BASH

It was early in the morning, and Alex was getting everything ready for Nyx's surprise party. Today, the pretty assassin girl was turning nineteen years-old. He still found it strange that such a tiny slip of a girl was older than him by three years, but, well, given everything he had seen since becoming Gabrielle's fiancé, this was probably the least surprising discovery he had made.

Of course, by getting everything ready, Alex actually meant he was preparing the food in advance of the party. He couldn't get everything ready right now because this was a surprise party. Nyx was still sleeping up stairs. So was everyone else, but if Nyx woke up while he was getting everything ready, it would make preparing a surprise birthday party pretty much impossible.

This would be the first birthday that Nyx had ever celebrated. Alex wanted to make it special.

At that moment, he was preparing the food that would be used for the party. Through careful observation, Alex had learned that Nyx's prefered cuisine was, of all things, gyros. He still remembered the way her eyes had lit up during the time she had tried one. They had been killing time in Mars City and came across a stand that had been making gyros. After that, whenever they went out, Nyx would find a gyro stand and gobble up at least six of them.

Alex was very glad that he'd had the sense to create his own vertical rotisserie. He didn't use it very often, so he kept it in storage, but he'd taken it out for this occasion.

As he was cooking the gyros on the vertical rotisserie, which was a long spit that rotated on a simple engine and was surrounded by nuclear cooking panels, the door to the kitchen opened. Alex looked up. Michelle was walking into the room, her long hair somewhat messy and sticking up in certain places. Her long-sleeved shirt was askew, showing off a hint of bare shoulder, and her pink pants were wrinkled. Her eyes were still slightly closed. However, she seemed alert enough to realize that she wasn't the only one present.

"Oh, Alexander. Good morning."

"Good morning, Michelle." Using a carving knife, he sliced the meat into thin shavings. These would make the base of today's meal. "I'm surprised you're awake so early."

"I set my alarm a little earlier than normal." Michelle smiled as she tucked a strand of hair behind her ear and walked over to him. "It's a special day today, isn't it?"

"That it is." Alex paused as he figured out what she was getting at. "Do you want to help me?"

"Yes, please."

"In that case, could I ask you to slice some tomatoes and chop at least two onions? Then I'd like you to saute them in a pan. Make sure the onions caramelize."

"Of course."

Michelle was not the most talented cook that Alex had ever seen. Actually, she was quite bad. While Alex was shaving meat off the rotisserie, Michelle had tears in her eyes as she tried to chop the onions with little success. He watched her for a moment as she cried while bringing the knife down in a chopping motion. After coating the meat in more fat so this new layer would become crisp on the outside, he wandered behind Michelle and gently took her hands in his own.

"Alex?"

"You're doing it wrong. You don't want to use those choppy motions. It'll make your chops uneven. Hold the onion like this... good. Now, when you first begin chopping an onion, you want to do it like this... yes, just like that. Nice. Now that we've cut the onion into slices like that, we can chop them up into tiny pieces. Here. Like this."

"L-like this?"

"Yes, just like that. You've got it."

Alex let go of Michelle's hands and walked back over to the rotisserie, nodding to himself as he noticed how the meat had turned a nice golden brown. He grabbed the knife and began carving out more shavings.

The next few minutes were spent like this. He and Michelle focused on getting all the food prepared. While they worked, they made small talk, but it wasn't about anything serious—at least, not until Michelle brought up that subject.

"I've noticed that Gabrielle hasn't been sleeping in her bedroom anymore."

After nearly choking on his own spit, Alex tried to keep himself from blushing as he answered the girl. "Th-that's right. Since she and I are, er, engaged and stuff, I told her that she could sleep with me."

"I'm glad." Michelle lifted her head long enough to smile at him. "Gabrielle has been longing to share such an intimate experience with you. It's why she used to slip into your bed after you'd gone to sleep."

"I know."

"She's been smiling a lot more, too."

"Yeah..." Alex smiled. "She has."

It took about fifteen minutes for Alex to carve the entire pork, during which time Michelle finished chopping the onions and the tomatoes. Alex carmelized the onions quickly. Then he stored all the food in the storage chamber. It was a lot like a fridge, except instead of keeping food cold, it kept them warm and ready to serve. The food would be good for up to twenty-four hours.

Just as he and Michelle finished using an air freshener to get rid the kitchen of the smell—he didn't want Nyx smelling the gyros when she woke up—Gabrielle burst into the room, a large, beaming grin on her face.

"Alex! I did it!" She waved a device that looked like a gun over her head, except it was larger, with a bulbous shape to the barrel. "Mr. Decorator! With this, I can have the house decorated in less than an hour!"

"Nice." Alex grinned as Gabrielle bounded up to him. Leaning over, he gave her a kiss on the cheek. "This will be a big help."

"Tee-hee!" Gabrielle blushed as her wings flapped and her ears wiggled.

"Can I count on you two to let Alice, Ariel, Jasmine, and Kazekiri in on this when they wake up?" he asked of them.

"You can count on us!" Gabrielle thumped her chest.

Michelle clasped her hands together and bowed. "Please do not worry. We will make sure that everyone knows what to do." She paused long enough to tilt her head. "You are planning to take Nyx out while we prepare, right? To keep her from realizing what we are doing?"

"That's right." Alex nodded, and then turned to Gabrielle. "By the way, how is Kazekiri?"

"There were no problems last night," Gabrielle said.

"Good." Alex sighed in relief.

Since Gabrielle and Michelle knew what to do, Alex began preparing breakfast for everyone, while the two sisters went into the living room and turned on the holovid. Alex didn't know what they were watching. However, the sound of explosions made him think it was some kind of operatic space adventure.

One by one, the others began waking up. Nyx was the first one up, but then Kazekiri, Jasmine, and Madison came downstairs and greeted him. He was pleased to see that Kazekiri looked well. She'd been having some problems sleeping. Nyx frowned when she had first entered the kitchen, her expression making him wonder if she could smell the gyros even though he'd used scent killers. However, she soon wandered over to the kitchen table, sat down, and began watching him.

"Hey, Nyx," Alex began casually as he stirred some eggs in a pan, "would you like to head into Mars City with me today? A new holo-drama that I wanted to see came out."

Nyx perked up. "You want me to see it with you?"

"Yes."

"Not Princess Gabrielle?"

"Gabby and I went on a date last week. Today, I'd like to take you on a date. After all"—he tried not to blush but failed—"you and I are engaged as well, right?"

Nyx remained silent for a moment, but only for a moment. "In that case, I will accompany you."

"Thank you."

"Hm."

Alice was the last person to wake up, and she arrived just in time for breakfast, and unlike the others, who were dressed and ready to begin their day, she was still in her pajamas. Well, it was Saturday, so that was okay. Alice usually spent weekends in her pajamas.

After breakfast, Alex and Nyx put on their boots, said goodbye to everyone, and left for the nearest shuttle stop.

He would leave decorating the house for Nyx's birthday up to the others.

1

Gabrielle didn't think she'd ever been more excited to celebrate a birthday before. She had certainly celebrated plenty of birthdays when she was younger, but they were always these big gatherings where lots of people that she didn't know attended. Most of those people had been old and wrinkly. At the very least, there hadn't been a single child present. All of her birthdays this far had sucked. The ones that she had celebrated for her sisters hadn't been much better either.

Maybe that was why she was so excited as she stood in the living room and adjusted the settings on Mr. Decorator.

She wasn't the only one who was decorating either. Ariel and Michelle were putting up a banner over the door that said, *"Happy Birthday Nyx!"* Alex had bought that banner last week. Well, it looked like the two of them were arguing about how high up the banner should go. She thought about breaking them up, but it didn't look like things would get serious, so she let them be.

Jasmine and Madison were also decorating... er... no, that wasn't quite right, was it? Jasmine was standing in place, one hand on her hip, the other near her face as she gave instructions to Madison.

"Oh ho ho ho ho ho! As the Queen of Decorating, I command you, Madison, to set up these tables! Oh ho ho ho ho ho!"

"Yes, Mistress!"

In either case, Madison looked really happy as Jasmine ordered her around. She was even wearing a big smile. Gabrielle guessed it was all good.

The plan for decorating was simple. Ariel and Michelle would set up the banner, Jasmine and Madison would put out the tables and prepare the games, and she, Gabrielle, would do the rest using Mr. Decorator. Alice was sluggishly helping Jasmine, but aside from breaking out some strange discs and a box from a cabinet, she hadn't done anything.

Mr. Decorator was her latest invention, and the name was self-explanatory. It shot out ribbons that would hang from the walls and ceiling to decorate a room. Gabrielle fiddled with the device, turning a knob and watching as the screen changed from green to purple. Nodding, she grinned, took aim at a spot on the ceiling, and fired.

BOOM!

Gabrielle's hand jerked as the gun exploded—not literally. It shot ribbons out of its nozzle so fast that the power was too much even for her. Maybe she should have worn her crisis suit for this? Gripping the gun, she tried to control where the ribbons went, but there were so many! They were everywhere!

"What the—?!"

"Mistress—mmmrrgglle!"

Jasmine and Madison received a face full of ribbons. It shot out and covered them from head to toe. Gabrielle jerked Mr. Decorator away from them. She had hoped it would stop them from being covered anymore than they already were. When Jasmine and Madison squawked as they were lifted off their feet, Gabrielle realized that they had become completely tangled in the ribbons!

Uh oh!

"Honorable Sister, you need to shut that—mmmphhhh!!"

"Oh, shiiiittt!!"

Her sisters were next. Both of them fell off the chairs they had been standing on while trying to put up the banner. They landed on the ground, where the ribbons quickly tangled them up. That wasn't good. She needed to shut this thing off! But she couldn't take her hands off the handle! If she did that, it would go even more out of control!

"Princess Gabrielle!" Azazel suddenly barged into the room with Kane and Abel. "I heard screaming, is everything—yaaaarrg!!!"

Azazel's words were cut off when he, Kane, and Abel were blasted off their feet by the ribbons. They struck the wall, which had been fortunately reinforced with durasteel plating after being destroyed so many times. The ribbons quickly connected to the wall as well, so they were struck there, forced to endure dozens of meters of ribbon shooting in their faces.

Gabrielly poked out her tongue as she tried to figure out how she could shut this thing off. Maybe if she encased it in her Aura of Creation... but no. That was a bad idea. Her Aura was still too unstable. She'd gone into the simulator the other day and took a large chunk out of the planet she had created while trying to control her Aura. Hmm... well, this might actually be a bit of a problem...

Even as the thought crossed her mind, Mr. Decorator sparked. The sparks skittered across the surface, growing increasingly more frequent.

"Huh?"

She had just looked down when Mr. Decorator exploded in her face. It didn't hurt, not really, but it did create a lot of smoke that caused her to cough. When the smoke cleared, Gabrielle blinked several times and looked around.

The room was covered from floor to ceiling in ribbons; Azazel, Kane, and Abel were stuck to the wall, their screams muffled; Ariel and Michelle were lying on the floor, flopping around like Mr. Snake after it malfunctioned; Jasmine and Madison were currently dangling from the ceiling. They looked like a pair of balls with arms, legs, and a head. In fact, the only person aside from herself who wasn't tied up in ribbons was Alice, who had miraculously avoided becoming entangled. She sat on the floor, no longer messing with the music box thingy.

"Hmmm..." Gabrielle murmured to herself. "That didn't work out quite like I had planned it to. Maybe I need to change the dimensional space so it doesn't release so much ribbon at once?"

"You are so troublesome," Alice said.

"Tee-hee!" Gabrielle couldn't really dispute that.

With a sigh, Alice stood up. "Come on, troublesome woman. We're gonna grab some knives and use them to cut these people down. Then we're going to redecorate the room."

"Okay! Just let me get Mr. Cut—"

"We aren't using one of your inventions."

"Fine..."

Gabrielle's shoulders slumped as she followed Alice out of the room. The screaming from the group who'd been trapped by her ribbons echoed behind her.

2

Alex felt a shiver crawl up his spine as he and Nyx sat down at the holo-theater. The air in this room was awfully cold. He was sure that was the reason for this spine tingling sensation.

Holo-theaters were massive buildings that contained several large rooms meant for mass entertainment. After getting their tickets, grabbing a bowl of lightly salted popcorn and a drink with two straws, Alex and Nyx had gone into their theater and sat down in the middle row.

Characterized by tertiary seating, the holo-theater featured a massive holovid. The seats were comfortable, made from a combination of memory foam and synthetic fibers, they not only regulated a person's body temperature, but could be reclined for extra comfort. When he and Nyx sat down, Alex had pulled the armrest up, so it wasn't in their way, and set the drink between them. Likewise, he set the popcorn next to the drink.

It was almost surprising how little had changed with holo-theaters. Before the new calendar, humans had gone to places called movie theaters. Alex had seen pictures of them during history class back in Primary, and aside from the holovid being replaced by some bulky screen, there wasn't that much of a difference.

"It has been a long time since I've been to a theater," Nyx said as she reached over and grabbed a piece of popcorn. She stared at it before popping it into her mouth. Her eyes widened before she came back and grabbed a handful.

"Do they have theaters in the rest of the galaxy?" asked Alex.

"They do." Nyx nodded as she grabbed another handful and popped each piece into her mouth. After she finished eating, she added, "They don't look too different from this, though most of them are bigger and allow for a three-hundred and sixty degree seating. Holodramas aren't as popular either. Theaters tend to feature either some type of sports game or gladiator fighting. Gambling is really big in the galactic community."

"I'll bet. Gambling is big everywhere."

Nyx ate some more popcorn. "I once assassinated a target while he was watching a space ball game."

Alex had no idea what space ball was, but he could feel the sweat trickle down his scalp when she mentioned assassinating someone.

The holodrama soon started with intense music blasting out of several speakers. Nyx jumped and transmuted one of her armbands into a sword. Alex pulled her back down.

"Relax, that's just the opening theme song."

Nyx still looked tense, but she relaxed once she realized that he was right. The opening theme song was being sung by a famous idol from Saturn. Alex didn't know her name, but he'd seen pictures of her on holoboards. The visuals on the holovid displayed an intense space battle as the music played in the background. Since the song was a sad one, it made all of the explosions from fighter craft being destroyed feel tragic.

The holodrama that Alex had taken Nyx to see was called Captain Carrick; it was a story about Carrick, the young captain of the Millenium Voyager, traveling the galaxy in search of his father. He ran into all kinds of trouble, from fights between two planets to alien space babes in sexy pirate uniforms. Through his wit and indomitable will, he managed to escape from all of the situations he found himself in, and he picked up a lover or two along the way.

Alex glanced at Nyx as the holo-drama played. He was pleased to see her glued to the holovid. Her eyes were wide open as she watched the drama unfold, her hand automatically going toward the bowl of popcorn. He grinned when she missed her mouth several times, spilling popcorn onto her lap... not that she had noticed. Realizing that Nyx was probably gonna eat all the popcorn, Alex contented himself with the drink.

As the holo-drama continued, the popcorn bowl was depleted, and Alex set it on the ground. Nyx immediately moved to fill the space. He wondered if she was even aware of what she was doing when she scooted so close their hips began touching. She probably wasn't. Her eyes were still locked onto the holovid, after all.

Deciding to let Nyx be, Alex leaned down to take a sip of his drink, but he paused when his head bumped against something. He looked to his right. He blinked. Nyx, who must have also had the same idea as him, also blinked several times as their eyes locked.

For a moment, Alex wondered if he should do something. Maybe he should kiss her? Would that be appropriate? He wasn't sure. It didn't matter anyway. The moment was broken when Nyx, her cheeks turning a surprising shade of red, jerked back in her chair and scooted away. He frowned at her, wondering if perhaps she was nervous. It would certainly explain her actions, though he could never imagine Nyx getting nervous about anything.

Picking up the drink after taking a sip, he offered the cup to Nyx, who stared at it for a second before, slowly, almost tentatively, reaching out to grab it. She brought the drink to her mouth and took a sip. He almost laughed when her lips puckered up like she had swallowed something sour.

"Is this your first time drinking a carbonated beverage?" he asked.

Nyx nodded. "I've had alcohol before, but aside from that and water, I haven't drank anything else."

"It takes some getting used to."

The holo-drama lasted for a total of two hours. After which, Alex and Nyx filed out with all the other theater goers. It wasn't long before they had exited the holo-theater and began wandering along a walkway. Alex checked his IDband. It was 1234. The surprise party wasn't going to happen for another two hours, which meant he needed to keep Nyx distracted with something else now.

"Hey, Nyx." Alex grabbed the assassin's attention. "Wanna try out the arcade?"

Nyx stared at him, her eyes bland, her expression blank. "Are you hiding something from me?"

A cold sweat broke out on his forehead. "W-what? No. Of course not!"

"Really?"

"Really."

Knowing better than to look away, Alex tried to maintain eye contact. He thought he did a pretty good job.

"Very well." Nyx looked away first. "I don't mind going to the arcade with you."

Alex breathed a sigh of relief. It looked like he was saved... for now.

There were quite a few arcades in Mars City's Entertainment District. Alex led Nyx by the hand, taking several warp pads, traveling up a couple of elevators, and stepping onto numerous escalators. Their path was marked by a lot of genetically modified plant life. Since Mars City couldn't generate its own atmosphere, they had to rely on other means of oxygenating the domed city.

The arcade that Alex took Nyx to was the one that he used to play at when he was younger. This was before Alex and Alice had moved out of the Metronome's house. Back then it had been easy for him, Alice, Selene, and Ryoko to hit up the arcade after school.

While the outside had the same appearance as most other buildings, the inside was marked by red carpet and numerous simulation games. There was everything from fighting games like the one that Alex and Arthur had competed against each other, racing games where someone sat in a cockpit to simulate a real space race, and even shooting games that involved putting on a VR system and using a fake gun to shoot at targets. Those weren't the only games, though. The arcade even had some that let people win prizes.

Arcades like this were another relic of the past that had survived into the future. Actually, Alex had heard that they had declined in popularity during the so-called 21st Century, but then there had been a huge explosion of arcades that popped up during the era of colonization. Alex guessed that the hardships of daily life had been so much that the people recreated arcades as a means of relaxing.

"What would you like to play first?" Alex asked.

Nyx looked around before raising her arm and pointing. "I want to try that."

"A racing game? All right."

While they started with a racing game, they didn't end with one. Alex traveled through the arcade with Nyx, playing everything from racing games to fighting games, and they even played darts and billiards. Actually, Alex found that Nyx was quite skilled when it came to pool.

"Billiards is another game that the galaxy plays... though we don't call it that." Nyx twirled the cue between her fingers after breaking the diamond formation. One of the balls, the two ball, had already fallen into one of the six holes. "We call it terme. Also, the billiards of your solar system is a lot more complex. There are many rules that I do not understand."

Setting up her shot, Nyx sat on the edge of the pool table, placed her hands behind her, and leaned back. Alex gulped when he realized how this pose emphasized the lines of her body. Nyx might have been small, but the way her modest breasts stuck out in this pose, and the vision of her thighs squished against the table, really hammered her sexuality home. She hit the cue ball, which struck another ball, the one she'd been aiming for.

It went in.

"And how did you get so good at this?" asked Alex as Nyx slid off the table, lined up another shot, and struck the cue ball. The next ball she aimed for went in as well. At this rate, he wouldn't even get to play!

"An assassin needs to have many skills." Nyx lined up another shot. It also went in. "Some of my targets would frequent bars. I learned how to play terme so people would accept me as a regular while I learned more about my targets."

"I guess that makes sense." Alex followed Nyx with his eyes as she walked around the table, lined up her next shot, and... missed. "Oh. It's my turn."

"..."

Nyx didn't say anything as she glared at the cue ball. Alex thought her slightly puffed cheeks were adorable.

He wandered over to the cue ball and studied the battlefield, noting where his balls were in correlation with the cue ball. It looked like the easiest to hit would be the three. On the other hand, it wasn't near a hole. The seven was near a hole, but it was also the farthest from him. Dang. This was a tough choice.

Time for a little risk.

Alex lined up his shot. He was going for the seven. Leaning over, he stared down his cue and eyed the little white ball. He calculated the distance between it and the seven ball, the angle, the speed that he needed to hit the ball with times the kinetic force that would be unleashed when his cue struck the ball. Everything was calculated down to a T. He could do this. No, he would get that ball in. Taking a deep breath, he pulled the cue back, and thrust it forward!

SCREEE!!!

Nyx and Alex watched as the cue ball flew off the table, bounced against the wall, bounced off a lamp, struck another table several meters away, and then hit some poor sap in the back of the head. Of course, the ball hit the guy hard enough that he was knocked out cold. He fell face first into his nachos.

As the man's friends began panicking, Nyx looked at Alex.

"You suck."

"S-shut up!" Alex tried, and failed, not to blush.

3

Alex managed to distract Nyx for another hour by playing games at the arcade with her. In fact, it might be more accurate to say that he was the one who had to remind her that they needed to return home. She had gotten so into a shooting simulation that it had taken nearly half an hour to pull her away. Now they were back in the Outer District, walking home, and Nyx was actually pouting.

Thanks to prolonged contact with her, Alex knew that Nyx was not as emotionless as she appeared, but it was rare to see her display her emotions so readily. Seeing the girl's cheeks puffed out like a squirrel was comical. It was also cute.

"Sorry, Nyx." He smiled apologetically. "But we really do need to return home."

"I'm not angry," Nyx muttered.

"If you weren't angry, you wouldn't be looking away from me like that."

"Hmph!"

Alex didn't know whether to sigh or laugh. It really was too much to see this badass assassin pout like a—well, like a teenage girl.

They arrived home; Alex opened the door to find an empty hallway. To keep up appearances, he called out that he was home, but of course, no one answered. Well, there was a muffled thump, but he guessed that someone had stopped Gabrielle from charging out to greet him, which would have ruined the surprise. He and Nyx took off their shoes. Nyx was frowning.

"It's too quiet."

"You think so?"

"I know so." Nyx pulled a pair of armbands off her wrists and transmuted them into swords. "Be careful."

"Uh huh."

Alex decided to just follow Nyx as she wandered up to the living room door. The noise had come from behind there. She raised her left arm. Panicking, he grabbed her wrist to stop her, but that might not have been the best idea. In her current state of alertness, she responded by dropping her swords, grabbing his wrist, twisting around, and throwing him over her shoulder.

He didn't even have time to scream as he slammed into the door, breaking it and flying into the living room. Shouts echoed around him as he smacked against the floor and rolled. He knocked into something, and then an object of some kind fell on top of him. Whatever had fallen on him was wet. He shivered as his body became drenched in ice cold liquid.

"A-Alex!"

As he sat up, Nyx rushed into the room and knelt before him. She actually looked kind of panicked.

"I'm sorry! I didn't mean to throw you! You just surprised me!"

"It's fine..." Alex groaned, holding a hand to his head. "Anyway, you may want to turn around."

"Turn... around?"

Nyx blinked several times, but then she turned around and finally noticed the people standing behind her. Alice, Ariel, Azazel, Abel, Kane, Kazekiri, Gabrielle, Jasmine, and Madison were all present. They were holding something in their hands. After a moment, the group seemed to realize that she had noticed them and pressed a button, causing the objects to shoot out decorative string with loud popping noises.

"Happy birthday, Nyx!" they all shouted.

"What... is this?" asked a stunned Nyx.

"It's your birthday party," Alex said, standing up. "You told me awhile ago that your birthday was today, so I thought we would celebrate it with you."

"But... why?" Nyx asked, staring at him with uncomprehending eyes.

"Because..." His eyes softened. "Today is an important day. It's the day you were born. That makes it a day worth celebrating, don't you think?" From the perplexed expression that she still wore, Alex knew she didn't understand. He held out his hand. "Come on. Let's have fun celebrating the day you were born, Nyx."

Still staring at him like she couldn't comprehend what was happening, Nyx reached out and placed her hand in his. The action was almost dainty.

It turned out that what Alex had knocked over was the table with the drinks. He asked Madison to get more drinks and fix the table. Meanwhile, he quickly rinsed off the carbonated beverages and got dressed in a spare change of clothes.

He entered the living room again to find that the party was, more or less, in full swing. There weren't that many people present. However, there was some music playing in the background, everyone was talking, and thanks to Gabrielle being her normal exuberant self, they weren't lacking in entertainment. She was twirling Alice around and laughing. Sadly, Alice did not look like she was having as much fun.

Surprisingly, Azazel, Kane, and Abel were engaging Nyx in conversation. It wasn't until Alex listened in more closely that he realized why.

"Say you were in melee combat with a skilled professional. He's better than you, but you can't put distance between the two of you because he has a special ability that allows him to stay in your guard. What do you do?"

"I would just use my alchemy." Nyx took a bite of her gyro. He wasn't surprised that she had already gotten herself one. "Even if they stay in my guard, it won't matter if I just squash them flat by transmuting the ground they're walking on."

"Er... yes, I suppose that would work."

"It's brilliant!"

"I wish I was an alchemist!"

"Don't say that! We are proud angelisians!"

"Nyx!" Alex walked over to her and grabbed the girl's hand. "Come on. Let's go talk with everyone else. You three." He looked at Azazel, Abel, and Kane. "Don't just stand there. This is a party. Mingle."

"Y-yes, sir!" Azazel and the other two saluted without realizing it.

Alex and Nyx joined Kazekiri, who engaged the girl in a conversation about her principals. Turned out that Kazekiri was interested in Nyx's philosophy of only going after wanted criminals. She wasn't the only one they spoke with that evening either. Everyone wandered in and out of the conversation, including Azazel and his two henchmen.

As the evening wore on, several more people showed up. Karen arrived first. Not only that, but she had brought whiskey. Alex would have scolded her, except he didn't even know how she knew about the party—until Gabrielle admitted that she had told Karen.

"It'll be more fun if more people show up!" she said when he asked why she had done that.

Darrick also showed up, as did Selene, Ryoko, Serah, and even Yumi, though Yumi nearly had a panic attack when she spotted Karen having a drinking contest with a swaying in his seat Kane. On a side note, she'd already drunk both Azazel and Abel under the table. They were passed out against the wall on the far side of the room.

As the party continued, Alex found himself being bounced from one person to the next. Sometimes he talked, sometimes he danced, and one time Karen had even tried to force him to drink alcohol. Yumi actually had to bail him out of that incident.

They also tried to play a game of Twister—except the game was an invention that Gabrielle had made, which sadly ended with their clothes being drenched in water. Turned out whenever someone fell, water shot from nozzles. At least half the girls ended up with see-through clothing and had to change. Alex had also ended up with see-through clothing, but he had already changed once and decided to let it dry naturally.

Jasmine had somehow gotten drunk off the smell of Karen's alcohol. Now she was laughing like a mad rich woman and trying to strip out of her clothes. Madison, bless her robotic soul, was trying to stop her. Sadly, both Serah and Ryoko were goading the girl on, while Alice was just watching with a *"it's too troublesome to interfere"* face. Gabrielle was talking to Selene and Kazekiri about her latest invention. Neither of them looked like they understood, but they were being polite and listening anyway. Darrick was also there, but he was nosebleeding over Jasmine, who had managed to pull her shirt off despite Madison's best attempts.

I'm so going to hit him.

Alex looked around, trying to spot Nyx in the crowd, which had grown a fair bit larger. With all the other people present, there must have been at least twice the size he had prepared for. They were already out of food.

He eventually found Nyx on the back porch. The door was open, so all Alex had to do was walk outside.

It was quite a bit cooler outside, probably because of how many people were in the living room. Even with advanced conditioners that could monitor the temperature, it didn't change what a bunch of warm bodies in the same room did.

"Don't want to be with the others? Have you grown tired of being around so many people?" Alex asked as he sat beside her. She had a gyro in her hand. It was probably the last one.

"It's not that," Nyx said. "I was just taking a break."

"I don't blame you." He looked back just in time to see Darrick get smacked in the face with a shoe. "They can be a handful."

"They can." Nyx nodded, and then paused. "But it's... fun. Being with all these different people. I have never quite experienced anything like it." She placed a hand against her chest. "It gives me this warm feeling, right here."

"Then I'm glad we decided to have this party." Alex smiled.

Nyx turned her head to look at him. "Why did you decide to have this party? I understand that it is the day of my birth, but I don't know why that is worth celebrating."

Alex would have cried at her words, but this was a special occasion, and he wasn't going to let himself get emotional like that.

He reached out and placed one of his hands over one of hers.

"The reason we're celebrating is because this is the day you were born." Alex squeezed her hand. "To me, that is one of the most important days of the year. After all, if you hadn't been born, then you and I would have never met."

"But I wasn't born. I was created."

"My point still stands."

Nyx stared at him for several seconds that seemed to stretch into an eternity. It wasn't an uncomfortable stare, so Alex bore with it. Finally, Nyx turned her head away from him, and then she did something unexpected.

She leaned her head on his shoulder.

"I think I understand now," she murmured. "Thank you. Hearing you say that the day I was created means a lot to me. No one else has ever said something so kind to me before."

There were a lot of things he could have said to that, a lot of things he wanted to say to that, but this was a special day. He didn't want this to become emotional. This was supposed to be a happy day, a day to celebrate the birth/creation of someone he loved.

"You're welcome."

Alex wrapped an arm around the assassin's shoulder, pulled her close, and together, they sat underneath the starless dome in peace—until an explosion from behind told Alex that his attention was needed elsewhere. He sighed. Nope. He just couldn't get a break.

AFTERWORD

Thank you all for reading A Most Unlikely Hero volume 8. If you enjoyed it, I would like to ask that you please consider writing a review. Books live and die by their reviews. The more reviews a book has, the more readers it will reach. If you liked this story, I hope you will help it find more readers.

I placed a very heavy emphasis on Jasmine and Kazekiri this volume. They didn't get much screen time in the last volume because Alex, Gabrielle, and Nyx were off gallivanting in another solar system. I thought it was about time I fleshed out their characters a bit more.

Jasmine and Kazekiri are interesting in that they sort of mirror each other in many ways. Both of them have a terrible home life. Jasmine's parents basically ignore her and only use her when they want to elevate their social status—such as the case when her father tried to force her into an arranged marriage—while Kazekiri and her brother escaped their parents care because their mom was a deadbeat and their father was sexually abusive.

Much as I would like to say everything you've read here is just fiction, the truth is these things happen in real life. While both characters are based on standard archetypes found in anime, their backstories are based on people I actually know. Don't worry. I got permission to use them as inspiration before I wrote this. I think adding this kind of realism helps give characters more depth.

One of the things I focused a lot on was the difference between Jasmine's and Kazekiri's personalities. Jasmine is a seemingly arrogant character who acts similar to Saki Tenjouin from To Love Ru. While she seems like nothing more than an arrogant himesama, Jasmine is actually really strong, both emotionally and physically. On the other hand, Kazekiri, who was inspired by Yui (also from To Love Ru), wants to be a strong role model to others, but the truth is she's emotionally weak. I wanted to showcase these differences in this volume.

I hope I did a good job and that everyone reading this series likes Jasmine and Kazekiri even more now.

Before I go, I would just like to give some thanks to the people who continue to make it possible for me to write.

I would first like to thank my editor and proofreaders. It's hard making the garbage I write readable. My stuff is always filled with errors, so I'm grateful they can help me get rid of all those pesky grammatical mistakes.

I am also very grateful to XuaHanNin, who continues to deliver quality artwork. Seriously. She does such an amazing job. All of the stuff she draws is super cute, and I cannot get enough of it.

Finally, I want to thank you readers. I can never say this enough, but thank you so much for reading my story. I sincerely hope you enjoyed it and will stick around to read the next volume. I've finally decided to develop Ariel and Michelle more. Volume 9 will be full of character development and intense battles!

~Brandon Varnell

SEE A SNEAK PEAK OF THE MANGA ADAPTION OF BRANDON'S AMERICAN KITSUNE SERIES!

HAVE YOU EVER EXPERIENCED ONE OF THOSE LIFE-CHANGING INSTANCES? AN EVENT SO MOMENTOUS THAT, YEARS LATER, YOU'RE STILL MARVELING AT HOW IT CHANGED YOUR LIFE?

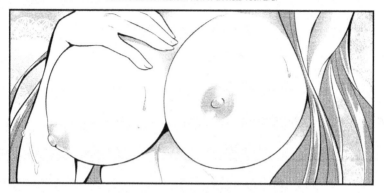

I HAD ONE OF THOSE. IT HAPPENED A WHILE AGO

EVEN TO THIS DAY, THROUGH ALL THE CHANGES THAT HAVE HAPPENED, THROUGH ALL THE EXPERIENCES THAT I'VE BEEN THROUGH, I STILL CAN'T BELIEVE HOW THIS ONE MOMENT CHANGED MY LIFE FOREVER.

NO MATTER WHAT CAME AFTER, OUR FIRST MEETING IS SOMETHING THAT I'LL ALWAYS REMEMBER.

ESPECIALLY SINCE, AT THE BEGINNING OF THIS TALE, I THOUGHT SHE WAS NOTHING BUT AN ORDINARY FOX WITH, UNORDINARILY ENOUGH, TWO BUSHY RED TAILS.

LIFE

.

.

.

.

.

.

.

.

.

.

IT HITS YOU WHEN YOU LEAST EXPECT IT TO.

coming soon!

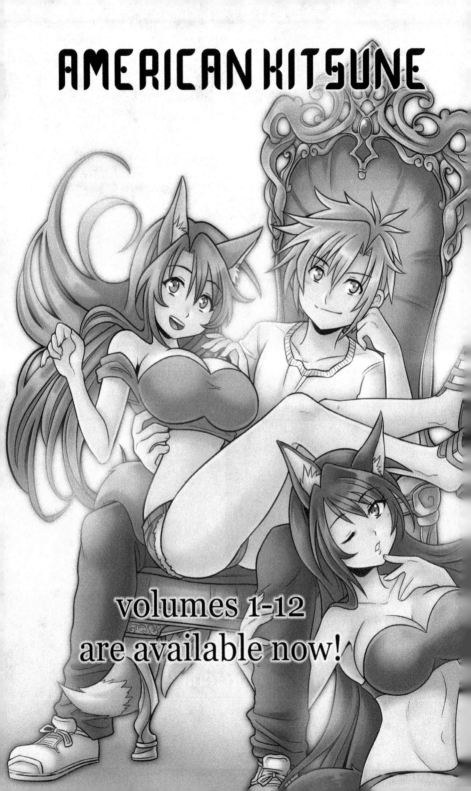

WIEDERGEBURT
LEGEND OF THE REINCARNATED WARRIOR

catgirl doctor

NOW AVAILABLE ON PAPERBACK,
KINDLE, AND KINDLE UNLIMITED!

NOW AVAILABLE ON
PAPERBACK, KINDLE, AND
KINDLE UNLIMITED!
MAN
MADE
GOD

Volumes 1-8
are available now
on paperback, kindle,
and Kindle Unlimited!

The Complete Series is available now on paperback and Amazon Kindle!

JOURNEY of a BETRAYED HERO

Want to learn when a new book comes out?
Follow me on Social Media!

 @AmericanKitsune

 +BrandonVarnell

 @BrandonBVarnell

 http://bvarnell1101.tumblr.com/

 Brandon Varnell

 BrandonbVarnell

 https://www.patreon.com/
BrandonVarnell

CPSIA information can be obtained
at www.ICGtesting.com
Printed in the USA
BVHW042238200920
589239BV00011B/138